'A Scottish crime thriller with a great lead in law ... Robbie Munro and a cast of reprobates to keep you guessing, laughing and on the edge of your seat - a cracking read.'

Gregor Fisher (*Rab C. Nesbit*)

'McIntyre's outstanding mystery featuring Scottish defense counsel Robbie Munro perfectly blends humor and investigation. Readers will want to see a lot more of the endearing Robbie.'

Starred review, *Publishers Weekly*

'*Last Will* is a reminder of how good Scottish crime writing is ... Robbie Munro, defence lawyer, struggling Dad, always flying by the seat of his pants, is great fun to be with.'

Paul Burke, *NB Magazine*

'A clever, absorbing and funny book ... an addictive page turner. I loved it!'   ***Mrs Bloggs' Books***

Present Tense

'Crime with an edge of dark humour ... could only come out of Scotland.'   **Tommy Flanagan (*Braveheart, Sons of Anarchy*)**

'Page-turning read, helped by a clear and crisp writing style. A fresh take for the Tartan Noir scene and I look forward to seeing where McIntyre takes Robbie next.'

Louise Fairbairn, *The Scotsman*

'This is dark humour, ironic humour, the kind you need when dealing with the things lawyers deal with.'

Liz Loves Books

'An entertaining novel with enough mystery threaded through it to keep crime fans gripped, and characters well rounded enough to carry a series.'   *... Magazine*

Good News, Bad News

'Take a plot that would knock John Grisham for six, season with a picaresque cast of supporting characters, garnish with one-liners that Frankie Boyle would kill for and you have a page-turner of the highest quality.'

Alex Norton (*Taggart*)

'Dry and pleasing wit which will surely see Robbie taking his place alongside Christopher Brookmyre's Jack Parlabane soon.'
Sunday Sport

Stitch Up

'A deft slice of Caledonian crime … rings viscerally true, thanks no doubt to McIntyre's lifelong experience in criminal law.'
The Times

'Nail-biting, dark-humoured writing, with twists and gut-wrenching surprises that leave you thinking, "just one more page please".'
Scottish Field

'A compelling, well-plotted mystery.'
The Herald

'A cracking read: cleverly plotted, engaging characters, humorous and McIntyre knows his subject matter well.'
Grab This Book blog

Fixed Odds

'Larger than life characters and a great story-line with a nice twist.'
Scots Magazine

'Full of wit … entertaining with a darker core, this is another winner in the Munro series.'
Live and Deadly blog

'A perfectly crafted Tartan Noir with mixed layers of hilarious moments and dangerous times.'
Meggy Roussel, Chocolate 'n' Waffles blog

'I just adored everything about Fixed Odds.'
Whispering Stories blog

William McIntyre is a partner in Scotland's oldest law firm Russel + Aitken, specialising in criminal defence. He has been instructed in many interesting and high-profile cases over the years and now turns fact into fiction with his Robbie Munro legal thrillers. He is married with four sons.

Also in the Robbie Munro series

Last Will
Present Tense
Good News, Bad News
Stitch Up
Fixed Odds

BAD DEBT

A Robbie Munro Thriller

William McIntyre

SANDSTONE PRESS

First published in Great Britain by
Sandstone Press Ltd
Willow House
Stoneyfield Business Park
Inverness
IV2 7PA
Scotland

www.sandstonepress.com

ISBN: 978-1-913207-30-4
ISBNe: 978-1-913207-31-1

Sandstone Press is committed to a sustainable future. This book
is made from Forest Stewardship Council ® certified paper.

Cover design by Two Associates
Typeset by Iolaire Typography, Newtonmore
Printed in the UK by Severn, Gloucester

This book was largely written late 2019 when Covid 19 was just a twinkle in a Wuhan bat's eye. That and the fact the book is set in 2021 is the reason there is no mention of the virus, but nonetheless, I would like to dedicate it to all the doctors, nurses, pharmacists, paramedics and other frontline staff, keyworkers and volunteers, who have worked so hard to keep the rest of us safe, not forgetting the forgotten lawyers, clerks, judges, sheriffs, police officers, social workers and prison staff who keep the wheels of our criminal justice system grinding.

1

You could tell it was summertime in Scotland by the longer intervals between the rain. It had started again. Fat drops splattered onto the page in my brother's hand. When he'd finished reading, Malky tucked the soggy sheet of paper inside his jacket and ducked his head under my big black umbrella. There were more people graveside than I'd thought there would be. As a rule, the older you were when you died the fewer mourners you could expect. I stared down into the hole. Made you think. One day you were having the time of your life: drinking with your mates, watching football, playing golf. The next you were being buried or burned.

I collapsed my brolly, stuck the spike into the ground and, along with my brother, stepped forward to receive one of the red cords the undertaker was distributing among the pall-bearers. There were lots of us, but then we weren't lowering a featherweight. Not in any sense of the word. Distant family members, old friends who'd dragged themselves away from busy schedules, even older friends who'd dragged themselves away from the Red Corner Bar, all took a cord. Last to receive was Sammy Veitch. A trip-and-slip lawyer, such was Sammy's encyclopaedic knowledge of the defects in West Lothian's pavements, he could identify the offending upraised slab even before you'd tripped over it. For once the wee man was clad in a sombre tweed suit rather than his usual Highland garb.

At the head of the grave, the minister droned on about life even more everlasting than his sermon had been back at the church. On his signal, we lowered the coffin into the ground, the thick hemp straps across the shoulders of the gravediggers taking most of the strain. Soon wood met earth. We let the red cords fall and stepped back. The man in the back-to-front collar stepped forward and stooped to pick up a handful of wet soil. As the dirt slipped through his fingers, there came a sudden stillness in the air, a flash of lightning followed by a loud clap of thunder. Someone up there was putting a No Vacancies sign in the window.

The service finished with a prayer, another roar of thunder and hailstones pelting the gathered throng. Many, like my brother, who'd been fooled by a bright start to the morning and come unprepared, scurried by us, casting soil into the grave as they went.

Malky and I were making our own departure, shuffling along, both trying to stay under the one umbrella, when Sammy came over, reached up and put a hand around each of our shoulders. 'I'll miss him,' he said. 'We all will. You can say what you like about the man, but he was a—'

'Dodgy, corrupt old shyster?' was my dad's suggestion. He'd come forward to toss an excessively large clod of mud into the hole and watched it splat against a coffin lid already lightly dusted with dirt and gravel. He turned to Sammy. 'No offence, of course. Sorry for your loss and all that. *If* you can call it a loss.'

'Dad, you're talking about Sammy's business partner. The man's dead. Leave it at that, will you?'

But the old man was on a roll. 'Leave it? No, I won't leave it, and don't go thinking you're any better than Eddie Frew the way you're headed.'

'And where exactly am I headed?' I said.

'Defence lawyers,' my dad spat. 'There'll be no snow-ball fights where Eddie "The Fixer" Frew's going.'

My father's view on the presumption of innocence and the right to a fair trial veered on the side of the lynch mob.

'You're retired,' I said. 'It's okay to stop thinking like a cop.'

'And start thinking like a crook?' he said. 'Like him? I mean, what's all that about?' He jerked a thumb in the direction of the minister, standing head bowed at the graveside. 'I'll bet the only time Eddie picked up a Bible was to check for loopholes.'

Sammy stepped between us. 'That's enough, Alex. Robbie's right. It's my partner's funeral. You didn't like him – Eddie knew that. He knew that and he didn't care. Now why don't you shut up and have a little respect for the dead?'

My dad snorted. 'Respect?' He turned on Malky. 'And as for you. I might have known Robbie would be here, but I expected more from you. Making speeches about what a great guy Eddie was. Always there to give folk a helping hand. Aye, so long as they greased his palm first.'

Sammy had had enough. 'Come with me, boys. You'll get soaked walking back in this.' He manoeuvred Malky and me away from my dad and led us in the direction of a man in morning dress who was waiting by one of two black limos, seemingly oblivious to the downpour.

'I'm sorry about that, Sammy,' I said, once the three of us had clambered into the back seat. 'I'll have a word with my dad later. Get him to apologise properly.'

Sammy, in the middle, turned to look at me. 'It's okay, Robbie. Me and your dad have always been sound. He never did like Eddie much, though,' he added, rather understating the obvious. 'Your old man and Eddie had too many run-ins back in the day. Eddie used to say your dad could make a bachelor confess to bigamy. Don't worry, we'll patch things up later over a dram.' He smiled. 'And Alex is right about one thing. Eddie was as bent as a Brexit banana. He was also as rude as hell to the punters. I could never understand why they flocked to him. There's me, buzzing about like a blue-arsed fly, chasing business all over town, while he just sat there, fighting off the clients. And as for legal aid? Not a chance. Cash was always king with Eddie.'

Like anyone who had known the late Eddie Frew, I couldn't disagree. A reputation was everything in criminal law. Especially a bad one. Some clients didn't want a straight-shooter. They wanted someone they thought would bend the rules in their favour, and Eddie 'The Fixer' Frew would bend them, break them and scatter the pieces about the courtroom if necessary, just so long as the money was right.

Sammy leaned across and patted Malky on the knee. 'By the way, I should have said earlier, thanks for coming and saying a few words, big man. It would have made Eddie's day knowing you were here.'

Come to think of it, why was my brother here? Sammy was the deceased's former business partner. A few of us local solicitors had pitched up out of professional courtesy. My dad had probably come along just to make absolutely certain Eddie was dead, and I suspected the large contingent from the Red Corner Bar had a lot to do with the free drink that was being laid on back at their local, courtesy of Frew & Veitch. But my brother? Was football legend Malky Munro, radio pundit and after-dinner speaker, doing guest appearances at funerals now?

4

'I'm here because Eddie asked me to come,' Malky said.

According to reports, Eddie had died from a massive heart attack. Dropped dead while on a visit to Queensbury House, a 17th century building renovated and integrated into the Scottish Parliament, where politicians and guests downed taxpayer-subsidised liquor. It was the equivalent of the old boys' clubs and smoke-filled rooms of yester-year, where affairs of state were discussed. Except these days there were a lot more women and a smoking ban. Many was the time Big Eddie Frew, a staunch unionist, had said he wouldn't be seen dead in the place at the foot of the Royal Mile. He was wrong about that. He'd been seen very dead. Dropping like the pound on the eve of Brexit, dram in hand and never spilling a drop. There would have been no time for him to call Malky before he hit the floor.

'When did he ask you?' I said.

Malky scratched his jaw. 'Would have been a few years ago now. Remember that time someone broke in and stole my Cup medal?'

How could any of us forget the wailing and gnashing of teeth that had followed? Or the fact that out of all Malky's trophies, that medal was all the more important because he'd scored the winner? A goal that had gone down in Scottish football legend as either the best or the luckiest cup-winning goal ever. An opinion that varied depending on the tint of the spectator's spectacles, light blue or shamrock green.

My brother looked out of the window at a West Lothian that was getting wetter by the minute. 'Eddie ... Well ... Let's just say he arranged for me to get it back and wouldn't take any money for it. All he asked was that I do him a favour. I thought he wanted a signed shirt or tickets to a game or something, but, no, he said to me, "When I die, say something nice about me at my funeral." I thought he was joking, but here I am.'

'Sounds like Eddie,' Sammy said. 'Sometimes I think he made more money out of court, than he ever made in it. He had the Scottish Parliament to thank for that, even though he hated the place. Closing all those police stations and turning the bizzies into call centre operatives. What did that lot in Holyrood think was going to happen?'

I knew what he meant. Close hospitals and there'd be fewer admissions, but people didn't suddenly stop getting ill. They looked for cures elsewhere: old wives and witch doctors. It was the same with police stations. For some, Eddie Frew was a justice medicine man – the cure to a failed system. It made sense in a twisted sort of a way. If you had serious people on the books, and Eddie had a client bank of some top-notch villains, why not hire them out? Someone stole your motor? Assaulted you? Maybe just a noisy neighbour? The police don't want to know, neither does the Council, so why bother to report it? Go see Eddie Frew. He knows a guy, who knows a guy. For a price, you'll get justice. Proper justice, without all the hassle of court and definitely no witnesses – at least none that will speak up.

Sammy was ten years Eddie's junior. Eddie had taken him on as a legal apprentice, and for years the pair practised in their hometown of Linlithgow, before deciding there was not enough business. So they'd diversified, opening offices in Edinburgh and Bathgate, with Eddie chasing the private money, Sammy chasing ambulances. Eddie had made a lot of contacts over the years, both high and low. He could eat at anyone's table. He had a map of where a lot of bodies were buried and was never afraid to exhume a few. Eddie always knew somebody who knew somebody. And the other somebodies those somebodies knew, were not the kind of somebodies you'd want to meet up a dark close.

'All the same, you must have done all right out of it,' I said to Sammy. 'You were in partnership for how long?'

Sammy thought about that. 'I'm sixty-four, so it must be getting on for forty years. Not that there was a lot in it for me. I fed off the crumbs from Eddie's table. He did occasionally pull a few strings for me, but we ate what we killed and shared overheads. After his illness, Eddie was very choosy and only took on a few new clients.' The richest few, I guessed. Sammy tugged at the seat belt and strapped himself in. 'Eddie might not have liked your dad, but he was Malky's biggest fan. Never missed a game. And he had a soft spot for you, too, Robbie.'

'I hadn't realised he was such a good judge of character,' I said. 'Unlike my dad.'

Sammy laughed. 'Och, your old man's all right. Dead proud of the pair of you he is.'

'Hides it well in my case,' I said.

Sammy leaned forward to give the driver some directions. 'What do you expect?' he said, reclining again. 'Your old man was a cop for thirty-odd years, doing his best to get folk banged up. Then you come along and start getting them out. But remember, he's still your dad. You don't judge a man like Alex Munro by his words. You judge him by his actions, and he'd never do you a bad turn, no matter how much he complains.'

The rain was still hammering down when the limo pulled up outside the Red Corner Bar. As the three of us alighted and hurried into the pub out of the rain, Sammy put a hand on my shoulder.

7

'I'm having to wind up Eddie's side of things,' he said. 'Once I've finished off his work in progress, the accountants will do the rest so that Wilma and the kids get what's due to them. He was semi-retired, and there's not that much to sort out. Most of it I can handle myself, but ...'

I wondered why Sammy thought it necessary to confide his business affairs in me. I was soon to find out.

'I've got a wee favour to ask you, Robbie,' he said, as, single file, we followed in Malky's slipstream, forcing our way through the crowd of happy mourners, on the scent of free whisky. 'Eddie's got this jury trial set to start soon—'

'How soon?' I asked, sensing the direction things were going.

'Day after tomorrow.'

'Wednesday?'

'Or possibly Thursday. Has to be called in by Friday or it'll time-bar. Who knows? It might not even start.'

That was the trouble with jury trials; they seldom started when you thought they would. When they didn't, you were left with a diary like a desert. When they did, it meant you were tied up for days. For a one-man-band like mine it caused havoc with the business calendar.

'It's in Livingston,' Sammy said. 'Your stamping ground. The case has dragged on for nearly a year. I know there's not that much time to prepare, but I thought you could maybe step in.' He sensed my hesitation. 'Honestly, it's a great defence.'

I'd heard the *it's a great defence* line many times. It was usually followed by *it's very straightforward*, and shortly before I was presented with the sort of thing Wile E. Coyote might gift-wrap for the Roadrunner. 'I'd like to help, Sammy, honestly, but—'

'I'd owe you one, Robbie, and, seriously, you'll thank

me for it. I'm almost tempted to do it myself, but I've done no criminal work for years. I couldn't find a jury in a courtroom these days, and Eddie would want me to instruct someone who knows what they're doing. You'd have been his first choice.'

While flattery has been known to work on me, this was one of Eddie Frew's clients, and I was sure Eddie's clients had expectations of acquittal directly proportional to the size of fee they paid. Just as I was sure they would not be magnanimous in defeat.

'Of course he'll do it,' Malky said. He was of the same view after he'd barged his way to the bar, scooped up three drams and returned to my side. 'Come on, Robbie. How can you refuse a dead man's last request while you stand there drinking his whisky?'

'Strictly speaking it's the firm that's paying for the drink,' Sammy said. 'And the food.'

'There's food?' Malky stood on his tiptoes and looked around until he spied a trestle table heaving with pies, sandwiches and sausage rolls.

'Who is this pal of Eddie's that's in bother?' I asked, after my brother had gone off in search of sustenance.

'Simon Keggie's his name.'

I knew the name from somewhere. 'The MSP? The one who battered the housebreaker?'

'He's not an MSP. He's Provost of West Lothian. That's not to say he wouldn't like to be an MSP. He stood in the election last year. The trouble is he's a Tory.'

I wondered why he'd even bothered. A Tory candidate in Linlithgow running for Parliament had about as much chance as Long John Silver running for a bus. In recent years the constituency had become an SNP stronghold, and before the Scottish Parliament, Tam Dalyell of Scottish

Labour had been MP for over twenty years. Although there had been a recent Tory resurgence, they were still a long way short of the mark.

'There was also the fact he was charged with assault the week before the election.' Sammy shook his head sadly. 'I really thought Keggie might have been in with a shout this time. The Labour candidate didn't know if he supported Karl Marx or Groucho Marx, and Simon Keggie is well-liked as a councillor. Very hands on. He's old school, and I don't mean old *private* school. Keggie went to Linlithgow Academy and he used to work for a living, and he lives locally. He's a man of the people.'

There were no prizes for guessing who Sammy had voted for. Tories wore kilts too.

'This has been a party-political broadcast on behalf of the Scottish Conservative and Unionist Party,' I said. 'But you're right. Being charged with assault on the eve of the election wouldn't have helped his cause. Anyway, I thought the case would have been well over by now.'

Sammy necked his drink and looked around for another one. 'Simon was an old pal of Eddie's, and he was determined to get him off.'

'When you say Keggie was an old pal of Eddie's ...'

'Don't worry,' Sammy said, reading my mind. 'This is Eddie Frew we're talking about. He didn't do mates' rates. The fee is all sorted out with the client.'

'How much?'

Sammy relayed the sort of hourly rate with which we at Munro & Co were entirely unfamiliar but would very much have liked to become better acquainted. 'Two-thirds for you, one for me,' he said. 'I've got to wet my beak.'

For a legal aid lawyer, even two-thirds of the figure quoted was beyond the dreams of avarice.

Sammy moved closer, putting a hand on my shoulder. 'What do you say, Robbie?'

I looked at him through the fog of pound signs swimming before my eyes. There wasn't much I could say, other than, raising my glass, 'Here's to Eddie.'

2

Since my brother and I had embarked on our new sports agency business venture, we'd had quite a few lunches together. To those mealtimes we'd invited promising young footballers, excited, but not nearly so excited as their parents, to be dining with former Glasgow Rangers and Scotland hero Malky Munro, at his favourite restaurant, Mr Singh's India on Elderslie Street, Glasgow.

So far, we hadn't signed up any major prospects, but lived in hope. Malky was a great frontman. To our prospective clients he might be a relic from another age, a time of muddy pitches and scary tackles, but to their fathers, especially those of the blue, red and white variety, he was a legend. Most were ready to have their sons sign with Munro & Co before the dip of the first pakora, and as for the mums, when my brother turned on the charm full blast, any reservations melted like a dollop of yoghurt on a chicken phaal.

It tended to be around coffee and mints, and, it has to be said, to noticeably less excitement from the mums and dads, that I'd be formally introduced into the proceedings to discuss what my brother referred to as 'all the legal stuff'.

Today was different. Our lunch guest had cancelled, so when Simon Keggie phoned for a pre-trial consultation, I'd invited him along instead. He'd brought his wife with him. I wouldn't say she was mutton dressed as lamb, but there was a definite whiff of mint sauce about Mrs Keggie. Hair cut in a severe fringe that along with the heavily painted-on eyebrows gave her something of an Egyptian look. My first impression was of an ambitious, go-ahead woman looking to the future. Keggie, on the other hand, grey hair swept back with Brylcreem, dressed in blazer and cavalry twill slacks, seemed to me like a man who'd had a glimpse of the future, didn't like it much and was happy to stay in the past.

Keggie didn't say a lot, and it was his wife who kept the chat going. If she'd come along because she was worried for her husband, she didn't look it. Neither of them did. Still, it was a pleasant change to have lunch guests less interested in listening to Malky's footballing anecdotes, than in what I had to say on the law. Not that we talked a great deal about the upcoming case. Keggie's position was already known to me and set out in detail in the precognition Eddie Frew had taken from him at the start of the case. Lunch was just a chance for me to introduce myself and, I supposed, to reassure the client that his money was being well spent. If there'd been anything terribly confidential to discuss, I'd have told Malky not to bother coming, but he'd made the booking and I was hoping he'd pay.

'It's terrible about Eddie,' Keggie said, pushing his empty plate to one side. 'So sudden. It's good of you to step in.'

Mrs Keggie smiled at me. 'Mr Frew's business partner was full of praise. He said you were the very man for the job,' and with that she sat back in her chair, waiting for me to confirm that, for the job, I was indeed the very man.

'Your husband has a fine defence,' I said, 'and I'm

told the Crown aren't bringing the jury in until Friday morning.' I turned to my client once more. 'If you'd like to meet up again tomorrow at my office in order to go over things more thoroughly—'

'Do we need to?' Keggie asked. 'I spoke with Eddie a week or so before he died, and we went over things then. I don't have anything to add and I'm sure you know the case inside out.' He gave me a solid wink. 'Eddie said it was a definite winner.'

Typical Eddie. Tell the client they're taking a walk, accept a large fee in advance and, when they get sent down, blame the jury and act surprised all the way to the bank. Personally, I'd always found predicting the outcome of a case to be a highly delicate business. Too optimistic and clients became blasé and appeared arrogant to the jury or, worse, were unappreciative of your efforts. Too pessimistic and they went off and found someone more optimistic. 'Yes, you do have excellent prospects,' I said, 'but, of course, it's a criminal trial, and anything can happen.'

He squinted at me across the condiments as though I'd suddenly lapsed into a foreign language. His wife reached over and gave my wrist a gentle squeeze. 'But anything *won't* happen, will it, Mr Munro? Eddie assured us—'

I cleared my throat. 'Like I say, I can't remember having had a better line of defence to present and am not thinking about anything other than an acquittal.'

She smiled, looked down at the tiny face of her gold watch, folded her napkin and laid it alongside her plate.

Keggie took the hint. Rising from the table he pulled his wife's chair out for her and she floated to her feet.

'I don't think we need to meet again before the trial, Mr Munro,' he said. 'Pat and I ...' He put an arm around his wife's shoulders. 'We have every confidence in you.' He shook my hand, then, with a nod to Malky and without waiting for coffee, left the table, settling the bill on the way out.

I watched him go. Was there ever a more perfect client? Not only a private fee-payer, but one with an actual defence.

Malky set down his knife and fork and tugged the napkin out of his collar. 'Let me get this straight. This Keggie guy struck somebody on the head with a baseball bat?'

It hadn't been a baseball bat. It had been a shillelagh walking stick, solid Irish blackthorn. Might as well have been an iron bar.

'How many times did he hit him?'

I wasn't quite sure how many times. Enough times for the victim to just manage to stagger out of Keggie's house, collapse in the street and subsequently be diagnosed with a linear fracture of the skull and a brain bleed that led to a medically induced coma. 'Repeatedly,' I said. 'In law that *could* mean only twice.'

'And was it twice?'

'Possibly three or four.' Malky raised an eyebrow. 'Okay, perhaps plus VAT,' I conceded.

'And Sammy told you that's a great defence?'

Non-lawyers don't understand what a great defence is. They think a great defence is being captured on CCTV having lunch with the Moderator of the Church of Scotland in Edinburgh, while your alleged victim is being assaulted in Inverness. In reality, there's no such thing as a truly great defence. If there was, there wouldn't be a prosecution. For defence lawyers, just having a story to tell the jury was about as great as it got. I ripped a piece of naan, dipped it in the last of my curry sauce, swirled it around the plate and stuffed it in my face.

'I'll admit,' I said, once there was room in my mouth for words, 'that the defence may not seem all that great to you. But it's sound enough, and what's especially great is that the client is paying privately. I wouldn't be doing it otherwise. I know I need to try and focus more on the sports agency side of things. It's just a pity there isn't more work coming in.'

'Do you really think you can get him off?' Malky asked.

I shrugged. 'It's a criminal trial. Like I told Keggie, anything can happen. It's pretty much fifty/fifty.'

'But that's not what you told him.'

'I told him his prospects of an acquittal were good.'

'No, you said they were excellent.'

'Look at it this way,' I said. 'He's at home one night, and someone breaks in—'

'How?'

'How what?'

'How did they break in?'

'What is this? Cross-examination?'

'No, I just wondered.'

'Well, it wasn't that much of a break-in. It looks like he came through the front door.'

'What? Smashed right through it?'

'Simon Keggie lives in the sticks. He doesn't always lock the door at night.'

'Let me get this straight. You say this burglar—'

'This is Scotland, Malky. We don't have burglars, we have housebreakers.'

'Whatever he is, you're saying he just opened the door and waltzed into your client's home?'

'That's right. And when confronted by this stranger

16

in his own home, late at night, my client was scared, apprehensive, and fearful for his own safety,' I said, in the same way I'd said it to Keggie over lunch, in the hope that he'd remember those words when it came time to give evidence. Once he hit the witness box he was on his own. I couldn't put words into his mouth. No leading questions allowed. 'You see, Malky, for a self-defence to work, three things have to be made out. Firstly, that the accused was fearful for his own safety, which you must admit is likely if a stranger comes swanning into your gaff at midnight.'

Malky shrugged his concession to that point.

'Secondly, without putting himself at a disadvantage, the accused must take any opportunity for escape without the need to resort to violence.' I felt a jury would think it a bit much to ask a householder to flee his own home. It was the third criterion I felt was slightly lacking, and that was the use of proportionate force. Malky had noticed the chink in the defence too. He leaned forward across the table, and, lowering his voice, said, 'Your guy whacked him repeatedly on the head with a big stick until his brain began to bleed. Was the burglar—'

'Housebreaker.'

'Intruder. Was he armed?' He hadn't been. 'Then you'd have thought one hit, maybe even two would have been enough, but—'

'Keggie panicked. What was he supposed to do?' I asked, I hoped rhetorically.

'Not smash his head in while he must have been trying to get away from your mental client,' Malky said, swilling at a pint of Cobra lager.

According to the medical reports, there had been minor injuries to the complainer's back as well as to his head.

'I suppose the intruder could have been running away ...' I said.

'Of course he was running away.' Malky set his pint down and wiped his mouth on a white linen napkin. 'He walks into a house and your client starts in about him with a dirty big piece of wood. Sounds like a running-away situation to me.'

'But he could have been running to find a weapon of his own,' I said. 'My client couldn't take any chances. He reacted instinctively, and the walking stick was right there by the front door. You have to take into account the heat of the blood.'

'The only blood seems to be coming out of the other guy's head,' Malky said.

'What would you do in similar circumstances, ladies and gentlemen?' I swept an arm at an imaginary jury, almost spilling Malky's drink. 'Until we could be assured all danger has definitely passed, who amongst us would not continue to protect ourselves, our family—'

'Does he have any family?'

'I don't think there are any kids, but you saw his wife.'

'I certainly did,' Malky said. 'Punching above his weight, isn't he? Shouldn't even be in the same ring. What is it about women and politicians? They're all over them like skin on a dumpling.'

'Mrs Keggie wasn't well and in bed. Seriously, who's going to find my sixty-year-old, no previous convictions client, guilty for assaulting a burglar in those circum-stances?' I said.

Malky corrected me. 'Don't you mean, housebreaker? Although he could just have been someone who'd got a bit drunk, lost their way, walked into the wrong house – we've all been there.'

'Not all of us, Malky.'

'And you really think you'll get him off?'

'By the time I'm finished with the jury, they'll probably award Keggie a medal,' I said. 'Anyway, I'll need to make tracks.'

Malky reached out and grabbed the hand I'd put on the table, ready to push myself to my feet.

'Sit down and have a coffee,' he said. 'There's something I need to tell you.'

He frowned and stared down at his plate. He hadn't been quite himself today. Unusually for him, he'd looked a tad worried. Not so worried that he hadn't managed to tuck away a lamb tikka ambala with a haggis naan on the side, but worried nonetheless.

'What's wrong?' I asked, when our plates had been cleared away and replaced by two coffees and a couple of after-dinner mints. 'It's not because of that painting again, is it?'

On the wall of Mr Singh's restaurant there was a large oil painting of a fantasy Scotland team, containing all the greats: Law, Greig, Baxter, Souness, Dalglish ... but no place for big Malky Munro. It was something of a sore point, and no visit to the restaurant was complete without Malky making a sarcastic remark to a member of staff along the lines of how the artist must have confused his profile with that of Billy McNeil.

Malky shook his head. 'It's not that. It's this.' He removed a piece of paper from the pocket of his jacket that was hung over the back of his chair. He unfolded it, laid it on the table and smoothed it out with the side of his hand. It was a letter. The BBC logo at the top right corner. 'It's a job offer,' he said.

'A job offer?' I picked it up. 'Sportschat?'

'It's a new programme they're launching on that Scottish channel. They say sports, what they mean is football. I'm going to be a regular. Starting next season, whenever there's a big game on, I'll be there, talking about the match before kick-off, at half-time and at the end. I'll even be interviewing the players and managers. You know the kind of thing.'

I knew exactly the kind of thing. Malky was already paid to host a twice-weekly football phone-in on local radio, for which he was paid to voice profound opinions such as, 'I thought the longer the game went without a goal, the more chance there was of a draw.' Not forgetting 'There's no game bigger than a semi-final', or my own personal favourite, when bemoaning Scotland's lack of world-class talent: 'That's the trouble with our football immortals – most of them are dead'.

I scanned down the page to where some figures were printed in bold. 'That number can't be right,' I said. 'They can't really be going to pay you that much.'

Malky shrugged modestly. 'If you want the best you have to pay for it.'

'But they could get someone who knows what they're talking about for this kind of money,' I said.

He snatched the letter back. 'What it means is, I'm going to be dead busy for the next wee while, and—'

'You're jacking in our sports agency business? The one that was your idea? The one that caused me to ditch most of my legal aid clients because I was supposed to work smart not hard? It's been six months and all I've got on my books are four female footballers who are paid boot money, and half a dozen overly optimistic schoolboys.'

'Little acorns,' Malky said, returning the letter to his

jacket pocket. He helped himself to one of the two after-dinner mints. 'Anyway, it's only temporary.'

'How temporary?'

'Just until the telly folk stop paying me silly amounts of money. Maybe they'll get fed up with me after a season.' He laughed at the absurdity of such a notion, and I had to agree. I watched a lot of football on TV. I was familiar with the so-called experts on show. My brother might be as bright as two in the morning, but he was the Bell Rock Lighthouse amidst the dimness of the competition.

Malky smiled at me across the table. 'Go back to doing what you enjoy, Robbie. Look at how excited you are about this latest case. A good defence, good fun and good money at the end of it. Sports agency,' he scoffed, as though my recent change in career course hadn't all been down to him. 'It's not for you. What you like doing is arguing with folk in court. Of course it is,' he said. 'You love it.' Reaching across the table, he ruffled my hair with one hand while nicking the last after-dinner mint with the other.

3

Sex. It's an expensive business. Not the act itself, which, somehow, I've always managed to avoid having to pay for. It's more the after-effects, which for me was the arrival of children; two, at the last count. And while they are the most precious things in the world, as my bank manager would tell you, they are a steady drain on already depleted resources.

One person who thought he'd found a way to make money out of sex, and, arguably, children, was Jeff Freeman, a scrawny young man with lots of hair and teeth, and a voice that made your skin want to crawl off in search of better digs.

Jeff had made some money mining cryptocurrency, whatever that was. He used that cash to further his various enterprises, for as well as excess hair, teeth, technological expertise and general creepiness, Jeff was also host to a lot of ideas, most of which, when tested, didn't sit full square with the Scots criminal law. It was when the Scots criminal law found out about Jeff's ideas, that he liked to call upon the services of Munro & Co., Linlithgow's finest, Linlithgow's only, criminal defence lawyers. Well, lawyer in the singular: me.

Most whisky aficionados still mourn the passing of St Magdalene's, which distilled its last drop of aqua vitae in 1983. But the Royal Burgh had four other lost distilleries, one of those being The Mains, a drop kick from Linlithgow Rugby Club, and which over the centuries had changed from distillery to brewery to film studio. Although, when I say film studio, that was what Jeff liked to call his recently refurbished two-bedroom flat.

'I have to say it doesn't sound to me like you were making an arthouse movie, Jeff,' was my take on things after he'd given me his side of the story. 'What I'm fairly certain you've just described is what we normal people call, a porno.' He looked hurt. I cut him off before he could protest. 'Tell me again the name of this movie the procurator fiscal has taken such exception to?'

'That's not important,' Jeff said, clearing his throat. From one of the light blue, looks-like-leather armchairs he lifted a cardboard box containing, amongst other items, a pair of flippers, a nun's habit and a coiled pink feather boa that spilled over the edge. He placed it on the floor and sat down.

'*Thongs of Praise*,' I answered for him. 'Directed by Jeff Freeman. Not exactly Ingmar Bergman's *Fanny and Alexander*, is it?'

'Fanny? Really? And Alexander? Is that a proper film? Great title,' Jeff said. I could tell he was making a mental note. 'Anyway, whose side are you on, Robbie?'

I'm on your side, Jeff,' I said. 'If—'

'If it's not legal aid?'

We'd already gone over this ground when he'd called me to ask if I'd come over. Jeff never called by phone. He always Skyped or Zoomed. Not that I minded internet video calls. They were free after all. I just preferred people not to see the faces I was pulling when I spoke to them.

'But, Robbie. I've no money.'

What he meant was he had no money for legal fees,

23

though I'd bet he had plenty stashed away for funding his dodgy enterprises.

'It's not fair,' he said. 'I've suffered enough. Look at the state of my flat. The cops have trashed it.'

I was going to point out that as the police raid had been nearly two weeks ago, there'd been plenty of time for a quick tidy round. Jeff didn't want to be interrupted.

'They took everything,' he said. 'My PC, my laptop, my phone. There's not a silicon chip left in the place.'

'Take away your director's chair and camera equipment too, did they?' I said.

It turned out Jeff's camera equipment amounted to an iPhone X, electrical tape and a tripod.

'How can you make a film with a mobile phone?' I said. 'Where's your sound system?'

He sighed. 'I was making a dirty movie, Robbie. Not *The Archers* omnibus. Honestly, I really am broke.'

One of the joys, and there hadn't been that many, of being in partnership with my brother in our fledgling sports agency, was the luxury of turning away legal aid cases, especially prosecutions under s.52 of the Civic Government (Scotland) Act 1982. Sometimes, however, the defence lawyer's love of a challenge kicked in.

'What's your defence?' I didn't sit down on the other armchair, because I didn't know where it had been, although I had made certain assumptions.

'The girls swore they were seventeen,' he whined.

'That's still not a defence to a charge of making child pornography,' I said. 'The girls would still be classed as children even if they were seventeen.' I could tell Jeff was confused. I didn't know why. Scots law was simple when it came to age. You could join the army at sixteen but you weren't to be trusted with fireworks. You could marry but not buy a bottle of champagne to celebrate. You could have sex but not be photographed naked. You couldn't watch a horror movie in the cinema, but you were free to watch the Parliament channel on TV.

'What's complicated about that?' I said.

Jeff was horrified on behalf of feminists everywhere. 'What! Are you telling me an independent seventeen-year-old burd can't —'

'It's probably best not to refer to young women as burds in court,' I said. 'Not unless these particular seventeen-year-olds actually *were* your burds, in which case you may have a statutory defence *if* you're in a relationship with both of them, they consented to being filmed and the film was to be distributed only to each of them.'

It seemed none of the above criteria applied.

'How could I make money off a film that only two people get to see?' Jeff said. You could fault his morals, but not his business acumen. He dropped his head into his hands and held it there for a while. 'Will you do it?' I heard his muffled voice say after a while. He looked up. 'Will you take on my case? Please, Robbie. What if I promise never to make another movie ever again? I don't care if Warner Brothers come battering at the door. All they'll get from me is *no thanks very much, go see what Ridley Scott's doing.*' He got up from his chair, brushed back his hair, and put all his teeth on display. 'Do this for me, Robbie, and I'll be in your debt big time.'

I had no idea what possible use I, or any right-minded individual, could make of a debt owed by Jeff Freeman, no matter the size of it, but now that Malky had bailed on me, legal aid beggars couldn't be choosers. 'When are you at court?'

'Tomorrow.'

'What is it? A bail undertaking?'

It wasn't. It was a cited case. From under his armchair cushion, Jeff produced a summary complaint. Just as I thought, it libelled two charges: one of making, the other of possessing indecent images of a child. The maximum sentence was twelve months.

'Tomorrow's no good for me,' I said. 'I'm busy. You'll need to go yourself.'

'I can't, Robbie. I wouldn't know what to do. What if they start reading out the charges in front of everyone? I've just had new double-glazing put in.'

I flicked through the pages of the summons. 'You can plead not guilty by letter,' I said. 'Sign on the line, date it and take it to the sheriff clerk's office this afternoon before four o'clock. They'll deal with it in chambers tomorrow and send you the dates for your intermediate diet and trial through the post. You can phone me with them later.'

I flicked back to the charge sheet. The girls were called Dani Quin and Layla McEwan. Their dates of birth showed them both to be seventeen years of age.

'What were you filming?' I said. 'A remake of *Rita, Sue and Bob Too*?'

Jeff's filmography knowledge didn't stretch as far 1980s British classics. 'I've not even seen *Rita, Sue and Bob One*,' he said. 'Tell me, Robbie. What are my chances?'

'What do they look like, this Dani and Layla?' I asked.

'I dunno. Normal I suppose. Dani's a blonde, Layla's got brown hair and … He cupped his hands and put them to his chest. 'A nice pair—'

'Do they look their age or older?'

'No, Robbie, definitely older. A lot older. You'd easily mistake them for seventeen and a half, eighteen. It's not fair. I was paying good money. Surely they've got a right to earn a living like those Formula 1 grid girls, and the ones at the darts.'

'Jeff, how about you stop whining for a second, and go get me a piece of paper?' I said.

He left the room and came back with a piece of lined paper that looked as though it had been ripped from a school jotter. I took out a pen and began to write on it. When I'd finished, I told him to sign at the bottom and date it. 'Put that in the same envelope as the form pleading not guilty, and hand it over to the clerk when you go.'

Jeff took the paper and folded it along with the form and stuffed them into the brown envelope that had come with his summons. 'Then what?'

'Then turn around and walk out of there before anyone can ask you any questions.'

'And after that?'

'After that …?' I said, 'After that we cross our fingers and wait for the trial.'

4

A lot of my clients wore suits. Simon Keggie was different. His suit fitted him. It was charcoal grey over a crisp white shirt, set off by a neatly knotted green, red and black striped tie that may have been regimental in provenance. Add to it a head of steel-grey hair and a matching clipped moustache, and he looked like the sort of chap who'd stand up if a lady entered the room and could call a bag of Werther's Originals into action at a moment's notice. What the man sitting in the dock at Livingston Sheriff Court that Friday morning didn't look like, was the sort of person who'd dent your head with a blackthorn walking stick. For that was the charge facing him, more legalistically set out in the indictment in which Her Majesty's Advocate alleged: *you Simon Edward Keggie did assault Angus MacDonald, seize him by the clothing, and repeatedly strike him on the head and body with a walking stick or similar instrument all to his severe injury, permanent disfigurement and to the danger of life.*

Keggie saw me looking round at him from my seat in the well of the court. I gave him a professional smile and received in return a polite nod of acknowledgement. He seemed just as confident as he had when we'd had lunch two days previously. I was pretty confident myself. So much so that I'd not bothered with any of the spurious pre-trial objections I normally employed to try and soften

28

up, or at least annoy, the Crown, represented today by Josh Wedderburn, a youngish procurator fiscal depute who didn't just look like he'd been handed this poisoned chalice, but like he'd taken a slug out of it as well.

The case was called, the jury empanelled and the ladies and gentlemen sent off to prepare themselves for the start of the trial. Forty-five minutes later they'd not returned. How long did it take fifteen people to phone their bosses and childminders, take off their coats and make a trip to the loo?

Eventually, a court officer came for me. 'There's a witness problem,' she said. 'Someone's not turned up or, at least, they're running late.' The two most hoped-for lines of defence in any court case are, one, the witnesses won't turn up, and two, if they do, they won't speak up. It looked like I was one-for-one already.

I returned to the courtroom, where the sheriff was being brought on without the jury. Another reason to be cheerful. Sheriff John Sibbald drafted in especially lest it be suggested the local sheriffs were biased in favour of a local politician. I'd come across Sheriff Sibbald once or twice in my travels and knew he was not the typical recruit to the shrieval bench. Yes, like so many others, he had not darkened the door of a Sheriff Court before donning the horsehair wig, and, of course, he had only the vaguest understanding of criminal law and procedure. In fact, I strongly suspected he'd never come across an actual crime, if one discounted the price of a G&T at the New Club. No, the difference between Sheriff Sibbald and most sheriffs was that he not only looked happy to be collecting his fat six-figure salary while accruing a copper-bottomed pension, but he was polite and almost courteous to us defence lawyers. How he'd slipped through the net of the Judicial Appointments Board selection process I had absolutely no idea.

It was when I'd sat down and looked across the table that I noticed for some reason the young PF depute was no longer facing me across the well of the court, but had been replaced by Hugh Ogilvie, the procurator fiscal himself

'Mr Munro . . .' Having just taken my seat, I stood up again on being addressed by the sheriff. 'You will be unaware of the situation, but I can tell you that while you have been elsewhere, no doubt studying your brief . . .' I'd been in the agents' room studying a batch of old Commando comics someone had dumped on the table, having a coffee and talking football. 'Your friend, Mr Wedderburn for the Crown, advised the court that he was not feeling at all well and required to withdraw. Although Mr Ogilvie has stepped in for the purpose of today's proceedings, sadly, neither he nor anyone else at his office is available to conduct the trial, and accordingly the Crown is seeking to postpone—'

'Would Mr Wedderburn's sudden ill health have anything to do with the absence of an essential witness?' I asked. The sheriff ignored my remark. I tried again. 'Is your lordship aware that this trial time-bars today?' It's the dilemma defence lawyers hated. It was all very well agreeing a fat hourly rate, but you had to put the hours in to earn it. If Keggie's trial was deserted at this stage, there was very little in it for me. Still, the basic instinct of the defence lawyer to have his client acquitted, tends to override the prospect of financial gain.

'As I was about to say before you interrupted me, Mr Munro—'

'And that the trial has been adjourned twice before on Crown motion?'

The sheriff closed his eyes and waited to see if I had anything more to say, in a manner that suggested I'd better not have. When he was satisfied I'd stopped objecting, he opened his eyes again, looked down at me and sighed.

'I am conscious that Mr Keggie has had this matter weighing heavily upon him for some time now, and—'

'A year,' I said, only trying to help.

'Thank you, Mr Munro. And, accordingly, is entitled to hold the Crown to its statutory requirement to prevent a delay in his trial. Since the Crown has been unable to commence this trial within the twelve-month period laid down by Parliament, I propose to desert the case simpliciter.'

I could scarcely believe it. Most sheriffs would have used the unavailability of the prosecutor through illness as a perfectly good reason to extend the time-bar.

Hugh Ogilvie jumped to his feet. In moments of high dudgeon his left eye tended to bulge. 'But my Lord. The trial *has* commenced. The jury is empanelled.'

The sheriff beat me to it. 'Yes, Mr Ogilvie, but no witness has yet been sworn. Which means that trial has not *formally* commenced.'

Ogilvie was upright again. I'd never seen his dudgeon higher. His face was red, the left eye protruding so far I thought the clerk might have to double as wicketkeeper. Voice raised, he said, 'Then if your lordship would allow the jury to return, I propose to call the first witness, Police Sergeant Raymond Collins.'

It was a clever move. The sheriff didn't seem to think so. 'I was of the understanding there was no one available to conduct this trial, Mr Ogilvie. Were rumours of your own unavailability greatly exaggerated?'

'M'lord, I would like to call Police Sergeant Collins,

have him take the oath, and then adjourn the case until Tuesday. It is a court holiday on Monday, and it would no doubt suit all concerned, in any event, if the trial could proceed and the jury hear the evidence without empty days in between. During the adjournment I have already arranged for one of my colleagues in a neighbouring jurisdiction to step into the breach. Miss Jordan will have read the papers and be fully prepared by Tuesday.'

The sheriff didn't seem entirely enamoured with that suggestion. Neither was I. The only procurator fiscal depute I knew from a neighbouring jurisdiction called Miss Jordan, was also known as Mrs Munro. Surely Ogilvie wasn't so desperate he'd instruct my wife to prosecute a case her husband was defending? But it looked like he was determined this trial would proceed. He ploughed on.

'Is it your Lordship's position that if Mr Munro were to take ill ...' Ogilvie looked across at me like he hoped I might suddenly be struck down with something debilitating, 'that in order to avoid the time-bar, you would insist the accused continued unrepresented?'

The old comparative justice angle was one often tried by the defence, though with little success. Usually sheriffs were prepared to grant a Crown motion to adjourn for the flimsiest of reasons, whereas if the defence sought a postponement there had better be at least a DEFCON 2 situation or threats of an imminent global pandemic.

'Of course, I could always call upon your Lordship to write on it,' Ogilvie said, which was legalese for *if you don't agree I'm going to appeal, and you can spend the weekend writing a note*. He was really sticking the boot in.

Sheriff Sibbald, still unhappy, eventually succumbed. 'Very well, Mr Ogilvie. There is no need to call the witness. I will send the ladies and gentlemen away until Tuesday and allow an extension of the time-bar until then. However ...' the sheriff said, looking over me to my client, 'if the Crown is not ready to proceed at ten o'clock on that day, I will desert this prosecution and Mr Keggie will be freed from this charge for all time.' And with that and a sympathetic nod to the man in the dock, the sheriff allowed the court officer to lead him off the bench.

5

'I wasn't expecting you back so soon,' Grace Mary said, sliding open a drawer in the reception desk and cramming a set of knitting needles and a large ball of pink wool inside. 'And there's no need to look at me like that.'

'I'm not looking at you like anything. If you want to take an early lunch at ... what is it ...? Half eleven? That's fine by me.'

'Lunch? What are you talking about, Robbie? You know I don't go for lunch until twelve. It's just that things were a bit slow and so I thought I'd catch up on some emergency knitting.'

I hurried to the window. 'What's up? Is there a fire across the street and you're knitting them a rope ladder?'

Grace Mary slammed the drawer shut like my fingers were in it. 'Joanna called. She said to remind you that she's going out tonight with the folk from the Fiscal's office. They're all coming through here and going to that new Indian place down the other end of the High Street.'

The Crown Office and Procurator Fiscal Service had once more decided that they could not do without the services of my wife, and she'd been given a new flexi-time contract to accommodate our childcare situation. The alternative had been for her to come to work with me. I felt she could have taken longer to consider her options. Those that made such decisions at the COPFS had ruled out a return to West Lothian, because that was where I plied most of my trade, so she was now prosecuting in the adjacent Falkirk jurisdiction. Nonetheless, Joanna had retained a lot of friends in Livingston Fiscal's office and was always invited to their nights out, events that happened whenever anyone had a baby, got engaged, retired or just if they hadn't had a night out in a while.

'Another one? What are they celebrating this time? Have they brought back the birch?'

'She didn't say.' Grace Mary stood, picked up a wire tray of incoming mail and followed me through to my office. The place looked so different now, redecorated to present a professional image to the potential sports agency clients my brother was supposed to be lining up for me. Thus far no one had been injured in the rush, and it didn't look as if anyone would be now that Malky had bailed. 'What she did say was to tell you that she's taken a change of clothes and is going straight from work. Your dad's got wee Jamie and he's picking up Tina after school. You've to leave early, collect the kids from your dad and give them their tea. She'll try not to be back too late. Got all that? Good.'

I stared down at the clutter of case files and unopened mail on my desk. How was I supposed to leave early?

Grace Mary didn't see the problem. 'Quit complaining,' she said, yanking open a cabinet drawer and stuffing letters inside files. 'You were expecting to be in court all day. Now that you're back early you can clear your desk, see your four o'clock appointment and be on your way. But before all that you'd better go see Brendan Paterson. He dropped in when you were at court saying something about a licensing appeal. He wasn't very happy. And make sure you get cash up front. You know what publicans are like. Worse than farmers for not paying bills.'

My day sorted, Grace Mary finished her filing and left. Hopefully my four o'clock client wouldn't take long. I checked the diary. It was Stephanie Meek, up on yet another breach of the peace charge. At least that was some good news. Murder, rape, armed robbery: you'd be forgiven for thinking those are what criminal defence lawyers are most interested in, but they're not. Murder is high-pressure work, invariably for low legal aid pay, sex cases are just icky, and thieves, the ones that get caught anyway, seldom have any money to pay a decent fee, which is often why they're thieves in the first place. Worse, you have to wait ages for serious cases to come to trial, and a lot longer to get paid.

No, while the occasional High Court case can be an interesting diversion, they are also stressful and terrible for cashflow. What a defence lawyer wants is a client-base consisting mainly of bams, or, to use the correct legal terminology, bampots. Bams come in all shapes, genders and ages, but what binds them together as a subset of my clientele is their ability to commit minor offences on a frequent basis. While in recent years the Scottish Government had cut back on prosecuting bams, instead sending them letters with orders for unpaid work they'd never do and fines they'd never pay, it was still the case that bams could be profitable. If a Scots lawyer can get a four-figure legal aid fee out of a rape or armed robbery they're doing exceptionally well, and with so few murders committed in Scotland, well, there aren't enough to go around. The fact is, an enthusiastic bam will earn a lawyer more in a good year than a serial killer, of which there are far fewer than crime fiction would have us believe.

Even though I'd been cutting back on legal aid work to concentrate on the fledgling sports agency business,

I'd kept on my regular bams out of loyalty more than anything else. Which was just as well because the fledgling had been shot down in a cloud of feathers.

Stephanie 'Meeko' Meek had been a bam of mine for years. A young woman with a blonde bob, a vicious temper and an unquenchable thirst for Buckfast tonic wine, Meeko's bamishness stemmed mainly from an irrational dislike of drug addicts. Most people aren't all that keen on junkies, but Meeko really, really hated them, and, whenever she came across one, thought it her public duty to carry out summary justice, something that usually involved the green glass container of the aforementioned tonic wine.

It's not everyone who complains about a spot of junkie-bashing; however, Meeko's problem was that after a couple of bottles of Buckie, she saw junkies everywhere. A person could be walking to church, Bible under the arm, and to Meeko's alcohol-befuddled mind it was just another junkie transporting their goods by innovative means. Fortunately for Meeko I'd had an inordinately high success rate when it came to court proceedings against her. Prise the bottle of Buckfast from her hand, sober her up, stick her in the dock, and when some drug-zombie, usually male, even more usually with a string of convictions, alleged that the cherub in the summer frock had kicked lumps out of him, reasonable doubts tended to abound.

That Friday afternoon, Meeko didn't show up for her four o'clock appointment. One thing I've possibly forgotten to mention while extolling the virtues of bams is their extreme unreliability. It's part of their charm. Reconciled to yet another Friday evening spent babysitting, I was all set to go home when I wondered ...

When I called my dad's house, as expected, Tina answered.

'How you doing, pet?'

'Fine thanks, Dad. Do you want to speak to Gramps?'

'Ehm, no, that's okay. Just tell him I'm doing something very, very important and that he's to give you and Jamie your tea and then take you home afterwards and wait until I get back.'

I heard my dad's voice in the background asking who was on the phone.

'It's Dad!' Tina yelled. 'He's doing something very important and—'

'Anyway, got to go, honey-bun. Tell Gramps I'll be back as soon as I can.'

I hung up and told Grace Mary to hold all my calls. My mobile phone buzzed in my jacket pocket a couple of times after that. Could have been business. Could have been my dad. To be on the safe side I let it ring out.

6

The Red Corner Bar of a Friday evening is a haven for those who seek to escape not only parental responsibilities, but loud music, political correctness and craft gins. Having given up on Meeko and made the necessary domestic arrangements, I adjourned there at half-past five. The first hour was tortuous with the proprietor, Brendan 'the Linlithgow Lion' Paterson, veteran winner of Commonwealth boxing gold, banging on about the possible loss of his pub licence. He'd been at me about it for weeks, ever since a police raid had found a team of underagers drinking in the pool room through the back. It was the final straw atop the Red Corner Bar's regular weekend punch-up, a local tradition to which the Licensing Board was keen to put a stop. The length of my bar tab and the fact that most of those having said punch-ups were clients of mine, were just two reasons Brendan had insisted I present myself at the upcoming Licensing Board hearing and plead his case. Tonight, I was being forced to mull over the finer legal points, albeit aided by one or two, or maybe it was five or six, on-the-house single malts, when I was joined by Sammy Veitch.

Sammy, though to a lesser degree than his recently deceased business partner, was something of a legend in the legal world of the Lothians. Short and dapper, a greying Van Dyke jutting from his chin like a permanent challenge, Sammy had correctly predicted the demise of Scotland's legal aid system many years before and transitioned into a no-win-no-fee personal injury lawyer. Sammy chased ambulances like a half-pint of heavy chased a fine single malt, and the same silver tongue that had charmed many a jury in the past, now assured the injured, and not so injured, that not only did they deserve compensation, but that he was the very man to make sure they received top dollar.

He reached up to where I was sitting on a bar stool and put an arm around my neck. 'If it isn't Linlithgow's finest criminal lawyer.' He paused, adding with immaculate timing, 'You are still the only criminal lawyer in Linlithgow aren't you, Robbie?'

At least Brendan found it amusing. 'What about you, Sammy?' he said. 'Fancy representing me at the Licensing Board? Robbie's not too hopeful about my prospects. You could persuade them to give me another chance, couldn't you?'

Another legendary thing about Sammy was his thrift. It was said he'd once found a sticking-plaster and gone off and self-harmed. If Brendan thought Sammy was likely to give away free legal advice, he should have known better.

Sammy looked at my empty glass, frowned and scratched his beard. 'Drinking alone, Robbie? Brendan, a dram of your finest malt for my young friend.'

'What you having, Robbie?' Brendan asked.

'He's having the same as me,' Sammy said, 'and I'm buying.' This wasn't like Sammy. The Sammy Veitch I knew was not a man inclined to strong drink. Not unless someone else was paying. He pointed to a bottle of twenty-one-year-old Springbank on the top shelf where it had remained for as long as I could remember. It was unopened. Unopened because Brendan's clientele would sooner buy a bottle of blended whisky than a single nip of Campbeltown's liquid gold.

'That's not for sale,' Brendan said. 'It's just for show.'

Sammy took out his wallet. 'How much?'

'It would need to be a tenner for a hauf,' Brendan said after a moment or two's mental arithmetic.

Sammy slapped a twenty on the counter. 'Set them up.'

Brendan called over Mickey, his probationary barman. Mickey was Brendan's sister's boy. Six foot three and built to last, he was newly released on licence after a six-stretch for armed robbery, and doing his best to keep in with his boss. Not the brightest, Mickey would have run through a brick wall if Brendan had asked him – so long as he'd pointed him in the right direction. He reached up to the top shelf and brought down the precious bottle.

'What are we celebrating?' I asked, after Brendan had blown the dust off and poured a couple of measures, careful not to spill a drop.

Sammy raised his Glencairn glass to eye-level. 'What we are celebrating, young Robbie, is your great success in court today.'

'Not that great,' I said. 'The case hasn't even started.'

Sammy admired the contents for a moment then poured them into his mouth with a lot of chomping in the process. 'And it never will.'

'What do you mean?' I said.

Sammy wiped his moustache. 'Well, it time-barred, didn't it?' He smacked his lips and set the glass down on the counter. 'Eddie's last case ... You know what? With Eddie gone, it's time for me to hang up the old gown and leave the law to you youngsters.'

Brendan rolled his eyes. Sammy had talked about retirement before, but if he was serious this time, I wasn't going to complain. Not if he was buying the drinks, and not just any old drink: no less than a Springbank with its very own key to the door.

Sammy slapped me on the back. 'Robbie is definitely the man for your job, Brendan. You want persuasive? This man could sell the Pope a double bed.' He rattled the base of his glass against the counter. 'Set up another couple, barkeep, and I shall consult with my colleague and give him the benefit of my advice.'

'That'll be another twenty, then,' Brendan said.

Sammy's moustache curled up at the edges. 'Let's call this one a consultation fee,' he said, leading me away.

'Eddie's last case isn't finished yet,' I said, when we'd taken our drinks to a table far enough away to avoid any requests for payment from the bar.

Sammy didn't seem to understand what I was saying. 'How's that then?'

'The PF took ill. It's been adjourned until Tuesday so they can find a new one.' Sammy looked at me, bewildered. 'But the time limit?'

'Extended,' I said. 'They do that a lot nowadays.' Sammy had been out of the criminal law game too long. Extensions to the time-bar period, once largely unheard of, were now a common feature of the Scottish courts. 'And you'll never guess who's going to be prosecuting it – Joanna. Don't worry, I'll try and talk her out of it.'

'Joanna, as in your wife, Joanna? Does she not work in Falkirk now?'

'She does, but she keeps in touch with her old pals in Livingston PF's office. She's on a night out with them at that new curry place that's just opened down the town.'

Sammy said nothing. He sipped at his drink, deep in thought, possibly at having purchased a couple of highly expensive and premature retirement whiskies. He left shortly thereafter, and once he'd gone the subject changed, as it always did, to sport. Tonight, it was the Red Corner Bar's never-ending debate on the best ever middleweight. Brendan, as usual, plumped for Marvin Hagler. Mickey, the probationary barman, agreed with the boss, while I preferred the flamboyance of Sugar Ray Leonard. As more of the patrons joined in, touting their favourite fighters, the discussion grew less theoretical. When two or three of Brendan's more inebriated regulars looked ready to throw left/right combinations in support of their pugilistic opinions, I thought it time to leave. A short taxi-ride home would allow me to relieve my dad of babysitting duties, and Joanna need never know.

I had it all worked out until I stepped through the front door of the bar and onto Linlithgow High Street, where I happened upon my missing client. Tonight, she was dressed in jeans, T-shirt and a bright orange hoodie. Meeko liked bright colours, inadvisable though they were when committing crimes, tending as they did to stick in the minds of eyewitnesses. But tonight, Meeko's choice of attire was not the only thing noticeable about her. There was also the terrified young man she had at the end of one arm, and at whom she was spitting fury whilst presenting the jaggy end of a broken Buckfast bottle with the other.

No one likes witnessing crime. This goes double for criminal lawyers. It's not that we're overly sensitive, it's just that having watched your client commit an assault, certain ethical issues may arise later when you come to defend them in court. I considered the dilemma. I could have walked away, but a legal aid fixed fee wasn't worth the imminent bloodshed.

'Eh, Stephanie, what do you think you're doing?' I said, calmly, as though it wasn't blindingly obvious that mad Meeko was intent on doing some serious injury to the terrified young man who was pressing himself up against the wall of the building hoping the brickwork would absorb him.

'She ... she stole my phone,' the young man sobbed.

I looked at Meeko. She stared back at me through glassy eyes. I had assumed she'd recognise me and come to her senses, but she was too far gone; her brain addled by the concoction of caffeine and alcohol that is supposed to be a pick-me-up for little old ladies, but is more of a lock-me-up for a large contingent of Scotland's youth.

Meeko muttered something incoherent, the slurred words accompanied by flecks of frothy saliva. I grabbed the wrist attached to the hand holding the broken bottle and stepped between her and her victim. She tried to pull her arm free, but I had a firm grip, and was about to impart some pro bono legal advice when she kneed me somewhere soft, and not gently. I let go, managing to shove her away before I doubled over. She started forward again, bottle raised, just as the door of the bar opened, and Brendan strode out. He sized up the situation in an instant and gave Meeko a left jab to the face. What was left of the green bottle flew from her hand. She staggered backwards and fell off the edge of the pavement, causing a car heading along the High Street to brake sharply, swerving to avoid her, crunching over broken glass as it did.

'Would you quit mucking about?' Brendan said, pointing a finger at me. 'You're supposed to be stopping the bastards from taking my licence away, not helping them.' With that, a growl and a sideways glance at the girl in the street, he marched back inside.

I wasn't sure what to do. The young man was shaking. Having had a good look at him, I realised that although he was tall, he wasn't a man at all. He was just a boy, not more than thirteen or fourteen years old. He wore a waterproof jacket over what on closer inspection was a school uniform, though the colours were not the black and blue of my alma mater, Linlithgow Academy, which would have better matched his left eye.

After several attempts, Meeko rose unsteadily to her feet. The fight had gone out of her and holding her face she stumbled off, muttering and cursing her way down the High Street.

I asked the boy if he was all right. He took a few deep breaths, gingerly touched his swollen eye, wiped a cuff across his nose and nodded.

'Where are you from?' He was from Edinburgh. 'Are you lost?' He was. He'd been dropped off late afternoon to take part in choir rehearsals, and someone was supposed to be picking him up.

'Where are they coming from?' I asked.

'Glasgow.'

Great. Most Glaswegians needed a passport and malaria tablets to go further east than Glasgow Cross.

'Who is it that's coming? Your mum?'

'No.'

'Your dad, then. Do you have a phone?' Of course, he didn't. Not any longer. That was why Meeko had taken such an interest in him. She'd seen him coming down the Kirkgate from St Michael's Church and identified easy pickings. I took out my own phone. 'What's your dad's number?'

'It's not my dad who's coming, it's my mum's friend.'

'Look, son, I don't need the family tree, just the number of who I'm supposed to be calling.'

'That would be me,' said a voice from behind. I turned to see the unmistakably large figure of Stan Blandy emerge from a mineral-grey Range Rover that had eased silently up to the kerb.

Stan had once been a major importer of illegal narcotics. Cocaine and MDMA were his drugs of choice. He'd shunned heroin for the simple reason he didn't trust junkies, while marijuana was a bulky product with an insufficient mark-up. Stan's was a simple strategy. Top quality produce, at top quality prices, to top quality people. The people who could afford to buy Stan's drugs were the kind of people the police weren't interested in. These days, if you believed Stan, he was no longer involved in organised crime. He'd got out, something that's not easy to do unless, like Stan, you organised the crime in the first place.

'Did I not tell you to wait for me up at the kirk?' he barked at the boy. The boy nodded. Stan took hold of him by the shoulders, looked at the black eye. 'You got that at the school. Playing rugby or walking into a lamppost or something. Got it?' The boy nodded again. He was good at nodding. Stan jerked a thumb backwards. 'Get in the car.'

Head bowed, the boy obeyed.

'What happened?' Stan asked.

'Someone took a shine to the boy's mobile.' I looked over my shoulder. Meeko had disappeared. 'He got a fright, but he's not harmed. Well, not too much. Who is he?'

'His stepmother is a ... business acquaintance of mine.

The boy ...' Stan winced apologetically. 'He sings in a choir.'

'I've never seen you drive before,' I said. 'Where's your chauffeur?' I'd met Stan's usual driver many times previously. He didn't have a name, just a shaved head, facial scars and a propensity for extreme violence.

'His step-mum was supposed to be coming for him and then something cropped up. She asked me if I could help.' She must have been one hell of a business acquaintance if she could press Stan Blandy into working as an Uber for the night. 'I took a wrong turn on the way here and had to double back.'

'I know who took the phone,' I said. 'Stephanie Meek, she's one of my clients.' I wasn't going to let a little thing like a knee in the chuckies get in the way of our business relationship. Bams weren't that thick on the ground in Linlithgow. 'She's okay if you can catch her sober. I'll speak to her and try and get it back.'

'Don't bother,' Stan said. 'I'll get him another, before his step-mum finds out.' He walked over to his car. 'You going somewhere?'

'Home,' I said.

He opened the front passenger door. 'Get in.'

We didn't talk much on the short journey.

'Thanks again for helping the wee man out of a jam,' Stan said, as we pulled up outside my house.

'I didn't do much,' I said. 'I didn't have to. Brendan from the Red Corner sorted it out really.'

Stan laughed drily. 'I wouldn't have thought a spit-and-sawdust joint like that would be your usual Friday night haunt, Robbie.'

'What do you mean? I pick up half my clients in there,' I said.

'Business is business eh?'

'And I went to school with the landlord. He's a local celebrity. Won gold in the Commonwealth Games. Flyweight. I was down seeing him because he's got some trouble with the local Licensing Board. They're trying to close the place down. Too many unsavoury incidents like tonight's outside his premises. He's got a hearing coming up.'

'How's that likely to go?'

Not very well was the answer. Brendan's publican's licence was hanging by the shoogliest of pegs.

As I alighted, Stan took a hold of my arm and squeezed. 'All the same. Thanks. If there's anything I can do for you, just give me a shout.'

'Don't be stupid, Stan—'

'Stupid? You think there's something stupid about me wanting to express my gratitude?'

'Not stupid. What I mean is—'

'You should know by now that Stan Blandy is beholden to no-one.'

'Of course you're not. What I mean is ... I just did what anyone would have done. It was no big deal.' I stepped out of the car. When I turned to close the door, Stan was leaning across the passenger seat, the seat belt straining against his immense frame. 'Anything. You understand?'

7

It was after ten when I slipped silently through my front door. The plan was to send my dad packing, carry out a check on the kids to make sure they were safely tucked in, and give my teeth a brush so that when Joanna returned from her night out she'd be none the wiser about my trip to the Red Corner Bar.

'You've been drinking.' Joanna emerged from the kitchen carrying a mug of tea. 'Where were you? Red Corner Bar?'

'You're back early, darling,' I said.

'And just as well.' She sat down on the sofa. 'When I came home your Dad was sleeping in the chair, Jamie was in his cot crying his beads out with a dirty nappy and Tina was watching a slasher movie. What's all this about you working late with some important client – on a Friday?'

'Long story,' I said. 'Why are you not out with your Fiscal friends, bragging about all the folk you've had banged up?'

'The others went on for drinks. I just stayed for the meal.' She took a sip of tea and looked away.

'Is everything all right?' I asked.

'Of course.' She took another hurried drink.

'Are you sure?'

'Forget it.' She drained the mug. 'It's nothing.'

In my experience, when women say, "it's nothing," it's usually safe to assume it's very much something.

Joanna rose to her feet, mug in hand. 'I think I'll go put some more milk in this.'

I took hold of her arm. 'Did something happen tonight?' The sleeve of her blouse rode up to reveal some faded black markings on the back of her hand just below her wrist. 'What's that?'

Without a word, Joanna set the mug on the arm of the couch, sat down again and pulled up her sleeve. There, partially washed away, was some writing. It looked like a car registration number. I didn't understand.

'Did you have a bump with the car?' I said.

Joanna sighed. 'We were in the restaurant. I wasn't drinking. After the meal, I said cheerio to everyone and was at the door putting on my coat when this guy appeared from nowhere.' She paused, took a deep breath and continued. 'He was friendly enough to start off with and I thought he was ... you know, just trying to chat me up. I said I wasn't interested and that I was just leaving. He offered to give me a lift home. I said no thanks, I had my own car, and he said he'd walk me to it. He wasn't being aggressive or anything.' Joanna took a drink of tea. 'Not at that point.'

'Not at that point?'

She patted the cushion next to her. 'Sit down, Robbie. I'm all right. He followed me. My car wasn't parked far away. I thought he was just trying it on, and flashing my wedding ring would get rid of him, but ... Well, he grabbed my arm. Really tight. He wouldn't let go. He dragged me into a shop doorway. I screamed and tried to kick him, but he had me in a sort of bear hug. I couldn't break free, and when I tried to scream, he put a hand over my mouth. I kicked him on the shin a few times, really hard, and he let go.'

'And then what?'

'And that was it. He just walked away, got in a car and drove off. Some passers-by must have heard me screaming and came over to see if I was okay. They made sure I got to my car safely.'

'Did you call the cops?'

'I was going to. That's why I wrote his number plate number on my hand. Then I thought the cops had better things to do on a Friday night, and, even if they didn't, I couldn't be bothered with all the hassle of giving a statement, and what would have happened anyway? No one else saw anything. It would be my word against his.' Joanna laid her head on my shoulder. 'I told you it was nothing. He'd probably had a few too many. I've had to deal with quite a few drunken idiots in my time. I haven't been able to scrub the numbers off properly and I didn't want you to notice it ... Or the ...'

'Or the what?'

'I might have one or two bruises as well.'

I put a clenched fist to my mouth and bit down on a knuckle. 'Where?' Joanna pulled down the collar of her top to reveal red marks either side of her throat. I would have been on my feet again if she hadn't held me down by the shoulders. 'Did he give you his name?' I said between gritted teeth. He hadn't. 'Then what did he look like?'

'Forget it, Robbie. I mean it. Don't do anything stupid.' She finished her tea, lifting the mug to her mouth with a shaky hand. 'It's just one of those things. Promise you'll forget about it?' She waited and tried again. 'Promise?'

'I will if you will,' I said eventually.

Joanna smiled. 'Forget what?' She leaned across and kissed me.

From the bedroom young Jamie made his presence known.

'Stay where you are,' I said. 'I'll make him a bottle.' And taking her empty mug, I walked through to the kitchen to jot down that car registration number while I still remembered it.

8

Saturday teatime. It had been a sunny afternoon. Tina was in the garden getting creative with mud and twigs, I was in the kitchen making her something to eat and her wee brother was finding new and interesting places to stick mashed banana.

Joanna was sitting outside in a deckchair, reading her way through a large bundle of papers clipped into a ring binder.

'You can't go ahead with it, of course,' I said, after lifting Jamie from the highchair and carrying him outside to join his mum.

'Why's that then?' Joanna asked, not sounding terribly interested in any answer I might have.

'Because it's . . . well . . . it's highly irregular.'

'*Highly irregular?*' On many issues, my opinion and that of my wife often differed; nonetheless, throughout our married life she'd consistently recognised my inalienable right to be wrong. 'Would you stop and listen to yourself? Just about everything you do in court is *highly irregular*. Why can't I be irregular now and again?' She flicked over another page. 'Anyway, I don't see what the big problem is.'

'The big problem,' I said, wiping Jamie's face with one of the endless pieces of kitchen roll I now carried about my person at all times, 'is that there's an obvious conflict of interest.'

'Really? How's that then?' Joanna asked, not taking her eyes off the brief.

'You know perfectly well.' I brought out a playmat and laid my struggling son down on it for some tummy time. 'I'm your husband.' Ignoring my wife's fatalistic shrug, I continued. 'You can't prosecute a case I'm defending.'

'Why not? Do you think I'm going to go easy on you because we're married?'

Not for a minute, but it didn't matter what I thought. It was what other people thought.

She laughed. 'Robbie, when did you ever bother about what other people thought? You just want the case to time-bar, collect a fat fee for doing zilch and watch a guilty man go free.'

That did more or less sum up most of my professional goals, not that I was going to give way on the point.

'It's not even your jurisdiction,' I said. 'In case you've forgotten you were moved from Livingston to Falkirk *because* your bosses thought it wasn't a good idea for us to practise in the same court.'

'There are exceptions to every rule, Robbie, and the plain fact is that there are no deputes available in Livingston to do the trial. I promised Hugh Ogilvie I'd do it. I know you two don't get on ...' That was putting it mildly. Hugh Ogilvie, West Lothian's procurator fiscal, regarded me as the urinal splashback in his world of beige trousers. 'But he helped me get my part-time contract in Falkirk after wee Jamie was born. I feel indebted to him.'

Jamie, who was learning to crawl, had only mastered reverse gear and was slowly making his way backwards off the playmat and onto the patch of divots and dande-lions we impertinently referred to as the lawn.

'I take it Josh Wedderburn is still playing the sick-boy card, then?' I said, picking my son up and putting him down again on the centre of the playmat. 'Surely there's someone available in Livingston. Why can't Ogilvie do it himself? He is the actual procurator fiscal after all.'

Joanna didn't bother to answer. We both knew that Ogilvie only conducted trials where victory for the prosecution was a certainty, and media coverage likely. Keggie's case wasn't one of those, and, looked at objec-tively, Joanna was not only an extremely good prosecutor, she was also working flexible part-time on the basis that she could be parachuted into cases at times of emergency such as this. Still, I wasn't going to start being all objec-tive and reasonable when I'd much rather have faced off against Ogilvie or one of Joanna's colleagues.

'It's unfair of them even to ask you,' I grumbled, reaching over her shoulder and trying to close the ring-binder. 'Giving you a case like this to look at over a weekend. You're only part-time. If it starts on Tuesday, what if it spills into the following week?'

Joanna pulled the binder out of my reach. 'If it spills it spills, but it's not going to. There's only a couple of days in it, three tops, and, as I'm sure you are only too well aware, if it doesn't start sharp on Tuesday the case will time-bar.'

'Then let it time-bar,' I said. 'Who cares? No one can blame you. You're bombproof.' I made another go for the binder, this time snagging a corner. 'You can't be expected to pick up a stinker of a case like this and be ready in a couple of days. It's the weekend and you've got kids to look after.'

My wife didn't see that as a problem. 'Monday's a court holiday, you remember what holidays are don't you? That means if I can get a chance to read the papers today ...' She tugged the binder from my grip. 'I can have tomorrow and Monday off. You say it's a stinker, but it's not exactly complicated. Most of the material facts are not in dispute, and, anyway, why can't I be expected to be ready? You were only instructed a few days ago and you haven't exactly been knocking your pan in with preparations for the defence.'

'That's because the defence is extremely well focused,' I said.

'The whole case is well focused, Robbie. We're both agreed that the victim ...' She leafed back to the beginning.

'The trial is a matter of hours away and you don't even know the *alleged* victim's name,' I said.

'Everything in the future is hours away, Robbie, that's how time works, and what do you know about the case? You've barely opened that file you brought from the office.'

I knew enough. Sometimes it was better not to get bogged down with too many facts. 'I've read the witness statements and the medical stuff. I think I can say I have captured the flavour of the thing. Man breaks into accused's home. Accused hits man over head with big stick. Man is injured. Man deserved it.'

'And what about the police interviews? Have you even bothered to listen to them?'

There was a window envelope stapled to the inside cover of the case file. I could see it held some blue-and-white memory sticks which in turn would contain recordings of Simon Keggie's police interview as well as his caution and charge. There was no need to listen to them. Eddie

56

Frew had gone with him to the interview. According to the summary of evidence, there'd been a lot of questions, each met with no comment from beginning to end. I'd have expected no less.

Joanna flicked over a few pages to find the copy indictment. 'And the victim, whose name by the way is Angus MacDonald, didn't break in, he was invited to your client's home—'

Invited? What was my wife talking about? 'He wasn't invited. That's the most disputed part of the whole case. He broke in.'

Joanna pointed to a sheet of paper. 'Invited. That's what's down in MacDonald's police statement. He was invited to Councillor Keggie's home to discuss some important business.' She closed the binder. 'There's absolutely no evidence of a break-in, whatsoever.'

'Important business?' I laughed. 'What important business would that be?'

'I suppose we'll find that out at the trial,' Joanna said.

I was going to have to put Joanna right on this. It would save time later. 'My client doesn't know this MacDonald guy. Why would he invite a strange man to his house in the middle of the night?'

Joanna gave me a condescending look. 'MacDonald has no previous convictions and is a freelance wildlife photographer. He takes pictures of bunnies and wildcats and stags. He's not a housebreaker. There are probably all sorts of reasons why older men invite younger men to their homes late at night, Robbie. You've obviously led a very sheltered life.'

'A romantic rendezvous at Keggie's house when Mrs Keggie was a few yards away in bed with the flu or something?'

'And . . .' Joanna continued before I could interrupt further, 'it's reasonable to infer from the wounds to his head and back that he didn't whack *himself* with a walking stick. Therefore, the only contentious issue is whether your client acted in self-defence, and the Crown position is,' she held up a hand to silence further protests, 'that, even if MacDonald was a housebreaker, hitting the victim—'

'*Alleged* victim . . .'

'Repeatedly with a blunt object, after he must obviously have been incapacitated, was not a proportionate use of force.'

'Proportionate is as proportionate does,' I said. 'How proportionate should you be if you happen to meet an intruder late at night in your own house with your wife in her sickbed? Did you give that guy on Friday night a proportionate kick in the shins or did you kick him as hard as you could?'

Joanna sighed. 'The blows were to MacDonald's back. He was clearly trying to get away.'

'Or looking for a weapon of his own,' I said. 'Why should my client take the chance?'

'So, it's a case of beat senseless, ask questions later?'

'He's sixty-odd years of age with a dying wife—'

'She had a bad cold.'

'And some stranger enters his house in the dead of night – what's he supposed to do?'

'Not beat the person's brain to a pulp for a start,' Joanna said.

'He's alive, isn't he? And I don't see any mention of lasting brain damage,' I said. 'It's not even down as an attempted murder.'

Joanna came back with, 'Well, it should be in the High

58

Court if you ask me. Crown counsel probably went easy on him because your client's a politician.'

'No, Jo. It's more to do with the fact that my client is a very popular local politician, sixty years of age, with an exemplary character, and because your bosses don't like throwing big High Court money at a case that's a dead cert loser. They just feel obliged to go through the motions in case someone complains.'

Joanna sniffed. 'We'll see how much of a loser it is when we're facing off in court. You can give the Crown witnesses your usual bludgeoning, then I'll dissect your client's testimony like he's a frog in a high school biology lab. After that it'll just be a case of speeches to the jury.'

'Your usual one where you say you are prosecuting in the public interest and the horrible defence lawyer is trying to get a criminal off?' I asked.

'You'll find out when you hear it. All I can say is that it will be a sight better than yours, which I imagine will be along the lines of *housebreakers deserve all that's coming to them.*'

I didn't dignify the remark with a reply, close enough to the truth though it was.

'Anyway, it's a bit of a departure for you, isn't it?' Joanna said, airily, opening the binder and burying her nose in it again. 'You usually stick up for housebreakers.'

'I usually stick up for *alleged* housebreakers, and so did you once.' My wife had either forgotten her time as a defence lawyer, or else my dad's views on the presumption of innocence were beginning to rub off on her. 'Whatever you think, Jo, I still say you're taking a risk. If . . . or, I should say, when you lose horribly, people might say you lost so your husband could win.'

'Not people who know me,' Joanna said, not looking

up from the papers. 'And since I use my maiden name in court, no one in the public benches need know our relationship.'

'They might if they catch us snogging at coffee break,' I said.

'Right at this moment, I don't see that as being a problem,' Joanna said, marking a section of the medical records with a yellow highlighter pen. 'Just like I don't see myself losing, horribly or otherwise.'

There's no telling some people – my wife being one of those people. I went inside and rescued a pot of cheesy beans. I was about to shout my daughter in for her tea, when she burst through the back door trailing muck. Joanna followed with Jamie in her arms.

'There's a monster in the garden!' Tina yelled.

The imagination of a seven-year-old is a wonderful thing. My daughter would do well to retain it if she was ever to follow in her old man's footsteps as a defence lawyer. 'You mean there *was* a monster in the garden, but now she's come in for her favourite cheesy-beans on toast,' I said.

'No, really, Dad.' Tina tugged at my sleeve. 'There's something in the bushes up at the trees.'

Our garden was what I liked to call eco-friendly. Others called it unkempt. My dad referred to it as 'the jungle'. Sometime ago I'd made half-hearted attempts to tame the wilderness, until my enthusiasm for horticulture had waned a few yards from the back door, whereupon things deteriorated into a sea of long grass, wildflowers and gorse bushes before coming up against a copse of spindly birch trees that separated our property from the fields beyond.

The toast under the grill began to smoke. 'Go and see what she's on about, Jo,' I said, rushing to grab it.

'It's nothing,' Joanna said. I'd heard that line somewhere before. I hadn't buttered the toast before Tina screamed, 'Dad!', and, dropping everything, I ran outside to meet my daughter coming back in a hurry.

'What is it?'

'The monster,' Tina said.

I could hear Bouncer barking somewhere off in the distance.

'I'll go take a look,' I said. 'Tina, take off your shoes and go and wash your hands. And your face, come to that. We'll get to the rest of you later.'

Joanna stepped in front of me. 'There's no need. It's probably just someone out for a walk who's got lost. He's away now.'

'He?' I said.

Joanna shrugged. 'He, she? Difficult to know at this range.'

Bouncer was still barking. 'I'll go and bring the dog in,' I said, and edging past Joanna made my way outside. At the far end of the garden I could see Bouncer jumping about frantically, growling and yelping his head off. I called to him to shut up, and he eventually obeyed. Together we walked through the wilderness to the birch trees. When we made it to the other side of the copse, acres of grass stretched before us, and, in the distance, skirting the edge of the field, a tall dark figure trotted in the direction of the road. Whoever it was, they were too far away for me to chase after or even yell at, so I went back inside.

When Tina was fed, cleansed of mud and beans, story-read and tucked up for the night, I joined Joanna, who was sitting on the sofa with Jamie on her knee. The TV was showing a crime drama about a missing child. I always felt sorry for TV cops, spending all their time looking for lost kids or chasing serial killers, especially when they had their own personal demons to deal with, usually drink or a child custody battle with a divorced wife who secretly still loved them, not to mention the cost of maintaining an unusual motor car. I could tell Joanna wasn't really watching it. She was holding our son tight and staring out of the window into the darkness.

'You know that dancing programme's on, don't you? The one you never miss?' I said.

She stroked Jamie's head, looking past me out of the window. Then her eyes came back to mine. 'It was him,' she said.

'Who?'

'Out there. At teatime. It was the man from last night.'

9

Monday morning. A court holiday. It was just me and Grace Mary. I was in my office, checking my diary. She was in reception, bashing away at a keyboard.

I picked up the phone and rang through to her. 'Are you sure there's nothing happening today?'

'Absolutely zilch,' Grace Mary said. 'You've already asked me that twice. Now, can I get on with what I'm doing for five minutes without you disturbing me?'

She hung up. I flicked over to Tuesday and called her back. 'Looks like I've got some intermediate diets tomorrow. Could you give Paul Sharp a call and see if he can appear and knock them onto the trial date?'

'Anything else?'

'No, that's all.'

I turned the page. Wednesday. Keggie's trial was bound to last more than a day. I buzzed through again. 'While you're at it, Grace Mary, better see if Paul's free to cover my remand court cases on Wednesday too.'

'He's not your servant, you know,' she said.

He wasn't, but he was a pal, and I'd covered for him many times before when our roles were reversed. I began to sift through a basket of mail to see if there was anything in it apart from bills, then had a thought. Joanna wasn't working today. Maybe we could do lunch. I searched around for my mobile but I couldn't find it. I must have left it in reception.

'Do you ever get shooting pains like someone's got a voodoo doll and they're stabbing it with a needle again and again?' Grace Mary asked when I rang to find out if she'd seen my phone anywhere.

'No, why?' I said.

'How about now?'

'Just have a wee look around and see if you can find my mobile, would you?'

'I don't need to look around,' she said. 'It's here in your jacket pocket. It went off a minute ago. Mr Paterson wants to come in later to discuss his licensing appeal tomorrow. Though, if you ask me, the Council should have closed that dump of his years ago. It's like the OK Corral down there at weekends.'

'*Tomorrow*?' I said. 'Are you sure? I thought it was next week. It can't be tomorrow, I've got Simon Keggie's trial starting. You know that.'

'No, I don't. You told me the Keggie case was starting last Friday and might collapse.'

'No, it was *supposed* to start on Friday, but it didn't. Don't you remember? That's why I came back from court early to find you up to your ears in emergency knitting.'

'When you came back early, I thought that was because it *had* collapsed,' Grace Mary said. 'You never told me it had just been postponed. You were always going on about it being a slammed drunk. Anyway, Mr Paterson is keen to know how things are coming along.'

Coming along? Things had come along about as far as me opening a case file and writing Brendan's name on the cover. I needed to think. Fortunately, with the practice I've had over the years I could do that quickly. 'Phone him and tell him everything's going great.'

'But you haven't done anything.' One of Grace Mary's

more annoying habits was pointing out the actual facts of any given situation.

'I'm not finished,' I said. 'After that, phone the Council and find out the chances of having the hearing continued for a few weeks or even just a few days.'

'On what grounds?'

'My unforeseen unavailability.'

'But it wasn't unforeseen. The hearing date's been pencilled in the diary for ages,' she said, at it again with the facts.

'Then make something up.'

'I made something up the last time.' There had been a last time? 'Don't you remember? You had that case in Inverness for the road rage guy? I got the Board to put off the hearing. They didn't like it very much then and I don't think they'll like it any better now. What are you going to do?'

Other than allow Brendan the use of my head as a punchbag, I had absolutely no idea.

'Leave it with me. I'll think of something,' I said. 'Any other good news?'

'I meant to tell you: Mr Blandy called before you dragged yourself in this morning.'

'What did he want?'

'He never said. He's going to call back.'

'Don't suppose he left a number?'

'Never does.'

'And talking of numbers,' I said. 'I have one I'd like you to do some research on.'

'What kind of research?'

'I've got a car number plate here, and I want you to find out whose it is.' I dug in my trouser pocket for the piece of paper on which I'd written the number scrawled on my wife's hand on Friday night.

'And how, precisely, am I supposed to do that?' Grace Mary asked.

'I don't know … Try—'

'Magic? Robbie, if I could find people based solely on their number plate number, I'd have my own show at the Fringe.'

'The number must be in my jacket,' I said. 'Could you have a look?'

Apparently not. According to Grace Mary, she had better things to do than waste her time playing private detectives. 'The only important number today, is the telephone number for West Lothian Licensing Board,' she said.

She was certainly right about that, but, on the long established principle that it's never a good idea to try and talk a civil servant into anything before lunch, especially not on a Monday, I asked Grace Mary to phone the clerk's office at two o'clock and give them the old clash of court commitment routine. 'Tell the clerk that my business in the Sheriff Court has to take precedence over their kangaroo tribunal. Or words to that effect.'

Grace Mary came through five minutes later with my jacket. 'They're on holiday,' she said, hanging it over the back of a chair. 'Like everyone else apart from us.'

Part-timers. I'd need to phone the clerk's office first thing in the morning and give them a dose of Human Rights and denial of access to justice, and any other legal sounding rubbish I could think of. Around half-past three, I was thinking of ways to avoid Brendan, when the door to my office was thrown wide and he marched in, clutching a bottle of Springbank twenty-one-year-old single malt by the neck.

'Brendan, I'm glad you're here,' I said.

He waved a hand. 'Just a flying visit. I've only come to

say thanks and to give you this.' He plonked down on my desk the bottle that I'd last seen on Friday night, the fill level just below the shoulder.

'Thanks,' I said, lifting the bottle and checking it for a detonator. 'What's it for?'

Brendan leaned over and gave me a slow-motion tap on the jaw with his fist. 'Don't be modest. It's not like you. I just got a call from the chairman of the Licensing Board sub-committee half an hour ago. On his day off, no less. He said that in light of certain representations made on my behalf, the Board didn't think it necessary to uphold any of the complaints made against me. My slate's been wiped clean, just like your bar tab. We both get to make a fresh start.' He pinged the bottle with his finger. 'Don't drink it all at once.' And with a wink and a 'See you later,' he was gone, leaving me staring at the bottle of Campbeltown's finest and wondering if the world had gone mad.

Grace Mary rang through from reception. 'Mr Blandy for you.'

I picked up the receiver in a daze. 'Hi Stan. What can I do for you?'

'It's not what you can do for me, Robbie. It's what I can do for you.'

'Is this about Friday night? Really, Stan, there's no need . . .' I thought about Brendan's sudden Licensing Board reprieve. How wide did Stan Blandy's tentacles stretch? 'Actually, do you think you could try and find someone for me?' I said.

'Just give me a name,' he replied confidently.

Unfortunately, I didn't have a name, or even an idea as to where to start looking. 'In fact,' I said, getting out of my seat and rummaging around in my jacket pocket for the scrap of paper. 'All I have is a number plate.'

10

'There are no opening speeches in Scotland,' Sheriff Sibbald told the ladies and gentlemen of the jury, first thing Tuesday morning. 'Apart, that is, from this one where I tell you there are no opening speeches.' It wrung the usual polite smiles from the fifteen, and the trial started, as they usually do, with the prosecution calling a Scene of Crime Officer to speak to some photographs.

After being talked through shots of the exterior of the accused's house, showing no signs of damage to the doors or windows that might have indicated illegal entry, we moved onto snapshots of blood spatters and droplets in the porch, on the inside of the front door, on the doorstep and garden path. Then we were treated to some images of the complainer's injuries. After the jury was sufficiently warmed up, Joanna called the complainer. I could sense the ladies and gentlemen start to take interest, shifting in their seats, ready to weigh up the prosecution's star witness. And what a witness he was. Seriously. Could this trial get any better? Simon Keggie was in his early sixties, and although he was a hefty individual, the one thing that had concerned me was the possibility the alleged victim would turn out to be a six-stone weakling. He wasn't. He really wasn't. He was a big man with short dark hair and an expressionless face. His thick eyebrows were woven with thin white scars, his nose was spread and thick. It was a face that had caught a lot of fists in its day. Slip him into a stripy top, chuck a bag marked 'swag' over his shoulder, and you could have looked him up in the dictionary under 'V' for villain. How could a face like that not have a criminal record?

I looked over at my client with a thin smile of encouragement. He didn't respond. Keggie seemed different today. His previous confidence had evaporated, and he was not nearly so relaxed as he had been on Friday.

The man in the witness box raised a right hand the size of an oven glove and took the oath. The sheriff looked down to his right. Miss Jordan? Joanna didn't move. What was she doing? Building the tension? Or was she taken aback by the appearance of the man in the witness box? That was what was wrong with the Fiscal service these days. No preparation. Cutbacks meant that witnesses weren't precognosced in advance. Deputes like my wife had to rely on police statements that often relayed more what the cops wanted the witness to say than what they actually did have to say.

The sheriff tried again. 'Miss Jordan, are you ready to begin?'

I leaned forward. 'Are you okay?'

Joanna's only reply was a sickly half-smile. The sheriff was about to speak again, when Joanna stood, picked up her papers, cleared her throat and began leading the witness through the initial formalities. 'You are Angus MacDonald?'

'Yeah,' the witness replied.

'Do you mind giving your address in open court?'

'Not really.'

'And is it Wester Brigg Cottage, by Muiravonside?'

It was.

'Mr MacDonald, I understand you are forty-two years of age, single and a wildlife photographer?' Apparently so. 'And you have absolutely no previous convictions, is that correct?' Joanna tilted her head at the jury and gave them a never-judge-a-book-by-its-cover look. She was hoping that by confirming her witness to be the cleanest of totties, he was more likely to be accepted as credible and reliable.

Introductions over, Joanna got straight to examination in chief. 'Mr MacDonald, we are interested today in the events of the evening of Sunday the twelfth of May last year. Can you tell us where you were and what you were doing?'

And that's where the wheels started to come off the Crown charabanc for, apparently, the witness had no recollection whatsoever.

'Any reason why your memory is so poor?' Joanna asked drily.

MacDonald shrugged. 'It's a long time ago.'

Recalcitrant witnesses are about as unusual as a Tom Jones song; practically every Sheriff Court domestic abuse case has one. Women, for it is usually women, who call the police and are then separated from their partners by bail conditions for months on end, racking up debt and having to single-handedly care for the kids, often start to have second thoughts and poor memories when they realise a big fine or a prison sentence for hubby isn't going to help the household finances, or the prospects for future domestic relations. Sometimes, having a good memory of events isn't worth it. Still, I hadn't expected the complainer in this case to be backward when coming forward. His police statement had been clear enough.

Joanna must have thought so too. 'Mr MacDonald, do you recall giving a statement to the police?'

The witness shrugged.

'Please answer the question,' the sheriff said.

'Yeah, I remember talking to the police.'

Joanna turned to the bar officer. 'Crown production 8 please.' The bar officer handed up a police notebook to the witness. Joanna walked over to the witness box and pointed to a page held open by a large silver paperclip. 'Is that your signature?'

The witness shrugged and the sheriff had to intervene again. 'I've told you already, Mr MacDonald. Answer the questions verbally.'

The man in the box sighed. 'Yes, it looks like my signature.'

'Then,' Joanna continued, 'if the passage of time has so eroded your memory, can we take it that the statement in this notebook, signed by you, and given, let me see, three weeks after the incident while you were still a patient at St John's Hospital, is an accurate and truthful version of events?'

'Don't answer that question,' I said, rising to my feet, even though the witness was showing no signs of replying.

The sheriff looked down. 'Mr Munro?'

'My friend is asking the witness to say whether the statement he gave to the police is the truth or not.'

'Yes, I had gathered that much, Mr Munro. You'll be familiar, no doubt, with section 260 of the Criminal Procedure (Scotland) Act 1995?'

I was. Every criminal lawyer was. It was the most frequently used evidential tool in the Crown toolbox and hated by defence lawyers. Witnesses not keen to give evidence, but who had given a statement to the police

71

in the heat of the moment, were given the option to say either that their statement was true, in which case it was adopted as their evidence, or they could say it was untrue – and that they'd lied to the police. Even if the original statement was a complete fabrication, witnesses tended to stick to it rather than admit under oath that they'd wasted everybody's time and were willing to swap places with the accused in the dock.

'It's that particular section of the Act which I'd like to address your lordship on,' I said. 'You might want to hear what I have to say in the absence of the jury and the witness.'

The man in the wig smiled patiently. 'I don't think that will be necessary at this stage. Continue.'

I did. 'My friend is asking the witness if the statement he gave the police was the truth. There are really only two answers to that question. Either the witness will say he told the truth to the police officers – in which case I expect Joa ... I mean, Miss Jordan will invite the witness to adopt the statement as his evidence—'

'A daily occurrence in these courts, as you must well know, Mr Munro. What's your point?'

'My point, M'Lord, is that, on the other hand, if the witness says the statement isn't the truth, then that might indicate that he lied to the police. Unless of course the suggestion is that the police fabricated the statement.'

The sheriff turned to the jury. 'I don't think we need be concerned about that having happened,' he said with a light laugh.

'Then your Lordship will also be aware that wasting the time of the police with a false report, especially one that leads to solemn proceedings and great inconvenience to all concerned, the ladies and gentlemen of the jury included, is a crime. For that reason, I respectfully submit that Mr MacDonald should be warned that he needn't answer the question if he thinks it might incriminate him.'

It's amazing the number of acquittals that are missed because the defence lawyer overestimates the presiding sheriff's legal knowledge. It's a trap I never fall into. Nothing ventured, nothing gained. I'd tried that particular line many times before, usually to much hilarity from the bench; however, on this occasion, Sheriff Sibbald's benevolent smile turned to a frown, as though he were actually giving some serious thought to my objection. Why the witness was being obstructive I had no idea. I'd read his statement too. He'd been invited to the house to talk business, there'd been a falling out and he had been set about by my client and a blackthorn walking stick as he was leaving. That statement was the main plank in the Crown case. But if that plank was showing signs of rot, I was going to jump all over it like a music lover on a banjo. If the sheriff agreed that a warning should be administered, it would give the obviously reluctant witness a get-out from giving further evidence.

Joanna anticipated the danger. 'It's quite all right M'Lord, I'll rephrase the question.'

Sheriff Sibbald looked down at me. 'Will that do you, Mr Munro?'

It would have to. I sank to my seat again.

Joanna continued. 'Are there any parts of the statement with which you disagree?'

That was really the same question, but before I could object the witness had already answered.

'All of it.'

'Really? So, your name and address . . . those are incorrectly stated?'

'No, but—'

'And your date and place of birth . . .?'

'Okay, all that stuff is correct, but—'

'Then I'll ask you again. With which parts don't you agree?'

The sheriff cleared his throat. 'Miss Jordan, I think you've had the answer to the veracity of the police statement. The witness says he disagrees with it and, while I suppose you could spend some time arguing with your *own* witness and suggesting that he either lied to the police last May or he's lying to the ladies and gentlemen now, I can't see how showing he's a liar would assist his credibility or progress the Crown case any. Can you?'

Joanna's nostrils flared. 'With leave of the court . . .' And without waiting for such leave she turned to the witness again. 'Take a look at Crown production 1, please.' She nodded to the bar officer who brought over the book of photographs we'd gone through with the Scene of Crime Officer. Joanna waited while the jury was handed copies. 'Turn to the first photograph.' It was an exterior shot of Keggie's home. 'Do you recognise that house?' Apparently not. She asked him to continue to images showing the inside of the house. 'Ring any bells?'

The witness studied the photograph, turning it this way and that. 'It's difficult to say,' he said at last.

'Turn to photo D. It's the porch of the accused's home. Do you see the staining to the walls and the floor?' If he didn't, he was blind. 'We'll hear from a forensic scientist that the staining is blood spatter – your blood.'

'A question please, Miss Jordan,' the sheriff said.

Joanna had one ready. 'Looks like you were there, doesn't it? You were there and bleeding all over the floor and walls. I'll ask you again. Were you there?'

The witness nodded reluctantly. 'Must have been.'

'Can you tell us, then, *why* you were there?'

I was about to get to my feet, but the sheriff put out a hand to indicate I needn't bother. 'Miss Jordan, I have a feeling Mr Munro is about to point out that if, as you suggest, the witness was in somebody's house, late at night, there are a number of possible answers to your question. One could amount to the admission of a crime—'

'On behalf of the Crown I undertake—'

'No, Miss Jordan. Even if you feel sufficiently empowered to give a guarantee of immunity on behalf of the Lord Advocate, which I'm not sure you are, I think the ladies and gentlemen are more than capable of drawing a reasonable inference as to the purpose of Mr MacDonald's visit to the accused's home at . . .'

'Around midnight,' I offered helpfully, sounding like the teacher's pet.

The sheriff looked down at Joanna. 'Let's move on, shall we? I'm sure we are all anxiously waiting to hear if the Crown has some actual evidence in support of the charge against the accused.'

Joanna, face flushed, glared angrily at the bench. Meanwhile I was beginning to have warm and fuzzy feelings about the man in the horsehair wig. Procurators fiscal were not used to anything but support from the bench. Well too bad. Welcome to my world. The world of a defence lawyer. I'd told my wife not to take on the case. With me acting for the accused, she'd been handed the perfect get-out clause. Who cared if there was no other depute able to do the case? It wouldn't be the first case to be lost due to time-bar.

Undeterred, Joanna battered on. 'Keep looking through the book of photographs until you get to photograph K.

Is that you?' He'd shaved off a lot of facial hair in the intervening twelve months.

'Yeah, that's me,' the witness agreed, adding unnecessarily, 'I had a beard back then.'

'And does photograph L show an injury to the rear of your head?' Quite obviously it did. 'And is that injury shown from different angles and in close-up on photographs M, N, O and P?'

The witness flicked through the booklet. 'I suppose.'

'And how do you say you sustained that injury?'

'It's all a bit hazy now.'

'Turn to photographs Q, R, S and T. Those are injuries to your back, aren't they?'

The witness grunted in agreement.

'I take it you're hazy about those too?' Before the man in the box could answer, if he was ever going to, Joanna said, 'We may hear later from the police officer who took your statement, that you said you were in the porch shown at image D when you were attacked. According to your statement, you were leaving when you were struck on the head and when you tried to get away you felt blows to your back, and—'

'Miss Jordan, are you really taking the witness back to his statement – the one he disagrees with?' the sheriff asked.

Joanna threw a smile benchwards like she was throwing a dart. 'I'll withdraw that question, M'Lord.' She turned to the witness again. 'Here's a simple question. You ended up in hospital. Why?'

MacDonald scratched his beard. 'I don't remember. I remember being in an ambulance . . .'

Normally, sheriffs don't like it when witnesses don't remember things, especially if the things they don't remember are things likely to help the Crown case. Usually at this point the sheriff would be butting in with threats of sending the witness down to the cells for a few hours to see if it helped improve his memory, but there were no such words on this occasion.

'What *do* you remember about the injuries you sustained?' Joanna asked.

'I bumped my head and had to go to hospital.'

'Where you were put in a medically induced coma because your head injuries were so severe?' Joanna said.

I didn't bother to object to such an obviously leading question. It would only have seemed like my wife's examination in chief was going somewhere other than down the drain.

The witness grinned. 'I'm here amn't I? So, no harm done, then, eh?'

'No harm . . .?' Joanna sighed hugely, looked from the witness to me, then up at the sheriff. Finally, she threw her papers onto the table and sat down. 'I've no more questions, M'Lord.'

The sheriff smiled down at me and enquired, 'Mr Munro?'

What was happening? Examination in chief had been a disaster for the prosecution, and now the sheriff was smiling at me. Sheriffs never smiled at me. Not unless they were sticking several years up one of my clients. I had the horrible feeling that any moment now my old primary school teacher would arrive mounted on a unicorn asking me if this was the way to Amarillo and I'd wake up regretting a late-night cheese toastie.

I rose from my seat. 'No thank you M'Lord,' I said, and sat down again.

11

My wife was no quitter. The fact we remained married was evidence of that. For the rest of the day she continued to flog a horse that wasn't just dead, but stuffed, mounted and on display in the museum of hopeless cases. Next up to bat was Mrs Keggie. Immaculately turned out, she gave her evidence in a straightforward fashion. On the night in question, she had heard voices in the hall, and knew nothing else of the incident until the police arrived to take her husband away. Joanna's plan had been to have Mrs Keggie say that, apart from her, only her husband had been in the house at the time. That way, by a process of elimination, he must have been the assailant. Mrs Keggie wouldn't commit to that, and under gentle cross-examination agreed with me that, going by the voices she'd heard, she couldn't say whose they were or how many people they belonged to. There may have been only two persons present or several. All she could say with certainty was that neither she nor her husband had been expecting any midnight visitors.

After that we heard from a doctor who spoke to the injuries, ambulance men who'd taken MacDonald to hospital, cops who'd found blood stains on the accused's floor and walls, and lastly a forensic scientist who told us that the DNA from the blood samples taken matched that of the alleged victim.

At the end of the Crown case, and in the absence of the jury, I made a submission of no case to answer. It was true that even without MacDonald's evidence, there was more than enough to prove he'd been assaulted to his severe injury, but, I argued, there was insufficient to prove *who* had carried out the assault. The Crown couldn't even say with certainty how many people had been present at the time. Why blame my client just because he was the householder?

At that, Joanna jumped up and down a great deal, asking why a notice of self-defence and not incrimination had been lodged if the accused was denying he was the person who'd struck MacDonald. I was expecting the sheriff to agree with the Crown perspective – sheriffs normally did – and say that since the accused lived alone with his wife, and she was in bed at the time, in the absence of evidence to show there were others present, it was reasonable to infer that the only person who could have carried out the assault was the accused. But he didn't. 'It's not for the defence to prove self-defence, incrimination or anything else, Miss Jordan. It's for the Crown to lead a sufficiency of evidence to say the accused was responsible for an assault before I can fairly let the jury decide whether it was justifiable or not.' And, having upheld my no case to answer submission, he recalled the ladies and gentlemen and instructed a rather bemused jury to return a formal verdict of not guilty.

I met my client as he left the dock a free man. We shook hands. 'Thank you very much for that, Mr Munro. Mr Veitch was right about you. And particular thanks for arranging things at such short notice.'

It was a strange turn of phrase I thought, but without another word he left me, embraced his wife and the two of them walked out of the door.

My own wife was still in the well of the court, tidying up her papers. 'Win some, lose some,' I said, not wishing to gloat. Actually, I did wish to gloat, but didn't dare. Criminal lawyers on both sides of a prosecution tend to be very bad losers, and I had to live with my loser.

Joanna gave me a peck on the cheek, and we walked together out of the court building where we each went our separate ways. I didn't see her again until shortly after six when she came home to find me in the kitchen helping Tina with her homework, something I was managing to do while checking the Tuesday night TV football fixture list on my laptop.

I sensed relations were still frosty-to-glacial. She glanced out of the kitchen window to the side of the house and noticed my brother's car like a radiographer notices a spot on the lung. 'Is Malky here?'

'Yeah, he insisted on coming over to watch the Champion's League match. At half-time he wants me to ask him his views on the game. It's practice for when he starts his new job. Kick-off's not until eight. Unfortunately, he seems to be expecting corporate hospitality.'

'He'll be lucky. I've had no time to go to the shops.'

'It's okay, I can make scrambled eggs,' I said, opening the fridge. 'Or I could if we had eggs.' I closed it again. 'Tell you what – why don't I put Tina to bed while you nip out to the shop, and, when you come back, I'll make something for all three of us.'

Joanna dropped onto a chair.

'What are you looking so worried about?' I said. 'You're not upset because of the Keggie case, are you? He was acquitted. Big deal. I'd have hung up my gown if I'd lost that one.'

'How could you lose with a sheriff like that?' she said.

'And another thing. There was nothing wrong with Josh.'

'Who?'

'Josh Wedderburn. The man who was so terribly ill on Friday that he had to put off the trial. Someone told me that he'd sufficiently recovered to play at the Star & Garter that same night.'

'Play?'

'The guitar. He's a country and western or a blues singer or something.'

Tina jumped down from her chair and rammed her homework jotter into the schoolbag before I could check it. 'What's a blues singer?'

'Something you'll never be,' I said. 'You've had it too easy. Woke up this morning, got my breakfast made for me, was driven to school, where I had a great time learning stuff, came home and my dad helped me with my homework? Can't make much of a blues song about that. You need to suffer before you can sing the blues. Like me, having to listen to your mum cross-examining her own witness all morning.'

I laughed. Joanna didn't. 'Come on, Jo. You can't blame Wedderburn for dodging a trial like that. But now you know the truth, you can make the man's life a misery. Tell Hugh Ogilvie to give him the next ten JP cited courts to do. After a thousand road traffic cases he really will be sick.'

Joanna didn't say anything. I went over and pinched her cheeks together so that her lips pouted and kissed her. 'What's with the worried face? It wasn't that great a Crown case even if the complainer had stuck to the script.'

Joanna turned her head away. 'That's not why I'm worried,' she said.

'What's the matter, then? Are you all right? It's not one of the kids is it?'

She shook her head. 'No, it's the complainer.'

'Who? The complainer in the Keggie trial? MacDonald? What about him?'

Joanna reached for Tina's schoolbag, picked it up off the floor and removed her homework jotter.

'What about MacDonald?' I repeated.

Joanna opened the jotter and began to check the contents, while my daughter skipped out of the room. 'Tina,' Joanna called after her. 'Your writing is worse than ever. Take your time, and—'

I closed the door between kitchen and living room. 'Jo, what about MacDonald? And don't say it's nothing.'

She took a deep breath, replaced the jotter in the satchel, leaned back in the chair and said. 'It was him. The person at the back of the house on Saturday teatime. The man who—'

'Who assaulted you on Friday night? That was MacDonald? It must have been some kick in the shins to fend *him* off. What were you wearing? Steel toecaps? Why didn't you say anything?'

'I couldn't ask for the case to be put off, not for a second time in the same sitting. It would have time-barred.'

'Of course you could have,' I said. 'No one would have blamed you for chucking the towel in. First of all, your husband is acting for the accused, and secondly, the creep who molested you, and is now stalking you, is the complainer. How many more excuses do you need to back out of a trial?'

But there was even more of a reason. 'On Friday, he didn't just grab me. He threatened me. Told me to drop the case against your client. Said he'd see me all right if I did.'

'How all right?'

'Three thousand pounds.'

'And you never thought of telling me this?'

'I didn't know who he was at the time. I just thought he was a nutter. A friend of Keggie's. It made me even more determined to get a conviction.'

'But, when you saw him in court, why didn't you say something then? Why not put it to him when he was in the witness box?'

'Accuse my star witness of attacking a woman late at night?'

'Yes, and of attempting to defeat the ends of justice, by trying to bribe an employee of the Crown Office and Procurator Fiscal Service,' I said.

Joanna snorted. 'It was a bad enough case already. Anyway, why should I care? It's his head that got stoved in, not mine. If he didn't want your client convicted, why should the rest of us bother?' Joanna stood up to put her coat back on. 'Doesn't matter. It's all over and done with now.'

Not so far as I was concerned, it wasn't. 'We'll talk about this later,' I said. 'Meantime you're going nowhere while that nut-job is prowling about. Put the kettle on and make yourself a coffee. I'll go grab a curry or a pizza or something.' Joanna protested, though not enough to make me think she meant it.

On my way through to the living room, I met Malky coming out of the toilet, newspaper under one arm.

'Do you ever do a jobby and think it should maybe win an award or something?' he said, collapsing onto the couch. My brother was a man with very few unexpressed thoughts. 'I did this one on Boxing Day and I kid you not—'

'*Boxing Day*?' I said. 'That was nearly six months ago. Have you been keeping a diary?'

'No, it's just that you remember the great ones. And by the way, how were you after that curry the other day? Spicy or what? I had an arse on me like the Japanese flag afterwards.'

Tina ran over and jumped onto Malky's lap. 'I did a poo once and it had corn in it.'

'See what you've started?' I said, lifting Tina and holding her at eye level. 'It's not nice for young ladies to talk about . . . you know . . . the toilet and bottoms and things like that.'

'But it's funny,' Tina said. 'And Uncle Malky says—'

'Don't listen to what Uncle Malky says. The rest of us don't. Go and give your mum a cuddle, she's had a hard day.' I put my daughter down and sent her off in the direction of the kitchen, looking like she would have preferred to stay and swap tales of the toilet with her Uncle Malky.

I was about to start in on Malky again about suitable topics of discussion in front of my children, when there was a knock at the front door. I opened it to Stan Blandy's driver. I hadn't seen him for a couple of years. He hadn't changed much: as short and stocky as ever, with a shaved head and a face you could have punched all day and only made improvements to.

'You've to come with me,' he said.

'Where to?' I thought it only pertinent to inquire.

'You wanted someone found. We've found him.'

12

We sped through the town centre and at Linlithgow Bridge took a left under the viaduct and into the countryside. I was seated in the front of a Mitsubishi Outlander estate. Stan's driver's leather gloves were on the wheel and a much larger man sat in the back, smoking a cigarette.

'Where's Stan?' I asked. Silence was answer enough, if not the one I wanted. Stan prided himself on now being totally legit, having cut all ties with the drug importation side of his business which had made him the extremely wealthy man he was. Not that Stan had ever associated himself directly with anyone remotely involved in his former criminal activities. He gave the orders; others took the risks. The fact that he was absent was a cause for concern. Where were we going? I was getting a little worried by the time we slowed and turned into a B-road. I grew even more apprehensive when after a few miles we started down a rutted farm track, then through a gate and into a small courtyard serving a semi-derelict cottage. One or two of the windows were boarded up and there was an adjacent row of grubby, whitewashed concrete outbuildings. The man in the back seat rolled down the window and flicked his cigarette out. Then he and the driver got out, and I was told to go with them to one of the outbuildings. Its small, barred window and sturdy iron door made it look like a cartoon Wild West jail. There was a rusty six-inch bolt shoved through the hasp that was intended for a padlock. The driver removed the bolt and walked inside, beckoning me to follow. Inside the outbuilding it was dark and the place smelled like something had crawled in, died and was rotting in a corner. The driver produced a black rubber torch. By its light I could see work benches littered with rusty tools, a large wooden trestle table and, when the beam was swung downwards, a figure, bound hands and feet, lying on his side on the filthy floor.

'Is that him?' the driver asked. 'The guy you wanted to speak to? The one you told the boss had been stalking your wife?'

It was hard to tell because the man's mouth and most of his head was wound around with silver duct tape. If it was MacDonald, how on earth had Stan managed to track him down so quickly? I'd been expecting maybe a home address or a place of work, not a personal introduction and certainly not a meeting in a disused outbuilding in the middle of nowhere. Using the sole of his shoe, the driver rolled the man onto his back. In the light of the torch, I could see the man's face was streaked with dirt and there was a pronounced lump, turning from livid red to blue, on his forehead. Other than that, he seemed uninjured.

The driver ordered his big pal to guard the door and wandered away to the far side of the room, leaving me and the man on the ground in the dark. He returned with a pickaxe handle. 'What do you want done?'

The man on the ground's eyes widened at the sight of the pickaxe handle and he began to thrash around.

The driver stepped forward; pickaxe handle raised. I put out an arm to stop him.

'I don't want anything done,' I said. 'I just want to talk to him. Take the tape off his face.'

With a huge sigh, the driver handed me the pickaxe handle, and, using a knife, sliced through the layers of duct tape around MacDonald's head, ripping it away. 'That him?' he asked again.

It was. It was Angus MacDonald. Just as Joanna had said, the man stalking her had been none other than the man who'd given evidence, albeit not very well, at Simon Keggie's trial. He was fast becoming a serial victim.

The driver dragged MacDonald to the trestle table, pulled him to his feet and propped him against it.

I cleared my throat. 'Eh, sorry about all this,' I said, realising how pathetic I must have sounded. 'I wanted a word with you, but this isn't really how I imagined it going. Still . . . Anyway . . . Seeing as how we're both here . . .' I was beginning to come across like it was a chance meeting at the opera.

The driver shone the torch in MacDonald's face, simultaneously placing the point of the knife against the man's cheek.

Eyes screwed against the glare of the flashlight, MacDonald stared at the pickaxe handle I was holding, shook his head and coughed. 'I don't understand,' he croaked.

A solid blow to the face from the hilt of the driver's knife didn't seem to help his understanding any. MacDonald dropped to his knees.

'Would you leave him alone?' I said, prodding Stan's man with the end of the pickaxe handle. 'Step back and leave this to me.'

I moved closer and stared him in the face. 'The procurator fiscal at the trial today. She's my wife.' MacDonald said nothing, just stared at the ground. Drops of blood from his nose mixed with sweat and dripped onto the flagstones and down the pickaxe shaft. 'Why were you stalking my wife? If it was because you wanted the charge against Simon Keggie dropped, then you got what you wanted. It's over. Finito. Understand?'

The prisoner gave no indication that he did understand. He just stood there looking decidedly pissed off, as I imagine I would have if I'd found myself battered, bound and dragged into a room by a bunch of strangers. I threw the pickaxe handle into a dark corner and stood up. 'Cut him loose.' There was no need for further hostility. If, as seemed to be the case, he'd been instructed to put pressure on Joanna to ditch Keggie's case, then there should be no need for him to bother my wife any more. I turned to the driver again. 'I said, cut him loose. Go on. What's he going to do? There's three of us.'

With a couple of deft slices, MacDonald was free. I gave him a moment to get to his feet and rub the circulation back into his wrists. On one of his forearms was a tattoo I recognised. A thistle crest, with a boar on one side, a cat on the other and the motto 'Sans Peur'. My Great Uncle Jim had had one just like it, except his had been India ink, faded with age and barely visible through a thick mat of grey hair. Jim had fought the Imperial Japanese army in Malaya and Singapore. He'd been shot, tortured and starved half to death in a POW camp. He'd been a regular visitor when Malky and I were boys, and we'd been brought up on his wartime tales. Despite his terrible ordeals, Jim was the kind of guy butchers and tobacco companies loved. A fried breakfast every morning, twenty Capstan full-strength before lunch. If the Japs couldn't kill him, he wasn't letting little things like arterial plaques or lung cancer see him off. He'd lived to ninety-four and would have made it to ninety-five had he not been knocked down by a Honda 4x4 on the way to the pub one night.

I watched as MacDonald tore the rest of the duct tape from around his head. When he'd finished, he flattened his hair with a hand and brushed dirt from his clothes. After that, the rest was something of a blur. I remembered my legs being swept from under me and falling heavily onto the stone floor. I also vaguely recalled hearing a cry of pain and the driver's knife clattering to the ground followed by a shout, another cry of pain and the heavy metal door clanging shut.

13

I was awakened next morning by the sound of Jamie yelling from the next room. The arm that had broken my fall the night before was stiff and sore. Joanna caught hold of it by the elbow as I was getting out of bed.

'That's some bruise you've got there,' she said. 'Looks painful.' She tested her theory with a squeeze, and I confirmed it with a muted yelp. 'How on earth did you do that?'

Years in court have made me quick on my feet, even my bare feet, but I wasn't fast enough for my wife. 'Has this got something to do with you disappearing off last night?'

'I didn't exactly disappear,' I said.

'Yes, you did. You disappeared to the shops to buy something for tea and reappeared later with nothing.'

'I had to go see someone. I must have bumped my elbow on something. It's nothing.'

'Doesn't look like nothing to me.' She tried to give the arm another experimental squeeze, but I pulled it out of her reach. 'Is it really sore?' she asked.

I straightened my arm out. 'Only when I do that.'

'Don't do it then,' she said, throwing back the duvet and getting out of bed. 'What was so urgent it made you miss a game of football on the telly, anyway? Wasn't it the most important game since the last most important game?'

My wife has never fully understood the life-and-death

nature of football. 'Just a client in a spot of bother,' I said.

'Robbie, all your clients are in a spot of bother. If they weren't in bother, they wouldn't be your clients.'

Tina burst into the room. She threw herself onto the bed, bounced off again, lifted my wife's phone from the bedside table, hacked into it and started watching a music video on YouTube. 'I think Jamie's done a pooper,' she said, 'and it's your turn, Mum.'

Joanna snatched her phone back and ruffled my daughter's hair. 'Are you keeping a record?'

I winked at my Tina. When it came to Jamie's number two nappies, my daughter and I had an understanding based on love, mutual respect and clandestine ice cream trips to Sandy's café. I used the distraction of Jamie's faecal deposits to disappear into the bathroom. By the time I was washed, dressed and in the kitchen, concern for my bruised arm had given way to finding Tina's homework jotter and packing her schoolbag. I knocked up a couple of rounds of cheese and Marmite sandwiches and put them along with an apple and a biscuit in her wee lunchbox. After that Joanna and I went our separate ways; she to drop Jamie off at my dad's, me to run Tina to school and another day's toil at the Sheriff Court.

'What's on today?' I asked Grace Mary, when I dropped into the office to collect my case files.

Phone clamped between shoulder and jaw, scribbling something down on a notepad, without looking up she tilted her head at a bundle of files on the end of her desk. I flicked through them. I was still flicking through them when she stopped scribbling and put the phone down.

'Are these all for today's cited court?' I asked. 'What happened? Was there a crime wave two months ago or something?'

'Life is just a constant surprise for you, isn't it, Robbie?' she said. 'Maybe you should look at some of your cases occasionally and get to know them.'

I took the files and wedged them into my briefcase. Getting to know your case files was a luxury legal aid lawyers couldn't afford, not at this early stage in proceedings. I'd get to know them at the trial. That was when it mattered.

The combination of Sheriff Brechin, who wanted to go into the detail of every case, and a trainee Fiscal who spoke with the speed of a shifting tectonic plate, meant court dragged on until lunch. I was chucking my briefcase into the back of the car when Joanna called.

'Where are you?' she asked.

'Just leaving court and on my way back to the office,' I said.

'How about we have lunch together?'

I've never been a fan of working late, which was why lunch was usually a quick crispy bacon roll at Sandy's café. My arrival gave Sandy's female customers relief from his flirting, as he rambled on to me about football and the local team. The café owner might have a framed picture of the all-conquering 1990s AC Milan team on the wall, but everyone knew he was more Linlithgow Rose than Rossoneri.

'Where about?' I asked.

'At home. I've got the afternoon off to take Jamie to the doctor for his jags. We could have lunch before I pick him up from your dad's.'

It sounded like a plan. Lunch and who knows what else we could do in a peaceful hour without Tina jumping on our bed or Jamie letting the world fall out of his bottom?

Joanna was scrambling eggs in the kitchen when I

arrived home twenty minutes later. 'Good morning at court?' she asked.

'The cited court with Bert Brechin and a baby Fiscal,' I said, which was explanation enough.

The toast popped. Joanna buttered it, laid the slices on a plate, plonked on some properly stodgy eggs and set it down in front of me. We ate in silence, me stuffing the food away, Joanna pushing hers about the plate.

Joanna put down her knife and fork. 'Where were you last night, Robbie?'

'What do you mean where was I?' It was a poor reply, but one I hoped would give me time to gather my thoughts.

'It's perfectly obvious what I mean,' Joanna said. 'Where were you?'

I finished the last of my food and stood up. 'I told you. I had to go and see a client about something urgent.' I looked up at the clock on the wall. Too early to make an excuse and go back to the office.

My phone rang. Hallelujah. It was Grace Mary. 'Where are you?'

'At home having lunch,' I said.

'Well, the police are here. They want a word with you. Wouldn't say what about. How long are you going to be? I'll tell them fifteen minutes.' The line went dead.

I held my phone up to Joanna. 'The office. I've got to go. Thanks for lunch.' I leaned across and gave her a kiss, then walked through the living room to the hall and the front door, skirting Jamie's playmat and the toys scattered everywhere. Joanna followed. 'Tell me you had nothing to do with it, Robbie.'

I turned and saw tears in her eyes.

I put my hands on her shoulders. 'Okay,' I said, with a laugh. 'I had nothing to do with it. Whatever it is you're talking about. Absolutely zilch involvement on my part. Happy?'

Joanna shrugged me off. 'The police are at your office, aren't they? They're looking for you?'

I could only be impressed by my wife's acute sense of hearing. 'They think he's dead,' Joanna said, only deepening the mystery.

'Who's they and who do they think is dead?' She didn't reply. 'Listen, Joanna. I have absolutely no idea what you're talking about.'

With unerring accuracy, she thumped my elbow. The sore one. 'Then how did you get that?' she asked, ignoring my cry of pain.

'I told you, I—'

'No, Robbie, you lied to me. You said you'd bumped it against something last night.' She poked me in the chest. 'The same night you disappeared. Robbie, please promise me you didn't do anything stupid and I'll believe you.'

She was going to have to narrow things down for me.

'Angus MacDonald. The complainer from the trial of Simon Keggie. The man who was stalking me...'

At the mention of the name my mouth dried like water on the moon. I'd hardly slept for worrying that he'd phoned the cops, consoling myself that he wouldn't dare otherwise he'd have to explain why he'd been stalking my wife. 'What about him?' I said.

'He's been reported missing. The police have been to see me. Your name is down as one of the people the cops want to speak to.' Joanna grabbed the lapels of my jacket. 'Look me in the eyes and swear you know nothing about it.'

I was listening to her but all I could think of was a pickaxe handle and drops of blood on a flagstone floor.

Three letters kept dancing before my eyes. D, N and A.

'How can you even think—?'

She shoved me away. 'Tell me what I'm supposed to think.'

I put my right hand up. 'I swear I did not harm a hair on the head of ... What's his name again?'

'Angus MacDonald.'

'Okay, I swear I did not harm a hair on the head of Angus MacDonald.'

'Or any other part of his body.' That was the problem with being married to a lawyer.

'Or any other part of his body,' I said, with a sigh.

Joanna looked at me for a moment and then hugged me. She smiled up at me through teary eyes. 'I'm sorry if I ...' she shoved me away again. 'Then why do the police want to speak to you about him?'

Those three same letters began their dance once more. Why was I so worried? The cops didn't have my DNA on file. There had to be another reason for their interest in me.

'Why, Robbie?'

'Possibly because I tried to phone him.'

'But you promised you wouldn't do anything about it.'

'And I didn't, other than call him a few times. I never got through. It went straight to his answerphone.'

'How did you even get his number? Were you going through my case papers?'

'Well, if you will leave stuff lying around inside your briefcase ... Don't worry,' I said. 'They'll have checked his phone records and will be checking people who've called him recently. It's just routine.'

Joanna put a finger to her mouth and bit it. 'Except ...'

'What?'

'I was so angry with Josh Wedderburn that I told him about MacDonald stalking me. What if he told the police and they find out you were trying to phone the man who'd been stalking your wife? That's a motive right there. You know what the cops are like. If they've nothing else to go on, you'll be prime suspect and they'll start building a case around you.'

'But I didn't know he'd been stalking you. Even you didn't know it was him until the trial had started,' I said, resuming the hug. 'At the time I made those calls all I knew was that he was the chief Crown witness in a trial I was about to conduct. Why wouldn't I try to contact the complainer for a precognition?' I let Joanna go and lifted my jacket and car keys.

By the time I'd opened the front door the concerned look on her face had relaxed, but only slightly. 'There's no need to look like that,' I said. 'I'll explain that I was just doing my job and they'll be happy with that. It'll take five minutes at most. There's absolutely nothing to worry about.'

14

I hadn't only made DI Dougie Fleming's day, but his week, month, year, and, quite possibly, life. I'd sat in police interview rooms on a great many occasions, but never before in the seat next to the wall. Not the one where my clients usually sat.

'You're sure you don't want a lawyer?' Fleming asked for the umpteenth time. 'I'd feel better if you had a brief.'

The young female DC who was squashed up beside him on one of the two bolted-down seats across from me nodded in affirmation. 'We're just wanting to make sure everything's done fair.' She couldn't have looked more sincere if she'd been sincere.

'No thanks,' I said. 'The sooner you've started, the sooner you'll finish.'

The DC looked at Fleming. He looked at me. 'Have it your way,' he grunted. 'I'm just concerned that you take full advantage of your rights.'

Fleming's only concern was that if he was going to start throwing allegations at me, he might miss and hit the wall because of some legal technicality – like me not having had legal advice before interview. A few years ago, before the advent of video-recorded interrogations and the right to a lawyer, he'd already have had my confession in his notebook.

Fleming unfurled a roll of papers and spread them

across the table in front of him. For the past seven hours, while I'd been banged up with four walls and a plastic mattress for company, he'd been jotting down all sorts of questions to ask me, the answer to which he must have known would be, 'no comment.' No comment all the way and I'd be out in no time. After all, what was the reason for a police interview if not to try and secure sufficient evidence to convict? If they already had enough evidence, why bother?

'What do you know about a missing person called Angus MacDonald?' was his opener.

'No comment,' I said. 'And just to save any confusion, I'll not be saying any more during the course of this interview.'

The door flew open. 'Whoa, whoa! What's all this?' A burly little figure in a kilt bustled into the room, beard all a-bristle.

'Mr Veitch is here,' the civilian turnkey at his back said, as though Sammy's dramatic entry might otherwise have gone unnoticed.

'If you don't mind, officers,' he said, very slowly, careful not to slur his words, 'I'd like a word with my client before this goes any further.' With that he dropped into the seat next to mine. The DC looked from Fleming to me, I looked at her, we were all looking at each other, apart from Sammy who was looking at his sporran because it had jammed itself under the edge of the table.

Eventually, the DC took the initiative. She sniffed, cleared her throat and said, 'Have you been drinking alcohol, Mr Veitch?'

'No more for me, love,' he said. 'A cup of tea will be fine.'

'Mr Veitch,' Fleming said. 'I think you should know

that Mr Munro has declined legal representation.'

'Well, he can un-decline because his father sent me.'

Detective Inspector Dougie Fleming respected my father almost as much as he disrespected me. Ex-Police Sergeant Alexander Munro had been his mentor as cadet Fleming had risen through the ranks, and, despite my father's many years' retirement from the force, there had remained a bond between them like that shared by grandchild and grandparent, united by a common enemy: me. In this case, however, my old man seemed to think I needed rescuing. Sammy Veitch – it was like sending a petrol tanker to hose down a house fire.

Fleming sighed. 'Mr Munro, would you like a consultation with Mr Veitch before we go any further?'

'Aye, he would,' Sammy answered for me, jerking a thumb at the door, his invitation for Her Majesty's Constabulary to leave. Soon it was just me, Sammy Veitch and his whisky breath. 'What have they got on you?'

'Nothing,' I said. 'Much. I think.'

'Did you do it?'

'Do what?'

'The thing you're in here for?'

'They haven't actually told me what I'm supposed to have done, yet, but the answer is no.'

'Then tell them that, and we'll catch last orders.'

'I was thinking more along the lines of no comment,' I said.

'Why bother, if you're innocent?' He glanced down at the watch on his wrist, ticking off the seconds until closing time.

'Sammy, when you came here, did you ask for any background information? The grounds for me being arrested? What evidence the cops have?'

'Can you do that nowadays?' Sammy's career in criminal law had ended long before the right to legal representation at a police interview was introduced.

I stood up and opened the door. As I thought, Fleming and his sidekick were outside, prowling the corridor, huffing and puffing like a couple of wolves temporarily deprived of their little pig. 'Go out there, see what they've got and come back and tell me.'

'They think you've murdered some guy MacDonald,' he said, on his return.

My stomach heaved. 'What makes them think that?' I just about managed to croak.

'Someone reported him missing last night. And there's this witness. A Fiscal called Wensleydale...'

'Wensleydale?'

'Aye, or Weddingham or—'

'Wedderburn?'

'Quite possibly.' Sammy sat down heavily opposite me. 'He says your wife was assaulted on a night out. By the dead guy. While he was alive obviously. Couldn't really have...' Sammy coughed and continued. 'This Wensleydale says he wasn't there, but he said he heard about it.'

'Okay, that's hearsay. What else?'

'They've got a record of you trying to phone the dead guy. Somehow the cops have got a hold of your mobile number—'

'Sammy, everyone has a hold of my mobile number. It's on my business card.'

'Right, well, they know you phoned this MacDonald guy a lot in the days after he assaulted your missus, and they've also got your phone travelling to somewhere near Muiravonside last night. That's where the dead guy—'

'He's only missing,' I said.

'Whatever, that's where he lives. It's really Falkirk jurisdiction, but because Dougie Fleming seems keen on being in on the action, he volunteered to do the interview.'

Was that it? A few phone calls, my phone in the same vicinity as his house. 'Do they know MacDonald was the complainer in a trial I had last week? I could have been phoning to try and get a witness precognition from him.'

'Were you?'

'Yes.'

'And last night? Why was your phone out in the wilds near to his house?'

That I'd need to work on.

'Was there any mention of a pickaxe handle?' I asked.

'Should there have been?'

I didn't reply.

Sammy prised himself out of his chair and went to the door. 'No comment it is then.'

15

There was no early release to the relative comfort of the Red Corner Bar. Instead, I spent the night in a police cell, the only things keeping me company a plastic-coated foam mattress, a cup of milky tea and an ancient edition of a Harold Robbins paperback the size of small sliced loaf. At eight the next morning I was transported to Falkirk Sheriff Court. At ten o'clock I was shown into an interview room.

'Bad news,' Sammy said, as though things could get any worse. He slipped a petition to me under the security glass separating us. The first thing I saw was the first thing every accused person's eyes are drawn to, namely, the big black '*Bail Opposed*' stamp in the top right corner.

'What did you expect?' Sammy said. 'The last time I had anything to do with a murder case, bail was a non-starter. At least now the law's changed we can give it a go.'

I didn't reply, just read further down the page. 'You Robert Alexander Munro did in the grounds of Wester Brigg Cottage, by Muiravonside and at other places to the petitioner unknown and whilst acting with persons unknown, and by means to the petitioner unknown assault Angus Fraser MacDonald and did murder him.' No mention of a pickaxe handle.

'That's a lot of unknowns,' I said, sliding the paper back under the glass to Sammy. 'Why is there no summary of evidence attached to it?'

'What's that?' he asked.

I was beginning to appreciate the purpose of the security glass. 'It's the evidence. In the form of a summary. That should be attached,' I said, doing my best to remain calm.

'You don't have to instruct me,' Sammy said. 'There's other lawyers.'

I was aware of that fact. I'd pondered very little else after I'd read the first two chapters of *The Carpetbaggers* and decided Mr Robbins's book might be better employed as a bolster to the one-inch-thick strip of foam that pretended to be a pillow. Did I want a better lawyer? I knew many who'd have been pleased to help: my good friend Paul Sharp for one. Paul would have taken the case on, made it his own, carried out enquiries, investigated the evidence, done everything that could properly be done – and that was the problem. What if I needed things improperly done? At least one of the unknowns in that murder petition was known by me and that was the person who'd abducted MacDonald in the first place. There were enquiries I needed to make with a person who made it his job not to be enquired into. Stan Blandy wouldn't take at all kindly to some third party contacting him on my behalf. I needed a lawyer to be a conduit between myself and the Crown, someone to do the admin; but when it came to preparing the case, that was something I'd have to do myself.

'You'll do fine, Sammy,' I said. A loud rap on the door behind me indicated my case was about to call. 'There's no reason why I shouldn't get bail. I've a business, a family and no previous convictions. What's the Crown got? More unknowns than the last series of *I'm A Celebrity* . . . Do your best and we can discuss things over a pint at the Red Corner Bar in a couple of hours.'

According to the red numbers on the court's digital

clock, my hearing lasted twenty-three minutes, which is about twenty minutes longer than the average first calling of a solemn petition.

'I thought I had him persuaded,' Sammy said, when once again we were talking at each other through plate glass.

'You did your best,' I said, and he had. Sammy had given the sheriff everything, but still not enough to overcome the Crown's demand that the case be continued one week for further examination and I remanded in custody until then. Apparently, the prosecution didn't want me at liberty contaminating any potential evidence until the police had time to complete their enquiries. It was a common tactic.

'You'll get bail next week when you come back for full committal,' Sammy said. 'There's no reason why not to grant it then. This is just a wee seven-day lie-down. It won't be too bad. How many visits have you made to folk in prison? Hundreds probably. It'll be just like that. Except all at the same time ...' He tailed off, recovering with a cheerful, look-on-the-bright-side smile. 'Treat it like a holiday. Getting away from all those weans of yours for a while. Lie back, read a book, watch some telly. You'll be back here in no time at all, and then we can have that drink.'

I'd sat on Sammy's side of the security glass so many times, said the same sort of thing to clients off on a short break courtesy of Her Majesty. It wasn't the next seven days that bothered me so much as the rest of my life. Suddenly it was all very real. Sammy started to get up from his seat.

'Where do you think you're going?' I asked.

He shrugged. 'I think we're done here ... Aren't we?'

'No,' I said. 'We're not. Get your notepad out.'

'Why?'

'Because,' I said, 'I'm about to swear an affidavit.'

16

I was pleased to discover that on admission to prison these days there was a lot less bend over, spread your cheeks, cough and think happy thoughts. Instead they sat me down on the charmingly named Body Orifice Scanner and let technology search those places I'd rather not have had the chubby fingers of a burly prison officer go rummaging around in. I got up out of the big chair, had my hair riffled for rope ladders and having been thrown a pair of jeans and a red prison polo shirt, was shown to a cubicle to change into them.

My cell was a double, but thankfully I was the only occupant. That was soon to change. Next morning, I was lying on the bottom bunk, reading, when the cell door opened and a man was ushered in. He had grey hair, a slight stoop and the face of a laboratory beagle that had just quit smoking. The door slammed shut again and I wondered if I should have commandeered the top bunk. Which was the best, top or bottom? Were farts heavier than air? I should have watched more prison movies.

At first glance my new roomy seemed all right. He didn't look like a junkie. That would have been all I needed. Banged up twenty-three hours a day with someone rattling like a charity tin.

He put out a hand. 'Tony,' he said, in an unexpectedly crisp, polite voice, like we were being introduced on our first day at Fettes College. I closed my book, swung my legs around and stood up. I shook his hand, sat down and picked up the book again.

He poked a finger at it, tilting the book towards me so he could look at the cover. 'Agatha Christie. Is that the best they can do for you?'

I pointed to a battered volume poking out from below the bed. 'It was crime fiction or the history of steam locomotion.' I said.

He smiled. 'Personally, I'd have gone with George Stephenson. What's your name?'

I turned my attention to the book again, flicked over a page. 'Oh, I'm sure you know who I am and why I'm here.'

Tony cleared his throat. 'And why would that be?'

'When did you get in?' I asked.

He hesitated. 'Yesterday.'

'Really?'

'Yes, really. You know—'

'Yes, I do know,' I said. 'I know quite a lot. Like I know that this prison is so overcrowded folk are having to share single cells. There's no reason why I should have a double cell to myself on my first night. I also know you're well over forty-five, so what are you doing in this wing and not the old-timers hall? And I know that you've been in here for a while and have agreed to move in with me so we can become pals and later you can tell a jury how I confessed everything to you. You say you're Tony, but I'm guessing there are some people would prefer to call you witness number one for the prosecution. What did they promise you?'

He didn't answer.

'Listen, Tony or whoever you are. I've got a week to do and then all going well I'm out of here and I'm not coming

106

back. You seem a nice enough guy, polite, educated and I'm sure we'll get along. I'm happy to talk about football, politics, the weather, even the history of steam locomotion, but I've already sworn an affidavit to say I'll be talking to no one about my case and that if anyone says different it's because they're a plant. So, if you'd like to be transferred back to where you came from, that's fine. If you want to stay here for a week, that's fine by me too. But at the end of the week you're going to have to break it to whoever sent you, that the only confession you can speak to was made to Hercule Poirot, in the drawing room at the end of this book.' I tossed the paperback at him and he caught it. 'Understand?'

Tony placed the book on the top bunk, walked across the narrow cell and filled a plastic tumbler from the tap. He turned and leaned against the sink. He smiled down at me while he sipped.

'They didn't tell me your name,' he said eventually. 'Just that you're a lawyer.'

'What else did they tell you?'

'That you'd murdered someone. They never said who, and they never asked me to lie about hearing a confession. They just want me to try and find out what I can.'

'What are you in for?' I asked.

Tony puffed his cheeks and exhaled slowly. 'My business had some ... accounting problems. Irregularities with the working of certain figures.'

'How irregular?'

'A million pounds' worth, give or take.'

'And you're remanded?'

'There have been other irregularities ... Over the years. They said if I helped with you, they'd keep the case out of the High Court. A Sheriff Court five-year maximum will be discounted to forty months for an early plea, I'll only do half with remission and most likely be out on a tag after half of that.'

Ten months for stealing a million. That was a decent hourly rate. There had been no irregularities in Tony working out those figures.

We didn't speak much the rest of the morning. Mid-afternoon I was let out for exercise. There was a full-size Astroturf football pitch and a couple for five-a-sides, but there was no football for me, just a walk in a concrete yard with a fine view of four walls. It was really just another cell, only larger and with a net roof.

Back in my cell, Tony had gone, replaced by a younger man, taller than me but scrawny with that pale, yellowish complexion that suggested even Dracula couldn't have found a vein in him. He was sitting on the top bunk, picking at his fingernails with the plastic handle of a toothbrush that had been melted and honed to a point.

'Cup of tea?' I said, walking past him to the sink and filling the kettle. He didn't reply. I heard him jump down and turned to see him facing me, hands by his sides, the toothbrush in one, the *History of Locomotion* in the other. 'Robbie Munro, that's you isn't it?' he said. 'Robbie Munro, the lawyer?' He held up the book. 'You like books, eh?'

'Not that particular one,' I said, 'but yeah, I like books. Not much else to do around here all day, is there?'

'Here's what you're going to do, then.' He clearly wasn't one for small talk. 'You fill out a pro form for some books to be handed in for you. On your next visit, you tell whoever it is to take one of the books to my mate. Then when the books are handed in, you give that one to me.' He smiled like a corncob. 'Easy.'

'Certainly sounds it,' I said. 'The trouble is I'm on a seven-day lie-down. I don't know when my first visit is going to be and by the time the books are handed in and processed by the screws, I'll be long gone.'

He sniffed and did some more toothbrush-handle manicuring while he thought about that. 'When did you come in here?'

'Yesterday.'

'You'll be getting a visit today.'

'I'm not sure—'

'Aye you will. And you'll tell your wife, your burd, whoever it is, to write you a letter, take it to my pal and then post it first class. Awright?'

I couldn't see Joanna agreeing to take a letter to a lock-up somewhere so it could be dipped in a psychoactive solution made from alloy wheel polish, but neither did I think this the time or the place to tell my cellmate all about my wife's job with the Crown Office and Procurator Fiscal Service.

The hand holding the makeshift chiv twitched, and, as I stood there longing for those simpler, friendlier times with polite, arithmetically challenged, little Tony, the cell door swung open and a screw marched in. He looked to be around six foot five and, by the way his white shirt bulged, it was clear he spent a lot of his leisure time at the gym lifting heavy objects.

He pushed his way between us to the sink. If he noticed my cellmate's hand suspiciously shoot behind his back when he came in, he didn't show any sign of it. He poured a tumbler of water and held it out. 'Here.'

I reached for it.

He pulled the tumbler away. 'Not you. Him.'

There was only one hand my cellmate could use. He

109

dropped the book on the floor, but as he tried to take hold of the tumbler, the screw dropped it. I jumped back as water splashed around my feet, and it was because I was looking at the floor that I missed the punch. In fact, I was only aware one had been thrown when my cellmate toppled backwards, cracking his head off the ground as he landed, the toothbrush handle skidding under the bottom bunk. The screw walked over to him, grabbed his hair and lifted his head to reveal a smear of blood on the linoleum floor. 'That was a nasty fall,' he said, letting the head return to the floor with another bump. 'Gave himself a bad cut to the head and I wouldn't be surprised if he's cracked a rib.' He pulled the sheet from the top bunk, rolled it up, laid it alongside the prone figure and kicked it so hard, the unconscious man on the floor slid half a metre until he met the opposite wall.

The screw picked up the sheet again, threw it onto the bed and turned to me. I backed away.

'Looks like you'll be having the cell to yourself for a while,' he said. 'I'll get him taken away and bring you a mop so you can clean up that slipping hazard. Be more careful next time.'

He walked to the door, opened it and turned to me. 'Oh, and Mr Blandy says to remember who your friends are.'

17

I'd like to say that the week flew by in a blaze of steam locomotion and Agatha Christie novels, but it was the longest, most boring time I'd spent anywhere, and I'd once spent a rainy weekend in Dunoon.

'Bail's no longer opposed,' Sammy told me, when next we met in the Sheriff Court cells, his words accompanied, as it seemed, by an attendant chorus of angels. 'But they want some special conditions over and above the standard ones.'

'Like what?'

'You've not to contact your wife.'

'They're a bit late for that, aren't they?' I said. Joanna had visited me in prison. I'd spent so much time assuring her of my innocence that we'd hardly talked about anything else, and I'd told her one visit would be enough, since I was sure I'd be released in a few days. I'd not put down anyone else on the list for a visit. I'd be seeing my dad soon enough, and Malky's presence would only have added to the Soccer Star's Brother in Murder Charge headlines that had already appeared in some of the red tops and online.

Sammy shrugged helplessly.

'But,' I said, 'her only use to the prosecution is to confirm that I went out last Tuesday night and came back a couple of hours later with a sore elbow. She's already given a statement to the cops, what can I do to change that?'

Sammy sighed. 'It's not so much because she's a Crown witness. It's more to do with her being a Fiscal. They don't want you influencing her in any way, you know, putting her up to mischief when she's at work, tampering with evidence, that sort of thing.'

'Who's going to look after the kids? It's a two-person job.' I was starting to sound like a punter. Every accused seeking bail has domestic problems, sick elderly relatives, a pregnant girlfriend or a job starting Monday: as though a sheriff might be remotely interested.

Sammy shrugged. 'It's take it or leave it.'

I didn't bother to ask what would happen if I didn't take it. There was a slim chance the sheriff would refuse the Crown's motion and not impose the extra condition, but if not and I didn't accept the conditions of bail, I'd go back to prison and have to wait there for my trial date. It was a roll of the dice and I wasn't prepared to throw them. If I wanted to be reunited with my wife this side of a life licence, my best chance was to go along with the conditions of bail and prove my innocence, something I couldn't do from inside.

The full committal hearing took less than five minutes. After a further half-hour wait, while the bail order was printed and signed, I was on the streets again. Sammy gave me a lift to my new bail address, where my dad was sitting at his kitchen table reading the newspaper. He must have been expecting me because on any other Thursday afternoon he and his pals would be thrashing golf clubs at the undergrowth and inventing handicaps. He glanced up at me over the top of the page when I entered the room and watched silently as I went to the sink and filled the kettle.

'That's a fine mess you've got yourself into,' he said at last, in a resigned I-knew-this-day-would-come sort of a way. 'If your mother was alive it would kill her.' He folded the newspaper and ran the side of his hand against it firmly, pressing the pages flat against the table. 'What have they got on you?'

'How much do you know?' I asked.

'I know that you're supposed to have murdered some scumbag who was stalking your wife.'

It wasn't much more than I knew.

'Did you do it?'

'Of course not,' I said.

'Aye, well, you'd say that even if you had done it.' He stood up, pushed me aside and removed a bottle of Ardbeg Uigeadail from under the sink. Then he took down a couple of Glencairn glasses from a cupboard, filled a small jug with water and set the lot down on the table. 'You'll need something stronger than tea while you tell me everything.' This was new for my dad. First wanting to talk things over rationally, and now the good whisky. When it came to single malt, my dad was a great believer that whisky came in the wrong size of bottle – too much for one person to drink all at once, not enough to share.

I sat and told him what the cops had on me. 'They know that this Angus MacDonald guy was harassing Joanna. They'll be using that as a motive.'

'Why did she even speak to them?'

'She didn't know the importance of what she was saying when she was interviewed. She thought they were inquiring into MacDonald stalking her and then they made it sound like something bad had happened to me.'

'She should have known better than that.'

'Joanna's not like me,' I said. 'She's a PF. She thinks you can trust the police.'

My dad let that go. 'What else did she say?'

'That I'd left on Tuesday night without telling her where I was going and came back an hour or so later.'

'And?'

'They asked her if I had any signs of injury.'

'Did you?'

When I didn't answer, he shook his head, opened the bottle and poured us each a measure. After adding a drop or two of water, my dad raised his glass to the light and took a sip. 'At least they won't be able to use that against you.'

'Why not?' I asked.

'A person can't be made to give evidence against their spouse. You're a lawyer. You should know that. It's only right. You can't expect a wife to break the bond of holy matrimony. Love, honour and rat on your husband? I don't think so. They can do it in England, but not Scotland.'

'They can now,' I said.

'Since when?'

'Since they brought in the Criminal Justice and Licensing (Scotland) Act 2010,' I said.

My dad grunted and knocked back the rest of his drink. He'd not hear a bad word about the Scottish Parliament. Even when they'd put up the price of whisky, he hadn't complained, just drunk more of mine. 'What did you say to them?'

'Nothing, of course.'

'What else have they got on you?'

'They know I phoned MacDonald a few times, but I can explain why that was. They've also tracked my phone from my house to his on the night he went missing.'

'Where does he stay?'

'He was doing up an old farm cottage near Muiravonside Country Park.'

'Is that where the body was found?'

'There isn't a body. Just some blood in the kitchen and in an outbuilding.' There had still been no word about the pickaxe handle.

'Where's the body then?'

It was a good question, and one neither I nor the police knew the answer to. What I was more interested in finding out was why the cops had been so keen to investigate MacDonald's whereabouts. He couldn't have been missing for much more than twelve hours. 'When does that ever happen?' I asked my dad.

He snorted in agreement. 'Does seem strange. Fit, adult male goes missing? Standard police assumption is he's on a bender or got himself shacked up. Nobody's bothering their arse about him for at least a week, most likely a lot longer.' He poured himself another, larger than the first, stared into its depths for a while and then up at me. 'Did you do it?'

I held his stare.

'I told you, Dad. I didn't.'

He held the Glencairn up, rolling it gently. 'Anyway, you couldn't have,' he said, with a sniff, eyes watching the straw-coloured liquid swirl in the glass. 'How could you? That Tuesday night you were here with me, watching the football.'

'Dad...'

'Ajax against Liverpool. Good away win. You remember, don't you?'

18

The bail conditions being what they were, over the weekend, and with my dad acting as a go-between, Joanna and I made arrangements for childcare. It was decided that except on Joanna's days off, Tina would stay with me at my dad's, and Joanna would take charge of young Jamie, depositing him as usual with my dad on the days she worked. Monday morning, having taken Tina to school, I was sitting at my desk like it was business as usual – except it wasn't.

I heard Grace Mary arrive dead on five to nine. At nine she came through to my office.

'I'm innocent.' I thought we might as well get that fact nailed down from the start.

'Innocent? I don't think so, Robbie. Not guilty, I'm prepared to believe.' She placed a case file on the desk in front of me. Typed on the white label was HMA -v- Robbie Munro. 'I've emailed the procurator fiscal for disclosure,' she said, opening the file and handing me a pen. 'I've typed up the form 8.1-A. Who am I putting down as your legal representative? And please don't say Sammy Veitch. He was in here on Friday, having me make him cups of coffee and looking at your office like he was planning on moving in.'

'Put his name down and have him sign the form when he comes in,' I said. 'It'll be okay for just now.'

'And I've booked Miss Faye for the trial. Actually, she booked herself. She called last week when you were ... otherwise engaged. She said you were to call her for a consultation when you were ready.'

Fiona Faye QC was my go-to gal when it came to High Court work. Since I was now on bail, the Crown had around ten months to serve an indictment. They usually tried to work to a timescale of seven months, and, it being June, I wasn't expecting much to happen until the new year. It would be months after that before the trial. It was nice of Fiona to show interest at this early stage. Most senior counsel let the solicitor do all the spadework and only sat up and took notice of the case a week or so before the trial kicked off.

'Did she say anything about fees?' I asked.

'No, and I didn't bother to ask. You've sent her a lot of work over the years.'

I had, but most of it had been legal aid. I wasn't sure if that would be enough for Fiona to take on my case pro bono. Still, there was plenty of time before I'd need to involve her, and money spent on a successful defence wouldn't be wasted.

Grace Mary left the room. I picked up the case file and looked again at my name on the front cover. It was surreal. I'd been involved in a number of murder cases over the years, but I'd never thought I'd ever be preparing my own defence. One advantage I did have over all the others was that this time I knew for certain the accused was innocent. I also had another: I knew who the real culprit was. Why had I been so stupid as to ask for Stan Blandy's help? He might say he was now totally legit, but there was legit and there was what Stan Blandy called legit. Even though it had been me who had involved Stan,

I wasn't going to start blaming myself for MacDonald's death. How was I to know Stan would put his personal rottweiler onto the case of locating Joanna's molester? I should have insisted that Grace Mary track him down. After all, I'd only wanted a note of his whereabouts, not an execution. *Remember who your friends are.* Well, I was remembering. I was remembering all the work I'd done for Stan's "business colleagues" over the years, and thought I deserved more than just protection from some drug-smuggling nutter in prison. Why should that be enough to buy my silence, when I was looking at a life sentence? I needed to speak to him urgently.

My first problem would be finding Stan, for he was not a man who wanted to be found. His business thrived in a miasma of shell companies and proxy CEOs. I had absolutely no idea where he worked or where he lived, other than that it was to the west. Previously, whenever we'd done business, I'd never called him, he'd always called me. Even then we'd never spoken on the phone other than to arrange a meeting somewhere he could be sure we weren't being seen or overheard.

'What we need is a game plan,' Sammy said, coming in and gently rousing me from my thoughts by slamming his battered old briefcase onto my desk. 'And d'you know what? I think I've got one.' He pulled up the chair opposite, sat down and pointed a finger at me. 'You say you never done it—'

'Sammy, did you wink at me just then?'

'And if you didn't do it, we need to find some folk to say they saw you never doing it. I was thinking Brendan at the Red Corner might know some people. He owes you one for that licensing board thing you got him a result for. He's bound to know some boys who can back you up. Boys who know the score. Of course, you might need to ...' He rubbed his thumb and index finger together. 'But it'll be worth it in the long run. Just tell me the time when this MacDonald guy was bumped off and we'll have you put miles away and surrounded by friends.'

I leaned back in my chair, studied the ceiling for a few moments and then stood up and looked down at my lawyer. 'Sammy, this is not a dodgy personal injury claim. You're making it sound like I've broken a leg and you want me to find a suitable upraised paving slab so that I can say I tripped over it. I'm charged with murder and I don't intend to gamble the rest of my life on the testimony of some Red Corner Bar regulars with records longer than The Beatles' back catalogue. Try and get it through your head. I didn't do it. I'm innocent. I don't need some half-baked alibi defence. I need to find the truth. Or, if not, something very like it.'

'That's exactly what I wanted to hear.' I had been vaguely aware of a shadow hovering outside the door to my office and had assumed it was Grace Mary eavesdropping. It wasn't. It was Joanna.

'What are you doing here?' I said. 'You know I'm on bail with a condition not to contact you. If they catch you with me, I'll end up doing a hundred and forty days on remand.'

Joanna pushed me out of the way, took Sammy's briefcase, handed it to him and replaced the briefcase with her handbag. 'I'd like to speak to my husband alone, please.'

Sammy stood up, chin raised, ginger beard thrust forward. 'I'm your husband's lawyer and—'

'You're not,' Joanna said. 'Not any more.'

Both myself and Sammy were about to protest at the same time, until Joanna showed us each the palm of a hand. 'Sammy, thanks for your help to date, but it's time for you to take a back seat, and Robbie, yes, I am aware of the bail conditions. You're not to contact me or otherwise attempt to communicate with me or enter our home address. What you may have forgotten is that you're not to do any of those things without reasonable excuse. Well, now you've got a reasonable excuse. I've resigned from the Procurator Fiscal's Office and you've now appointed me as your solicitor. What's a more reasonable excuse than an accused person communicating with his lawyer?'

I looked at Sammy, Sammy looked at me. 'This is a mistake,' he said. 'You're too close to this, Joanna. You can't think objectively. I've been a lawyer longer than the pair of you put together. I know what I'm doing. Leave it to me. I'll sort it.'

Joanna was of a different mind. 'No disrespect, Sammy, but you *don't* know what you're doing. You're a civil lawyer and this is a criminal case. The most serious criminal case you can get. It's not that I don't trust you. I just trust myself more. Now, any questions?' Joanna asked in a manner that suggested she wasn't expecting any. 'Good.' She turned to Sammy. 'Tell Grace Mary to draft up a bail review application setting out my change in circumstances and asking for a hearing as soon as possible.'

'Tell her yourself,' Sammy said, after receiving an *are-you-still-here?* look from my wife. 'I'm not the office boy,' and with that, one kilted lawyer left the room, closing the door firmly behind him.

'That was a bit harsh, Jo,' I said. 'Sammy was only trying to help.'

'We don't need his kind of help,' she replied. 'I don't trust him to keep his mouth shut. A few drinks and every

120

pub in the town would know what crazy defence he'd thought up. He's a distraction and better out of the way.'

'I do have one question,' I said, feeling like I should be putting my hand up and asking permission. 'What if the cops see us together? The reasonable excuse is a great defence to a section 27(1)(b) charge, but I don't fancy spending time on remand waiting for the trial so you can present it.'

Joanna came around the desk and hugged me. 'Don't worry.' She ran her hand over my hair. 'There's nobody at the Fiscal's office going to mark a prosecution against you for breach of bail. I've made sure of that.' She kissed me and stepped away. 'But you're right. If some over-eager cop sees us together before the bail condition is formally lifted, you could end up in the cells for an overnighter, and I'm not having you spend any more time behind bars.' She picked up her handbag and kissed me again. 'You've got a lot of explaining to do, but it can wait a few days. After that I want to hear the truth. That's the *whole* truth, Robbie,' she said, emphasising her remarks with a poke to my chest. 'Not just something like the truth.'

19

'Are you and Mum not talking to each other?' I was at my dad's kitchen table supervising Tina's homework, which as usual had been left until five minutes before bedtime. My daughter's teacher, Miss Closs, was very big on homework. Tina never came home without some. Occasionally there would be projects to do: on history, nature or far-flung corners of the globe. Each came with a strict deadline attached. A deadline that Tina was extremely poor at detaching and communicating to her parents, with the result that Joanna and I had spent many a long evening printing stuff off the Internet while our little project-writer slept on, waking in the morning to find a jotter stuffed full of pictures of Robert the Bruce, the fish of UK coastal waters or the Panama Canal. Still, Miss Closs's pupils always seemed to do best. She was only in her early thirties, but her name combined with platinum blonde hair, round rimless specs and a figure that was more love handles than *Love Island*, had led the kids to nickname her Santa. Some parents said it was because she delivered. Personally, I thought it was because the parents did all the work while she took the credit.

Unfortunately, Tina had inherited her father's inde-cipherable handwriting. Today Miss Closs had sent her home with some sheets of words, the letters printed in dots that Tina was supposed to trace around. My daughter held up for my inspection the first attempt, which had taken her all of twenty seconds to complete. On this sheet the words were to do with climate change, and, so far as I could see, any direct hits on the dotted letters had been about as accurate as an internet weather forecast.

'Yes, we're talking. I was talking to Mum today at work,' I said, flipping to the next page, all to do with fruit, and pushing it under her nose. 'Now why don't you try again, and take your time with it?'

'Is it because of that man you killed?' Tina asked, picking up her pencil and gripping it like it might try and escape.

I ruffled her hair, which didn't make her writing any neater. 'What are you talking about?' I laughed. 'I haven't killed anyone.'

'Then why isn't Mum here and why are we staying at Gramps's?'

'Because ...' I said, pulling her towards me and whispering in her ear, 'he gets lonely sometimes and he likes it when people come to stay with him.'

Unconvinced, she pulled away and continued to plough the page with a blunt HB. 'Why's he going away out tonight if he likes it when people come to stay with him, then?' Bad handwriting never made for a bad cross-examiner.

My dad came into the kitchen to say cheerio, kissed the top of Tina's head and left.

'Was it a bad man you killed?' Tina asked, after he'd gone. 'My teacher says there are bad men who try and steal wee girls and you should never talk to them or take their sweeties. Was it one of them? Was it a pedalo? If it was then I suppose it was okay to kill them. Unless it was Uncle Malky. He always gives me sweets and ...' Tina stopped, pencil poised over a dotted banana, and looked up at me. 'Does Uncle Malky steal wee girls?'

'No,' I said. 'It's the big girls Uncle Malky has difficulty keeping his hands off. You wee girls have nothing to worry about. And who told you this nonsense about me killing someone?'

'Natasha.'

I thought it might have been. Natasha. Seven-and-a-half years old and already with the face of someone who'd stick a knife in your football if you kicked it over her fence.

'She said her dad read it in the newspaper and he was laughing about it.'

'That's because it's all a big joke,' I said.

'But it's not funny.'

'I know. It's hard to explain. You'll understand why it's a joke when you're older and we'll all laugh about it then. Okay?'

Bouncer scratched at the back door to get in, which was an excellent excuse to break off the conversation. I waited until I thought Tina should have finished and returned to the table to find out she was now colouring in the illustration of a bowl of fruit at the foot of the page. Using all the dexterity of her attempts at neat handwriting, she'd managed to mark the tabletop liberally with felt pen. I took a cloth from the draining board and looked under the sink for some cleaning solution. There was a bottle of Cif behind the bottle of Ardbeg we'd drunk from the previous Thursday. The level of the whisky hadn't changed. I'd say one thing for my dad: he never touched a drop when he was watching the kids. But I'd have to speak to him about moving the stuff under the sink to a higher cupboard out of Jamie's reach. I was moving the green whisky bottle out of the way, when I thought about another type of green bottle. Not a bottle full of fine Islay malt, but a tonic wine bottle, smashed and with jagged edges.

Tina was long in bed when my dad returned from the Red Corner Bar's Monday night domino competition, clutching six cans of McEwan's export. 'Silver medal again?' I said. 'Who won the speedboat?'

'It was a steak pie and who else but Sammy Veitch? I swear the man can see through walls. I stopped wearing my specs when I played with him, because I used to think he was reading my hand from the reflection. Now I just think he has X-ray vision. Hope he's as good at finding you a defence as he is at finding the double-six every shuffle.'

'Did he say anything about me?' I asked, hoping Sammy, a few drinks under his sporran, hadn't been holding forth on my case to the clientele of the Red Corner Bar.

'Not much. He did say he'd been sacked. I hope you know what you're doing. I mean, I'm sure Joanna's a fine lawyer and all that, but she's ... Well, she's ...'

'My wife?'

'No, not just that. She's ... Och, you know.'

Someone who didn't know my dad might have formed the impression he was referring to Joanna's sex, and that like some of my criminal clients, who didn't want *a burd* representing them in court, he thought Joanna wasn't up to the task. Anyone who did know him, would be aware that nothing could be further from the truth. My dad didn't believe in equal rights for women. Why should they lower themselves to our standards? For my dad, the battle of the sexes had been lost a long time ago. Old-fashioned male manners and chivalry were not patriarchal, but an attempt by men to retain some vestiges of pride. No, what the old man was referring to was what he considered to be Joanna's one weak point when it came to criminal law.

'You mean she's honest?' I said.

125

'It's not that.' He screwed up his face. 'Well, it is that. This is the justice system. Sometimes you need to give it a bit of a hand. The truth is all very well, but—'

'Not the whole truth?'

'All I'm saying is that Sammy was reminding me how we were all watching the football down at the Red Corner bar, the night it happened. You, me, Sammy, Brendan. I haven't spoken to Malky yet—'

'And what about the CCTV cameras?' I asked. 'The ones that cover the High Street and won't show me either entering or leaving the pub.'

'Ach, it was just one idea. Sammy's full of them. I don't know if he was trying to help or just making a point. He's not happy about being sacked.'

'I know that, Dad. And I am grateful for what he's done. But if Sammy's best idea is an alibi that will burst like a fat man's breeks at a buffet, then it's no good to me.'

Without another word the old man headed through to the kitchen to put the cans of beer in the fridge. After that I saw him bending over at the sink. 'And don't bother touching that bottle of Ardbeg,' I said. 'You'll have had enough to drink tonight and I've got to go out and see someone.'

'At this time? Who? You're not going home, are you? It just takes one person to drive past and see your car parked outside and they'll lift the phone to the police. A man's got his needs but wait until this bail thing's been lifted. You said it would only be a few more days.'

'It's okay, Dad,' I said, closing the cupboard door and handing him the kettle. 'I'm not going to see Joanna. I'm paying a visit to another woman. Don't wait up.'

20

The other woman was Meeko. She'd mugged Stan Blandy's 'business acquaintance's' son, and taken his mobile. There'd be a contact number on that phone, if not for Stan then certainly for this new woman in his life. All I needed to do was track down Meeko, get the phone and set up a meeting with the big man. What I would say to him at that meeting was something I hadn't quite thought through yet, but would be along the lines of, *You got me into this, now get me out.*

On a Monday night, the streets of Linlithgow were quiet. I drove out of the town centre and eventually found Meeko's door. There was no answer and no neighbours around who might be able to shed light on her whereabouts. Next stop was the corner shop she was known to frequent: an outlet for alcohol where age was regarded as a social construct and nothing to do with what was on your actual birth certificate.

'Meeko's barred.' The proprietor was quite adamant about that. 'She's not getting back in until she starts paying for the stuff she takes.' It seemed a not unreasonable position for a shopkeeper to take.

His wife, dressed in brightly patterned salwar kameez, was sitting on a stool in a corner behind the counter, watching a portable TV. 'Last time she stole from us we called the polis and the next night our big window got broken,' she called over her shoulder, eyes fixed to the screen. 'What are you wanting her for? Is she in trouble again? Good. Maybe if you got her locked up, we'd get some peace around here.'

Like most Scottish towns there wasn't all that much for young people to do in Linlithgow. The days of youth clubs and other such voluntary organisations were largely gone. If young people didn't want to join the Scouts, Guides, Boys' Brigade or other such pseudo-paramilitary organisations, their other options were to stay in and play video games or hang around street corners and parks, waiting until they looked old enough to sneak into a pub without anyone asking too many questions. So I drove around town, checking everywhere I thought Meeko might be loitering. I had almost given up when I encountered a bevvy of neds, if that's the correct collective noun. One of them peeled himself away and sauntered over to me. He had lank greasy hair, a face you could have lost in the snow, and by the way the bright red cotton tracksuit hung from his scrawny fame, I reckoned the only actual tracks he saw were the marks on his arms.

'You looking for that wee bitch Meeko?' he asked, in a manner that suggested he might once have been given a close-up of the heavy end of a Buckfast bottle by my missing client. He certainly seemed like her target audience. 'What you want her for? She on the game now?'

'She stole a mobile phone. I'm looking to get it back,' I said.

He cracked a laugh. 'Good luck wi' that.'

He was about to walk away, until I pulled him back by the shoulder. I tugged a tenner from my pocket. 'Any ideas where she might be?'

He shrugged out of my grip. 'Hey, boys,' he called to

the group. 'Anyone know anything about that wee slag Meeko and a mobile?'

No one did.

'Too bad,' I said.

The young man didn't move, just stood there watching as I carefully folded the ten-pound note and returned it to my pocket.

'She'll have it in her house. I know where she lives,' he said, which was a fat lot of good because so did I.

'Not much good to me if she's not in,' I said.

He sneered up at me. 'How's that, then?'

Under normal circumstances I would have drawn the line at housebreaking, but housebreaking was only a crime if the security of the premises was overcome with the intention of theft. I wasn't stealing. I was recovering stolen property for the purpose of returning the item to its rightful owner, at least that was what I kept telling myself. Under cover of darkness, or as dark as it gets in Scotland around eleven o'clock on a late May evening, which is to say not very, I pulled up outside Meeko's place. It was a four-in-a-block and she had the top left flat which was entered by a door at the side of the building. There was no knocker or bell, just the pane of frosted glass that I'd been banging on earlier to no avail.

'What's the plan?' I asked. Fortunately, upon looking around, there didn't seem to be anyone who might be interested in us, and anyway, Meeko's immediate neighbours would be used to noisy comings and goings. 'You done this before? What is it, a Yale lock?'

'Calm yoursel',' the young man, whom I now knew only by his nickname, Bop, said. 'I've done this hunners of times. I did four months last year for tanning the bowling club.' He studied the door, gave it a push to test its strength, shook the door handle a few times and then took off his tracksuit top. I put out a hand to take it from him, but instead he wrapped the clothing around his arm. Before I could fully risk-assess the situation, Bop had stuck his elbow through the glass in the door. In hindsight it would probably have been best to instruct a housebreaker who didn't get caught quite so often.

'That's us in,' he said, reaching through the jagged edges and taking the snib off the door.

'No, that's *me* in,' I said, handing him the tenner. 'You stand over there, Raffles, and keep edge. I'll be back in a minute.' I needed that phone. What I didn't need was the boy called Bop charging about, switching on lights and generally attracting the sort of attention that would get both of us lifted.

Through the door, I ran up the internal stairs and straight into a living room strewn with fast food wrappers, crushed beer cans and empty bottles of cheap sherry and tonic wine. From there I went through to the only bedroom. It was dark and I didn't want to switch on a light. The police had taken my phone as a Crown production, but I had an old one with me. It had a torch. I used it to scan the room. In the narrow beam I made out an unmade bed, a small dressing table with make-up piled high in a little wicker basket, an empty munchy-box, an overflowing ashtray, a jewellery box and a burst-open pack of tampons, but a distinct lack of any handheld telephonic communication systems. Keeping the light on the move, I could see that, apart from the bed and dressing table, the only other items of furniture were a small bedside table with a pint glass half-full of water on it, and a pine wardrobe with a green hoody hung over one of its doors. On the floor below was a bunch of dirty underwear, leggings and socks. I opened the other wardrobe door to reveal a row of coat hangers, most of them empty. I took a step back. To search the place properly would take time and that was in short supply. I stood, frozen, not knowing where to start, or even if I should start. I just wanted to get out of there, but I needed that phone. I took a deep breath and turned to face the door I'd come in. There, hanging from a hook, was a bright orange hoodie, filthy and torn. That was because it had skidded across Linlithgow High Street and almost underneath a passing car. Just how drunk had Meeko been that night? Too drunk to do anything other than cast aside her damaged hoodie and crash out on the bed? Too hungover in the morning to remember robbing a terrified teenager of a mobile phone? I really hoped so.

Thirty seconds later, mobile in hand, I was back downstairs and onto the street. I reckoned my first housebreaking had lasted all of three minutes. The same length of time it had taken Bop and my tenner to disappear.

I headed for my dad's, stopping en route for a closer look at my ill-gotten gains: a mobile phone in a pink case with sparkly bits on it. A strange choice for a schoolboy, but it looked like the kind Grace Mary used. The screen was cracked, and it was hard to tell if the phone was broken or if the battery was dead. First thing to do would be to try and charge it up. Grace Mary might have a charger somewhere and, if not, back at my own house there was a tangled box of cables that probably contained jump leads for the Space Shuttle. But that would have to wait. I'd taken enough risks for one night. I wasn't going to chance returning to my home address in case the cops carried out a routine check and caught me breaking bail.

The old man was in bed when I arrived back at his place. Next morning I'd get a charger from somewhere, check the contacts on the phone, call the boy's mum and ask her to put me on to Stan. We'd arrange a meeting and I'd talk some sense into him. Stan was anything but stupid. He was a businessman. I'd been his lawyer for years, ever since I'd been at Caldwell & Craig. When I'd left, the old established Glasgow law firm had retained Stan's commercial business, but the criminal side of things had followed me to Linlithgow. There was no logic in throwing me to the wolves when we both knew who the real culprits were. Stan could hire any old muscle to chauffeur him around. He wouldn't want to see me, his favourite lawyer, go to jail for a crime I didn't commit. Would he?

21

I was still trying to reassure myself on the integrity of the man who'd made a fortune out of illegally importing drugs into the UK over many years, as dawn broke on a new working day. I did eventually manage a couple of hours' fitful sleep, but was up, washed, dressed and pacing around by six-thirty. Tina didn't wake for another hour. I had her breakfasted and ready for school in record time.

'It'll be great,' I said, dropping her off. 'You're first in the playground, so you can meet all your pals and have lots of time to play before school starts.'

Next stop was the office. In the drawer of Grace Mary's desk I found the charger I was looking for. I took the mobile, plugged it in and it soon booted into life. To operate the phone required fingerprint ID. Either that or a six-digit passcode. I had neither. Mobile phones feature a lot in criminal cases, and I knew that without some pretty sophisticated gear I might as well try and crack a walnut with a damp sponge. Still, anything was worth a try. I was busy punching in random numbers at nine o'clock when I heard my secretary arrive.

'Grace Mary, bring your finger through here, will you?' I called through to reception.

'Which one?' she yelled back, sounding like she had a particular finger in mind.

I didn't respond, so she walked into my room and stared down at me. 'Is that my charger?'

'Put your finger on here,' I said.

The charger cable was only two feet in length and the plug was just above the skirting board, so she had to hunker down to do it. Even after I'd made her use all ten fingers, the phone stubbornly refused to comply, no matter how much she wiggled her digits.

'Who do we know who can crack open phones?' I asked.

'There's Geode Forensics, who we normally use,' Grace Mary said, as with the help of a hand on my head she hoisted herself back onto her feet. 'Though they're not cheap.'

'This is my case we're talking about,' I said. 'Expense is irrelevant.'

'And they might have some concerns.'

'About what?'

'About a few things, like whose phone is it, do you have permission to bypass the security, data protection, the right to privacy. Oh, and reset of stolen goods.'

'Who else do we know?' I said.

'There's what's his name, Jeffrey Freeman. He's got an intermediate diet coming up soon. Maybe you could speak to him about it?'

Jeff would certainly know how to crack open a phone. And he owed me one for taking on his case. I brought up Skype on my laptop and clicked on the avatar that made him look even more hairy and toothy than in real life, if that were possible.

'I hate to correct you, Robbie. But I don't owe you anything,' was Jeff's toothy on-screen response. 'Up until now all you've done is scribble something on a piece of paper for me to hand into the court.' An unclothed female figure scampered across the background and a voice yelled at Jeff telling him to hurry up and something about nuns' costumes being itchy. The screen went blank for a moment thanks to Jeff's finger over the camera, then he returned. 'And as you can see, Robbie, I'm very busy at the moment, so sorry if I don't drop everything to help you get into your phone because you've forgotten your own passcode. Try your date of birth. That's what everyone else uses.' A long rectangular box on my laptop screen told me the call had ended.

'Maybe Joanna will know someone,' was Grace Mary's next suggestion.

Until yesterday Joanna was a procurator fiscal depute. The people she knew who could break into phones were police officers. Me breaking into a phone associated with Stan Blandy was a big enough risk. Having the cops do it was suicide.

'Joanna's not coming into the office today, is she?' I said. 'We agreed not to see each other until we have the bail condition removed.'

'Relax. Joanna took a load of files home last night and said she'd go straight to court after she'd dropped wee Jamie off with your dad.'

I sat thinking while I left the phone to charge and, no brilliant ideas springing immediately to mind, at the back of eleven I trudged round to Sandy's café, or Bistro Alessandro as nobody but Sandy called it, for a coffee and crispy bacon roll. What was I going to do? Stan was my only hope.

'Got yourself in some real trouble this time, haven't you, Robbie?' Sandy said. He set down my order on the table in front of me and pulled up a chair opposite. The only other customers were two older women having coffee and sharing a cake in the faraway corner. Sandy's voice was loud enough for them to hear. 'Murder. I suppose if you're going to start off on a life of crime you might as well start at the top.' He put two fingers to his brow. 'Tia saluto.'

If Alessandro's AKA Sandy's coffee was as good as his third-generation Italian, I'd have been drinking somewhere else. I tucked a paper napkin under my chin. 'Forgive me for lapsing into two of the handful of Italian words I know, Sandy,' I said, but it's not tia saluto, it's ti saluto.' I lifted the lid of the roll and squirted on some brown sauce.

Sandy scowled. 'That's what I said. Anyway, ti, tia, it's the same thing.'

Was it? My own Italian was pretty much based on repeated viewings of *The Godfather*. 'What about Tia Maria?' I said.

The women at the corner table ordered another vanilla slice. They'd worked out that by eating only half a cake they could save enough calories to eat another half. 'And by the way, Tia Maria is Spanish,' one of the women called over to me, wiping cream from her lips with a napkin. 'It means Aunt Maria.'

There then ensued a discussion as to why an Italian liqueur had a Spanish name.

'Why you always showing me up in front of the customers, Robbie?' Sandy said, sotto voce, not that he'd have known what that meant. 'Are you in a bad mood today?'

'Yes, Sandy,' I said, 'I am in a bad mood today. I was in a bad mood yesterday, I'll be in a bad mood tomorrow and, quite possibly, I'll be in an extremely bad mood for the rest of my life, or until I get parole.' That was how it was going to be if I couldn't prove my innocence. Not that an accused person was required to prove their innocence. There were two sides to every trial. The scales held by Lady Justice were equally weighted, but into the defence's pan was dropped the golden feather that was the presumption of innocence. Or so they said. I'd seen enough verdicts to wonder if the people in the jury box had been watching the same trial as me. I blamed the media. In Scotland, justice wasn't done unless someone was convicted. Even Police Scotland's boast that they'd solved every murder allegation since the Force was unified, included those accused who'd been found not guilty. So far as their statistics were concerned, they'd charged the right person, it had just been the wrong verdict.

'I'm sorry, Robbie. I was just trying to cheer you up,' Sandy said. 'If there's anything I can do to help...' He screwed up his face and shrugged. 'I don't know...' he glanced around in case the women at the corner table were undercover cops; they were certainly eating enough pastries. 'Maybe... you know... you were at my place watching the football that night.'

If I'd bought a ticket and gone to the game, there wouldn't have been as many people watching it with me as were now volunteering to give me an alibi.

'Thanks, Sandy, but I wouldn't want to get you into any trouble.'

'It's no trouble,' he said, getting up and making his way around the counter. 'You can count on me. I'll not let the Carabinieri put you away.'

I was taking the first bite into my crispy bacon roll – was there even such a thing in prison? Bacon rolls inside, if they existed at all, were probably all flubbery fat and tomato ketchup. As I mulled over this hellish scenario, the bell over the café door tinkled and a couple of uniforms marched in.

'Robbie Munro?' the first in the door asked.

'Over there,' Sandy replied helpfully, pointing me out.

The first cop came over. 'Robbie Munro?'

I stopped chewing and nodded.

'Mr Munro, I am arresting you on suspicion of housebreaking. You don't have to say anything, but anything you do say will be noted and may be used in evidence. Do you understand?'

I did. Only too well. I untucked the paper napkin from the collar of my shirt and stood up. The second cop started to unclip a set of handcuffs from his belt, but his colleague shook his head, and he put them away. 'No need for that. Mr Munro isn't going to cause any problems, are you, sir?' He gestured towards where the second cop was now standing holding the door open. 'You can bring your roll with you if you like. We've had a lot worse than a few crumbs in the back of our unit.'

But the food of the gods might as well have been food for the dogs. I couldn't have swallowed a bite. I laid my roll down and let myself be escorted outside. By the stares from the faraway table, some people now had more to talk about than the origins of coffee liqueurs.

'We'll contact your lawyer when we get to Livingston,' the first cop said, when I was safely in the back of the patrol car.

Lawyer? Charged with housebreaking while on bail for murder? I didn't need a lawyer. I needed an escapologist. How could I prepare my defence to a murder charge from behind bars? As the patrol car eased into the High Street traffic, reality bit. Was this it? Was I starting my life sentence now?

22

'Murder, now housebreaking, you're becoming an old hand at this, Mr Munro,' the custody sergeant said cheerily, as I was brought up to the charge desk where, details taken and rights read, I was all set to be processed for the second time in a fortnight. Once again, I chose not to seek legal advice. Sammy Veitch wouldn't have a clue what to do, and I couldn't face Joanna. The ten-mile journey from Linlithgow to Livingston had given me time to think. If I was officially charged with housebreaking, I'd most likely be prosecuted under summary procedure. Since I was alleged to have broken bail, that meant a maximum forty-day remand before I had to stand trial. Providing I was acquitted, I'd be out before the murder charge was anywhere near a trial date.

They kept me waiting in a cell for what must have been a couple of hours: lightning fast by Police Scotland standards. After that there was a short trip from the cell area to the corridor containing the interview rooms. I was shown into the first of these by the same cops who'd arrested me and told to sit down. They asked if, before they started the interview, I wanted something to drink. I asked for a glass of water and they left, locking the door behind them.

What did they have on me? A neighbour who'd seen me and Bop break in? Or just my car's number plate? Maybe someone had recognised Bop and he was already arrested and spilling his guts. Or maybe the wee rat had thought it too good a story to keep to himself and the whole world now knew how he'd helped Robbie Munro, lawyer and murderer, break into Crazy Meeko's house. A hundred possible sources of evidence leapt into my mind, accompanied by a hundred and one possible explanations I could use in my defence. After all, if it had been Meeko who reported the crime, what could she say? That someone broke in and stole the mobile phone she'd stolen two weeks before? No, I was confident I'd be found not guilty of any housebreaking charge. I just didn't want to languish in prison as a bail-breaker while awaiting my chance to secure an acquittal.

An age later one of the cops came back, minus his partner or my glass of water. 'Looks like you're out of here, Mr Munro,' he said.

'I'm being released?' I said, trying not to sound too surprised.

'Grounds no longer exist, apparently. Don't think the Inspector was so very happy about it. She got a call from HQ. Looks like you have friends in high places.'

Not that I knew of; however, like the song, I did have friends in low places. One friend in particular. Did Stan's influence reach as far as the upper echelons of Scotland's unified police force?

I returned to the charge bar, where I signed for my few belongings. 'We'll let you out the side door,' the sergeant said. 'There's a car waiting to take you back.'

Released and chauffeur-driven home? Something didn't seem right. Were the cops being wary because I was a solicitor? I'd lodged many a complaint over the years on behalf of clients lifted out of their beds in the dead of night, only to be released barefoot and penniless at horrible o'clock in the morning and expected to make their own way home. Not that it had done anyone much good. Complaining about the police was like complaining about the weather. You felt better after a rant, but it still rained the next time you had a barbecue.

The sergeant came from behind the charge bar, led me through the main door from the cell area and along a corridor towards the glass door through which I'd been brought a few hours earlier. There was an unmarked saloon car waiting. Why the special treatment? Escorted out, not by a member of civilian staff or a bobby, but by the custody sergeant, and to what wasn't a blue and yellow liveried patrol car, but what turned out to be a very comfortable-looking, sapphire black BMW 7 series. Something was definitely wrong.

I stopped, turning to the sergeant. 'It's okay. I can find my own way home, thanks.'

Two figures in plain clothes, one male, one female, exited either side of the beamer and stood waiting, staring straight at me. The front passenger was female, forties, tall with an athletic build and a craggy face that had forgotten how to smile. Her male companion, standing by the driver's door, was older, fatter, with greying stubble on his head and chins and a face that had forgotten how many sausage rolls he'd had for lunch.

The female produced a small plastic wallet. She flipped it open and held a warrant card in front of my face. 'SCD. We'd like a word.'

The Specialist Crime Division investigated organised crime. It was formed in 2013 when Scotland's police forces amalgamated, and was successor to the former and highly controversial Scottish Crime and Drugs Enforcement Agency. The SCDEA had been a separate police force from the previous eight regional outfits. It didn't have a Chief Constable, rather a Director who reported to the Scottish Ministers. It had been called the Scottish FBI and was thought by many who moved in the same legal circles as I did, to have people working for it who were bigger crooks than the people they were trying to catch.

The custody sergeant gave me a gentle nudge in the back. 'I don't think finding your own way home is an option.'

I climbed into the back of the car and we set off. Neither of the police officers spoke, not even to accept my stilted thanks for the lift home. When, having emerged from the Avon Gorge, the BMW continued a mile or so along the A810 and took a right turn down an undesignated road, I thought the driver must know a shortcut. It was only when a little further on we swung left onto a country lane, that I knew exactly where we were headed. Officers from the SCD weren't here to discuss a break-in. They were here to talk about murder.

23

'Remember this place?' The male cop asked, as the car braked sharply and came to a halt, half on gravel, half on the thin strip of grass that marked the edge of the single-track road.

Remember it? The buildings on the far side of a hawthorn hedgerow were ringing more bells than a campanologist at Christmas.

'Muiravonside Country Park is a mile or so down the road isn't it?' I said. 'I've passed by this way before with the kids.'

'And at night-time with your phone, it would seem.' He shifted awkwardly in his seat to look at me. Due to his bulk he could only half-turn and I could only see one side of his face; below the left spectacle lens was the faintest memory of a bruise. 'Get out,' he said.

I remained seated, staring straight ahead.

'Get out now or I'm turning this car around,' he said, glaring at me with one piggy eye, like I was his six-year-old son misbehaving in the back seat. 'And then you might find grounds suddenly exist again for that housebreaking charge.'

He alighted and yanked open my door. I looked up at him. His stubbly head and face were obscured by the roof of the car.

'If I get out, I expect to hear no more about that

housebreaking rubbish,' I said to the Paisley pattern tie that was lying almost horizontally over the paunch in the white cotton shirt. 'That's the deal. Okay?'

He ducked his head under. 'If you say so. Now get out.'

The two of us walked together a few metres further along the road to a field gate now festooned in blue and white police tape. If there was forensic work still going on, the male cop didn't seem to care. 'This place was derelict for years before Angus MacDonald bought it. Ideal for a murder locus, don't you think? Location, location, location.' He pushed the gate open and led me up the path, past the front of the cottage and across the courtyard to the outbuilding. There was police tape across the door, and it was still secured by the rusty six-inch bolt. The cop stripped away the tape and removed the bolt from the hasp. Inside, the smell was just as bad as before, and the place almost as dark, illuminated only by the open door and small window, the bars casting stripes of light across the stone floor. At a quick glance I could see the lengths of duct tape and electrical ties that had been used to bind MacDonald had been removed. On one of the flagstones, white chalk circles had been drawn around a few dark-coloured splodges that I took to be MacDonald's blood. There was no sign of the pickaxe handle. I really hoped Stan's men had tidied up behind them. Otherwise, tape, bag and pickaxe handle would all have been sent for examination to the Police Forensic Science Lab on whose database, since my arrest, my DNA and fingerprints were now to be found.

The cop pointed to the chalk outlines. 'MacDonald was brought here bound and gagged. It's not clear where exactly he was killed. From the blood on the kitchen floor it looks like it was done in the cottage, but he was here before or after and his body later taken away.'

Clearly, MacDonald's bid for freedom had been short-lived. Stan's men must have come back after dropping me off at home. They'd killed MacDonald and got rid of the body. Why hadn't he called the police before they got to him?

The cop looked at me expectantly. Did he think I was going to break down and blurt out an admission of guilt? Who were these people who had the power to release me from police custody and put a pen through what was, on paper at any rate, the crime of housebreaking committed whilst on bail? Why had they brought me here? I'd already appeared in court on the murder charge. I was now fully committed for trial and under the protection of the court. The police had no authority to question me further about MacDonald's murder. They'd had their chance and received a big fat no comment. Anything they might attribute to me on this impromptu visit would never make it as far as a jury. Even Sammy Veitch could pluck the fruit from this poisonous tree and throw it in the face of the prosecution.

'What's your name?' I asked. 'Just so I know when I send in my formal complaint.'

'I'm Detective Inspector Dicker and my colleague is Detective Chief Inspector Sandeman,' he said.

'Then, as experienced police officers, you must know that bringing me here is a waste of your time and mine.' When he didn't reply I took a step towards the exit, only for the female cop to appear framed in the doorway, feet apart, hands behind her back, daylight streaming around her.

Dicker brought his face close to mine. His glasses needed cleaning. 'Why was Angus MacDonald murdered?'

I took a step back. 'I refuse to answer that question on the grounds that I don't know the answer,' I said.

Dicker smiled through the stubble, chubby cheeks lifting the frame of his glasses. 'We'll see how smart-arsed you are after they stick twenty-five years up you.'

'Look,' I said. 'You've got to see how ridiculous and ineffectual you bringing me here is. If this is some kind of an attempt to fit me up, and I don't see what else it can be, it's only strengthening my case.'

'Oh, that your defence is it?' Dicker said. 'A police stitch-up?' It was certainly fast heading to the top of my list of possibilities. 'If we really wanted to, we could fit you up for this MacDonald murder faster than a Singapore tailor. That's not why you're here. You're here for an off-the-record chat.'

In my experience off-the-record chats with cops had a habit of metamorphosing into on-the-record admissions when it came to the trial.

'Good, then you can put this on the record,' I said. 'I have absolutely no idea why someone would want to kill Mr MacDonald. Honest.'

'Honesty is exactly what we're looking for. We'll be honest with you, if you'll be honest with us,' Dicker said.

Seriously? Was he trying the *help-us-to-help-you* routine with a solicitor, veteran of a thousand police interviews? When cops said that, what they really meant was *help-us-to-help-you-convict-yourself*.

'Okay,' I said, 'but before we go any further – you've done all the talking so far, and been reasonably polite. Your colleague hasn't said anything yet. Am I to take it you're the good cop?'

Something clattered off the stone floor at my feet. A pickaxe handle. It was inside a thick plastic production bag, sealed with translucent blue tape, but with no crime label attached.

Sandeman walked over and stood so close to me that I could smell the perfume she wasn't wearing. It was time for the bad cop to speak for herself. 'What'll they find if they run that under the microscope?' She poked the production bag with the shiny point of a sturdy no-nonsense shoe and slid it across the ground to Dicker.

He picked it up and gave me a close-up through the thick polythene bag. There were a few thin, dark streaks on the side of the pickaxe handle: the blood that had dripped from MacDonald's face after he'd been struck by Stan's driver. I said nothing. That was why I'd been brought here, wasn't it? In the hope that I'd say something stupid. And talking of stupidity, how stupid was it of Stan's men to leave the DNA-ridden pickaxe handle at the scene?

Dicker's face broke into a wide smile. That and the smell of the place reminded me of gutted trout. 'Looks to me like it could be blood, ma'am,' he said.

Sandeman feigned a sigh. 'I suppose we'll only know for certain *if* we send it to forensics.'

Dicker turned and sauntered towards the door, taking the production bag with him.

'I take it you know the way home from here, Mr Munro?' Sandeman said. She pressed a card into my hand. 'My number. I don't think you killed MacDonald. But I do think you know why he was killed and who by. That means you have a choice. You either decide you want to talk to us, in which case we'll help you get out of this, or you don't, and that production bag gets sent to the scientists.'

24

It was way past Tina's bedtime. I'd called her in from the garden several times, but to no avail. Joanna, young Jamie on her hip, joined me, in the hope that our combined authority might succeed where my vocal cords had failed. It was so good to be home again. Earlier that day, while I'd been trying not to help the police with their enquiries, Joanna had provided the Crown with an affidavit confirming her police statement. She'd already resigned from the Procurator Fiscal Service and was now officially instructed by me as my defence solicitor. Those were sufficient changes in circumstances for the review of my bail order to be sanctioned, and the prosecution hadn't even bothered to oppose the motion to remove the special condition of bail that we should not communicate with one another.

'Just five more minutes,' Tina said, pre-emptively, when she saw us standing at the back door. Taking the rubber bone from Bouncer's mouth, she hurled it as far as she could down the garden before girl and dog bounded after it.

'Watch out for any monst—' I began to shout. But there was no monster. The monster had been Angus MacDonald. No need to watch out for him any more.

'What are we going to do?' I asked Joanna.

She kissed me. 'The first thing we do is get the kids to

bed and then have an early night. After a good eight hours we'll see things a whole lot clearer.'

'Jo,' I said. 'I've been a legal aid lawyer for fifteen years, I am on the duty lawyer scheme, I have two young kids and now I'm charged with murder. The last time I had a good eight hours I had an umbilical cord attached. We need to talk now. Listen to me.'

I'd given things a lot of thought, mainly about the alibi offers and who I thought might not crack while giving evidence. My dad was the best bet, though there were pros and cons. As a cop he'd have credibility, lessened to an extent by being the accused's father, of course, but on the upside again, he'd had plenty of practice lying in the witness box. I rummaged in my pocket and produced a crumpled piece of paper on which I had jotted down some notes. I smoothed it out on the palm of my hand.

'Okay, let's hear your plan,' Joanna said, as she watched Tina rampage among the undergrowth. 'But it better be good. What we need is a properly thought-out defence. No hare-brained alibi schemes, nothing left to chance. Every move carefully thought through, every countermove by the Crown anticipated and neutralised.'

'You know?' I said, crumpling the paper into a ball and casually slipping it back into my pocket. 'I think I'd be more interested to hear what you have to say.'

Joanna took a deep breath. 'Okay. We've got to assume your DNA is on that pickaxe handle. If the deceased's blood is on it too—'

'Why would the cops from the Specialist Crime Division be holding onto it if it was?' I said.

'I suppose they could be bluffing,' Joanna said. 'Why else take you to the murder scene? The pickaxe handle may have been tested for DNA and come up negative.

They've no body and without a murder weapon linked to you, what have they actually got?'

We hadn't yet received anything like full disclosure of the evidence but, from my wife's enquiries through various channels, she'd gleaned some important pieces of information. There wasn't much more I could tell her. It went without saying that, like any husband, I only kept from my wife those things I didn't want her to know, but when it came to criminal law, only a mug didn't tell their lawyer everything – even the bad stuff. Everything I said was confidential. Lawyers, like naughty children, have selective hearing. I'd told her about asking for help to track down Angus MacDonald, how I'd been taken to his place by two men whose names I didn't know, and what had taken place in the outbuilding. I'd even told her about my strange encounter with Dicker and Sandeman from the Specialist Crime Division. The one piece of information I hadn't divulged was any mention of Stan Blandy. It wasn't that I didn't trust my wife. I just didn't trust her not to do the best for me, and she might think that doing the best involved telling the jury the whole truth. I couldn't do that. I'd make my own inquiries with Stan, and very carefully. If Stan thought my predicament might prise a chink in his armour of respectability, a life sentence would suddenly seem like a trip to Disneyland.

Joanna placed Jamie in my arms. He was dressed in a chunky blue cardigan which either Joanna's mum, Tina's Gran or Grace Mary had knitted for him. I'd mixed up some of the baby presents and had been forced to keep things vague when sending out the thank-you cards. I'd even sent a thank-you card to one of Joanna's relatives who hadn't sent a gift – though embarrassingly one did arrive shortly afterwards. Joanna tugged the collar snugly around the wee man's neck. It might have been a sunny evening in May, but there was still a chill wind blowing around chez Munro. 'Let's see…' She counted off the sources of evidence on the fingers of one hand, starting with her thumb. 'First of all, they've got what they think is a motive – you wanting to sort MacDonald out for stalking me.'

'That's easily explainable,' I said. 'He was a witness in a trial that was thrust on me at short notice. I had to prepare and, obviously, I'm going to try to precognosce the alleged victim.'

Joanna waved aside my intervention. 'We're not viewing this from a reasonable doubt standpoint,' she said. 'We're taking the Crown case at its highest.' She lifted her index finger. 'Two: MacDonald hasn't been seen alive since he was in court giving evidence. Before then you didn't have his address. The witness list only gave him care of Police Scotland.' Middle finger: 'Three: they have your phone travelling from here to his house at around eight o'clock.'

'Yeah, my phone. Not me.'

'Seriously, Robbie. Stop talking like one of your clients.' Ring finger: 'Four: they have MacDonald's blood on his kitchen floor. Also…' Pinky: 'Five: they've got a statement from me saying that you went out of the house shortly before eight and came back later with an injured arm.' I hadn't blamed Joanna for speaking to the police. She would have been worried when they came to the door asking questions and thought I'd been involved in an accident or something. She thumped me on the arm that wasn't cradling Jamie. 'That's for lying to me about that.'

'Still, it's all very thin, don't you think?' I said, ever the optimist.

'Without the pickaxe handle?' Joanna shrugged. 'Maybe

you didn't go to the shops. Maybe you went somewhere else, and maybe you just happened to pass near to MacDonald's home. You know what these police mobile phone experts are like with their triangulation reports. If the Crown wants, they'll triangulate you into a seat in a particular room in a building or half a mile away in a car.' It hadn't taken my wife long to start thinking like a defence lawyer again. 'You could have been going anywhere. Wester Brigg Cottage isn't that far out in the wilds.'

I thought I saw tears begin to well in my wife's eyes.

'You do believe I'm innocent, don't you Jo?'

She blinked a few times. 'Speaking as your defence solicitor, it doesn't matter what I believe,' she said. 'It's what the evidence shows that I'm interested in. With mobile phones the prosecution has the best of both worlds. If you have it with you, it's the spy in your pocket. If you don't, they say you left it behind because you were up to no good. Let's hope we can use the fact you did have your phone and spin it to your advantage.' Joanna tugged her bottom lip. 'I just don't get it. If you've been charged with murder and the Crown don't know about the pickaxe handle, they must have a card up their sleeve.'

'Like what?'

'How do I know, if it's up their sleeve?' She came closer and kissed me again. 'Sorry for snapping. Maybe me acting for you isn't such a great idea.'

I kissed her back. 'I wouldn't have anyone else. Who can I trust more than my own wife? So, what should we do?' I asked, deep down knowing the answer.

'You give the cops the people who tracked down MacDonald for you ...'

'I can't do that.'

'It's the truth.'

'I don't know for certain they did anything.'

'Robbie ...'

'Really, I wasn't there. Anything could have happened.'

'Like a zombie attack or something?'

'No, but someone else could have got to MacDonald. It's not like that was the first time he'd been assaulted. Look at the Keggie case. Whatever happened to proof beyond reasonable doubt?'

'Robbie, when are you going to stop thinking like a defence lawyer and start thinking like a juror? If a man goes missing for no reason and his blood is found in his house along with a bloody pickaxe handle that's been chucked in an outbuilding, that just so happens to have a stranger's DNA all over it, a stranger who had a grudge against him and whose phone can be put at the murder scene – put two and two together for once and make four. No juror is mulling that over for long and wondering if they have a reasonable doubt. Not when it's Friday and they're wanting to get off to the pub or have to get home and make the tea.'

I laughed. 'Five minutes out of the Procurator Fiscal Service and you've become very critical of the criminal justice system.'

'This isn't funny, Robbie,' Joanna said, as though I needed reminding. 'You said one of the cops from the SCD was a Detective Chief Inspector. When does a DCI ever get from behind the desk and hit the mean streets? If the SCD are involved it's because they think what happened to MacDonald had something to do with serious organised crime. You've not told me the full story. There's something missing. Those men you were with were sent by somebody. You've got a name. The SCD want it. You need to give it to them. Let them take care of things.'

I shouted a final warning to Tina, then turned to Joanna again. 'What are my other options?'

Tina and Bouncer, four legs trotting, two legs trudging, came down the garden toward us. Joanna took Jamie back from me and kissed his head. 'There aren't any,' she said. 'You've got the number of the SCD – call it.'

25

I did have DCI Sandeman's number, but I had no plans to call it. Not yet. Instead, I called a different number and arranged an appointment to see one of my former business partners.

Maggie Sinclair, a woman with more sides to her than the Hope diamond and twice as hard, was now semi-retired and a consultant with Caldwell & Craig. Setting up an appointment hadn't been easy, and I could only be afforded ten minutes of her valuable time, and then only after I'd mentioned it was a confidential matter to do with an important client of the firm.

It was during my time at Caldwell & Craig that I'd first made the acquaintance of Stan Blandy. He was a client of the then senior partner, who'd specialised in corporate law, and the firm still handled all Stan's legitimate business interests. I doubted very much that the grand old legal beast that was C&C would have helped launder the money that was used to fund these legitimate enterprises, but wouldn't have been surprised if it had turned a sleepy eye. All I knew of Stan's affairs was that occasionally he would refer a client to me, usually on drugs charges. The private fees that followed, never directly attributable to Stan, of course, kept the other partners happy. Unfortunately, in criminal law, rich, private-paying clients like Stan were few and far between. It was Maggie who had persuaded the other partners that crime law didn't pay, not when a criminal trial at legal aid fixed-fee rates netted the partnership only the price of a decent lunch. Unfortunately, criminal law was what I did, so I'd been given a choice: change what I did or go and do it somewhere else.

That was when I decided to return to my hometown of Linlithgow. With perfect timing, hardly had I pinned my brass plate to the door than the powers that be moved the local Sheriff Court from the Royal Burgh and sent it ten miles south to the new town of Livingston. Other than the additional commute, it made little difference to me. Linlithgow had never seen a crime wave, in fact scarcely a ripple, and to a criminal lawyer location isn't all that important. What is important is reputation. If you're selling a house or making a will, people look for the cheapest and nearest option. Those who have concerns over their liberty ask around for recommendations and are prepared to travel. Which was not to say that I'd been inundated with work these past five or six years. Few defence lawyers were nowadays, not with the drop in prosecutions. In a reversal of the adage about sticks and stones, punching someone or nicking their property was fine; call them a bad name on social media or use an incorrect pronoun and the procurator fiscal would throw the book at you. Well, perhaps not the book, but certainly the iPhone. It meant that victims of crime looked for other ways to redress wrongs. One way had been to visit Eddie Frew.

'I hope you didn't mind using the side entrance, Robbie,' Maggie said, fixing me a smile as weak as a politician's promise. 'But as you know, there's been some publicity surrounding you. We've asked our friends in the press not to get us involved—'

'But you aren't involved.'

Maggie would have wrinkled her face if the Botox injections had allowed it. 'All the same. Coming in through the front door and past the waiting room would have been ... awkward, in the circumstances.'

'You do know I'm innocent?'

Maggie smiled condescendingly and sat herself down behind a desk that wasn't quite the size of a tennis court. 'Now, why are you here and what is this about an urgent matter to do with a client of Caldwell & Craig?'

'I need to contact Stan Blandy.'

'Impossible.'

'I don't need his home address, just a phone number or an email will do.'

Maggie leaned back in her big chair and released a sigh that would have inspired a Venetian to build a bridge. 'Robbie, even setting client confidentiality aside, you have come across the General Data Protection Regulations, haven't you?'

I had, and I'd taken the view that they were just an excuse for civil servants and other pen-pushing bureaucrats not to release helpful information.

'Tell you what,' I said. 'How about you give him a call just now and pass me the phone. All I want to do is speak to him.'

'Concerning what exactly?'

'Are you suddenly forgetting about client confidentiality and the GDPR?' I asked.

'No, I'm not.' Maggie leaned across her enormous desk at me. 'If Mr Blandy *was* your client, you'd have his contact details. Now tell me why you want to speak to him.'

'Maggie, lift the phone, get Stan Blandy on the line

or I'm going to take a seat in the waiting room and tell everyone in there all about how I was once a partner here and am now a murder suspect. If ...' I said, putting up a hand to deflect her protests, 'you try to have me removed, and who in here is going to do that? I'll cause an almighty scene. Now, is all that unpleasantness really going to be necessary for the sake of a phone call to someone to whom I'm bringing good news?' It was a bluff. On bail, as I was, and already just having dodged a housebreaking charge, I'd have thought twice about dropping a toffee wrapper.

Maggie's hand moved towards the phone and then withdrew.

'What kind of good news?'

What difference would it make if I told her? I delved into my pocket and placed the mobile on the desk. I still thought it strange that a teenage boy would choose a pink sparkly wallet as a phone cover.

'I have a phone belonging to him,' I said.

Maggie sat up straight. She picked up the phone and stared at the sparkly cover, turning it over in her hand like it was some archaeological find. 'No, Robbie ...' she said, voice raised but showing no outward sign of emotion, though that may have been down to the Botox. 'What you have there is *my* phone.'

There are times that even amidst the impenetrable confusion, basic instincts kick in. I reached out and grabbed the mobile out of her hand.

'And you can have it back,' I said. '*Once* you've made the call.'

26

The call was made. I met Stan the next day. Stan didn't like meetings with criminal lawyers at the best of times. He liked being seen meeting criminal lawyers about as much as the average Scottish Nationalist likes being seen in Union Jack underpants. For that reason, anywhere with CCTV coverage was a no-go, thus ruling out most of central Scotland's public areas. Which was why I had returned to the offices of Caldwell & Craig. I arrived via the side entrance around half-twelve, the arrangement being that Stan would give me a maximum of thirty minutes before he took Maggie to lunch, and I went back to Linlithgow and a bacon roll at Sandy's.

Maggie met me at reception and guided me through to the boardroom, where two rows of empty chairs stared at each other across a wide expanse of mahogany. I pulled one out and sat under the gaze of her late father, Tom Sinclair, whose oil painting hung on the walls alongside some former senior partners of the grand old law firm.

Maggie herself had for a short time been senior partner of Caldwell & Craig. Moneywise, she no longer needed to work. Which was good because she'd always preferred others to do that for her. She'd been married three times, most recently to Alasdair Brodie, aka Lord Bantaskine, who, like his father and his father before him, was a High Court judge. The ancestral Bantaskines had each at one time held the position of Lord President of the Court of Session, Scotland's senior judge. It was only a matter of time for Alasdair. In Scotland, when it came to the justice system, we liked to keep things in the family. Thus far for Maggie, all three of her marriages had been financially advantageous, the two divorces even more so. How she managed to lure so many wealthy men into her web, I didn't know. For me, the thought of romance and Maggie Sinclair was as irreconcilable as peanuts and chewing gum. I was sure her two ex-husbands now felt the same. Some said the excellent divorce settlements had been all down to her legal expertise. Personally, I thought anyone unfortunate enough to find themselves wedlocked to Maggie would be happy to pay the ransom money just to escape. Why the present incumbent was still hanging in there, I couldn't understand. Just as I couldn't fathom why Stan Blandy had been chauffeuring Maggie's stepson across Central Scotland on a Friday night. Surely, it couldn't be love.

The Stan Blandy I knew was a hard-nosed businessman, in the same way Ben Nevis was a bump in the road to Fort William. Relationships were dangerous and an unnecessary distraction from the business of making money. I'd heard him say many times before that women were not to be trusted. Stan must have an angle, for there'd never been so much as a whisper of an affair or the possibility of a Mrs Blandy. Stan loved himself too much. It was said that he'd have sex with himself, if he could turn around quick enough. But people change with age. Now in his late fifties and with enough cash to sink one of the ships that he'd sailed into UK harbours transporting Colombian cocaine via Antwerp or, occasionally, premium MDMA from the Netherlands, had Stan decided it was time to relax, sit on his piles of money and experience all the things he'd missed out on – like romance? No, I couldn't see Stan falling into that trap. And certainly not with Maggie Sinclair.

'It's complicated,' Stan said, when I asked him about it.

'I've only got a law degree, but try me, I might understand,' I said.

'Maggie had to go to some do for judges with her husband. She lives in Edinburgh now…'

I was aware that Maggie had moved in with her latest marital victim to his modest eight-bedroom mansion house set in a manicured acre-and-a-half somewhere in Wester Coates. She probably thought she was slumming it. Less than twenty-five minutes east of my own home, it was way too close for comfort.

'She dropped the kid off earlier and asked if I'd go back for him. He must have taken her phone with him.'

'You and Maggie…' I said. 'Are you…?'

'Maggie's a married woman, and we're not here to discuss her personal affairs. What do you want?'

What did I want? Was he for real?

'What I want, Stan, is for you to get me off the hook for this murder charge,' I said, as calmly as I could.

Stan mulled that over. 'I could maybe put some pressure on a few jurors, when the trial comes around…'

'You said you owed me a debt for stopping Maggie's son getting bottled.'

'And you asked me to find the guy who was annoying your wife.'

'That's right. *Find* him. Not have your guys abduct and murder him, leaving me to take the rap.'

Stan's face widened to accommodate his smile. 'You wouldn't be doing anything stupid like recording this conversation, would you?' he said.

My lungs were too fond of oxygen to try anything like that on with Stan Blandy.

'Didn't think so,' he said. 'Not that it matters. The man you asked me to locate was located. Anything else that happened is down to you.'

'Stan, the meeting I had with MacDonald lasted all of five minutes. What happened afterwards had nothing to do with me. I never saw him again. He ran away, your guys killed him and yet it's me who ended up on remand at Lowmoss.'

'Where I made things as comfortable for you as I could,' Stan reminded me.

'I know that,' I said. 'And I'm grateful ... I suppose ... in a way, but I should never have been there in the first place. Your man, the driver—'

Stan shook his head. 'He did nothing. Trust me. I've asked him. If he had done something, he'd have told me. He rids the world of some scumbag? I don't see that as a sackable offence. But all my employees know there are some things I don't forgive. Lying to me is one of them.' He looked at his watch. 'Was there anything else?'

'Yes,' I said. 'You still owe me.'

Stan failed to understand why. 'I found the man for you. That was the favour you asked for saving the boy. It's a shame things didn't work out, but—'

'I'm talking about returning Maggie's phone,' I said.

'It was good of you. That's the only reason why I'm here.'

'She asked me how I came by it. I haven't told her. Not yet,' I said. 'I haven't mentioned that her stepson, probably a future judge if his family tree is anything to go by, almost got carved up by a Buckie bottle on Linlithgow High Street because you couldn't be relied on to pick him up on time.'

The kind of people who threatened Stan Blandy were usually trying to save themselves the 7,000 Swiss francs to pay Dignitas. He looked at me in the way a child looks at an injured fly and wonders what would be the most fun: pulling the wings off or just a straightforward splat.

'*Stan Blandy is beholden to no one.* That's what you told me,' I said.

Stan's lips barely moved. 'Don't bring me into this, Robbie. Do and prison will be the least of your worries. Bottom line, I found a man for you. That's all.'

'Really? Well, you found him very quickly. I know you have ways and means, but locating him inside twenty-four hours, and all you had was a number plate? That's impressive even by your standards.'

'Not really. I took the reg, gave it to someone I know, and they came back with the name and address of the person it was registered to.' Stan stood up, walked around the table and stared down at me. 'I'm sorry, Robbie. Truly, I am, but there was no reason for me or my boys to kill MacDonald. I did what you asked. We're quits.' He walked to the door and turned to look at me again. 'And just in case you're wondering, what that means is that you don't ever try to speak to me again on this or any other subject unless I want to be spoken to. Understand?'

27

'And you believed him?' Joanna handed me my baby son and placed the changing mat on the floor in front of me. 'This mysterious underworld figure whose name you're too scared to even mention to your own wife who also happens to be your solicitor?'

Strangely enough I did believe him. Stan was no liar. He could afford not to lie because no one was ever going to challenge him, whatever the truth. There were people like that. Untouchable people who were always right, even when they were wrong. In the legal world we called them judges.

As soon as the nappy was off, Jamie commenced his impersonation of an untethered firehose. Tina shrieked with laughter and threw her mum the terry-towelling nappy, kept for such emergencies. When Jamie was born, we'd bought a bundle of them for the sake of the environment. We'd saved the planet for nearly a week before moving on to disposables.

'Why would you believe someone like that?' Joanna said, throwing the towelling nappy over the offending member like she was putting out a chip pan fire.

I asked Tina to go and fetch Jamie's PJs. She screwed up her face. 'Go on, I'll time you,' I said. 'See if you can do it in less than ten seconds. One, two ...' and off she went. I wondered how much longer she'd fall for the old I'll-time-you routine. 'I believe him because if he'd had MacDonald killed, he'd have told me. What's it to him? He knows I'd never incriminate him. Even if I did, and I told the truth, imagine how well that would go under cross-examination? *So, Mr Munro, you asked a person you say is a criminal client of yours, to track down the man who was stalking your wife, because you just wanted a little chat? And that was before you and a couple of his henchmen took Mr MacDonald to a secluded spot and interrogated him with use of a pickaxe handle?*'

Joanna shrugged. 'Are you saying it was just coincidence that he was in town the very same night MacDonald put the squeeze on me to drop Keggie's case? And just a coincidence that he could track MacDonald down for you so easily, just using a number plate?'

'Coincidences happen all the time,' I said. 'It's only the cops and prosecutors who don't believe such things exist. The man we're talking about has ways and means to do lots of things. He also has other people to put on the squeeze, and, trust me, if they'd squeezed you, you'd stay squeezed, not get away by kicking some shins. And, anyway, how would he know to threaten you? You'd only just been given the case.'

Joanna handed me the baby wipes. 'I keep coming back to Josh Wedderburn. One minute he's too sick to prosecute Simon Keggie's trial, the next he's giving it the Lonesome Cowboy Blues at the Star & Garter Hotel.'

Tina crashed into the room and threw a little yellow all-in-one at me. 'Nine ... ten,' I said, loudly. 'Well done, ten seconds. You're getting *really* quick. Now why don't you go and start running the bath for Jamie? I'll bet you can do that really fast – one ...!'

'I think Wedderburn tried to have the case time-barred,' Joanna continued, after Tina had departed at speed. 'First of all, there was a huge delay before the indictment was served, then there were two spurious motions by the Crown for adjournments. After that he called the trial in on the last possible day, when he just happened to come down with an extremely short-term illness, and the witness who never turned up was Angus MacDonald. That trial was never starting on time. When Wedderburn heard I was taking over the case, he could have contacted MacDonald and told him not to cooperate.'

It was a theory I could warm to. There was just one problem with it. 'If the plan was to have Keggie acquitted, it worked. Why would someone want to kill MacDonald afterwards?'

Faced with that dead end, I took Jamie through to the bathroom where Tina was playing with a temperature float shaped like a boat, sailing it through a sea of steam and bubbles. The reading was 46 degrees.

Joanna followed me into the bathroom. 'Maybe I am wrong,' she said, 'and if I am, you'll need to find someone who had a better motive than you for killing him.'

'Which is why I was thinking of putting Sammy Veitch onto the case,' I said, adding cold water. When the correct temperature was reached, I lowered my son into the water. 'If he's as good at chasing down leads as he is at chasing ambulances, it's got to be worth a try.'

'How much would we be paying him?' Joanna asked.

'As little as possible. He hasn't paid me for the Simon Keggie trial yet, so we could work something out later.'

When wee Jamie was bathed, filled with milk and in his night attire, I carried him through to our room and laid him in his cot. According to my dad, when it came

166

to the job of being a baby, Jamie was just like my brother Malky had been. Give him something to drink, let him have a good burp and he'd sleep all night. Some things never changed.

Next morning, I braved court for the first time since I'd been in the dock. Some fellow solicitors welcomed me back, others stayed well away. Jeff Freeman, ex-porn film director, met me outside Courtroom 2 where his intermediate diet was about to call. He was looking worried and wanted to know 'the plan'. I find it best, if you do have a plan, not to tell the client about it. That way they don't go blabbing and have it filter back to the prosecution.

The prosecution was represented that morning by the subject of my discussion the night before, Josh Wedderburn. I hadn't seen him since his sick-boy routine at Simon Keggie's trial. He had a little plan of his own.

'How are you, Robbie?' he asked. 'You'll have a lot on your plate just now, and I was thinking, this Freeman business. It all boils down to whether the video footage is indecent or not. If your client's still determined to go to trial, how about we agree the routine police evidence of the search, et cetera, by way of a joint minute of admissions? Then it'll just be a case of the sheriff watching the video and coming back with a verdict. That way we can shorten the trial and save you a lot of hassle that you don't need right now.' Wedderburn was a relatively new depute and had not quite mastered the art of fake sincerity. I, on the other hand, had had years of practice.

'Thanks, Josh,' I said. 'How about we just knock the case on, and you can bring the joint minute along to the trial?'

His attempt at a sympathetic smile needed work. 'No problem, Robbie,' he said. 'Anything to help.'

At lunchtime I found myself in the café on the ground floor of the Civic Centre, eating cheese and onion toasties with good friend and fellow solicitor, Paul Sharp. It didn't take long to get around to the subject most on my mind. I'd already explained to Paul that Joanna would be acting in my defence, and, because I knew that whatever I told him would be kept in strict confidence, had filled him in on what I understood to be the Crown case, minus mention of the pickaxe handle.

'Seems reasonably thin to me,' he said. 'Have you consulted with Fiona Faye yet? I'm assuming that's who you've instructed.'

'It is, but I've a few things to sort out before we consult,' I said, moving my mouth around some molten cheddar. 'I wouldn't want to waste her time until I've seen everything the Crown is going to throw at me.'

'Well let me know if there's anything I can help you with,' Paul said, starting in about his toastie, burning his lip in the process.

'A defence would be good if you've got one handy,' I said.

Paul didn't say anything. Just looked at me, food poised warily at his mouth.

'You believe I'm innocent, don't you?' I said.

'We can all do stupid things in the heat of the moment,' he replied, once he'd tentatively bitten another corner off his toastie.

'Paul, I didn't do anything stupid. At least not so stupid that I killed someone.'

'Then why is there a case against you at all? Why would

168

the Crown go off half-cocked with a prosecution against a solicitor, if it only had the bare threads of a circumstantial case? Are you sure you're not keeping anything back?'

At the top of the stairs leading from the court complex, I noticed Hugh Ogilvie looking down at us. I jerked my head up at him, and said to Paul, 'Loose lips ... It's probably better if we don't talk about my case any more. You know what he's like. You're not my solicitor and if he thinks we're talking about it, he'll have you hauled in for questioning in case I've blurted out a confession.'

'Why would he do that?' Paul laughed. 'Other than because he hates you, I mean.'

Ogilvie began his descent.

'Let's talk about football or something,' I said, and as Ogilvie walked across the lobby towards us, we both tried our best to avoid eye contact by digging into our toasties. He walked to the counter carrying his own reusable bamboo drinking vessel and ordered himself a coffee to go. Cup in hand, he strolled in our direction once more, this time stopping when he reached our table.

'Everything all right, gentlemen?' Paul stuffed the rest of his food in his mouth and got to his feet mumbling something about having to see a client in custody. Ogilvie remained standing, looking down at me. 'Congratulations on the Keggie case,' he said, like he had a pain in his side.

Hugh Ogilvie was the procurator fiscal for Livingston. Political allegiance on his part had always been more for career furtherance than any point of principle, which was why he was currently a nationalist. Simon Keggie was a Tory councillor, and to hang a political scalp like that on his belt would not have harmed the ambitions of a procurator fiscal seeking elevation to the bench, one little bit.

'You've got a dog, haven't you, Robbie?' he said, lifting

the lid off his coffee and sniffing it. 'Me too. Sometimes I take mine for a walk in Kirkton Park of a Friday evening – if the weather's nice.' He lifted his head to look past me across the stone-floored atrium to the sun spilling in through the glass frontage of the Civic Centre. 'I usually go around seven o'clock.' Then, taking a sip of coffee, he continued on his way.

28

There are plenty of places to walk a dog near to where I live, but at seven o'clock that evening I was eight miles from home, over the Bathgate Hills, and walking through the stone archway into Kirkton Park. Ogilvie, a boy about Tina's age and an excitable little spaniel were loitering by the wooden totem pole that served as a signpost. Leading the way towards them, Tina was towed along by Bouncer, happy at being somewhere new.

When Ogilvie saw us coming, he started to walk along the path near to the tennis courts, and we followed. When we came to a children's play area, Tina handed me Bouncer's lead and she and Ogilvie's boy were off like a shot.

I walked over to where Ogilvie was standing and stood by his side while our dogs got better acquainted in the way that dogs do. Bouncer was on a short leash. He was a friendly enough dog but could get overly excited and didn't always play well with others. I'd rescued him as a puppy from the not-so-tender care of Jake Turpie, full-time scrap dealer and psychopath. Bouncer had settled in with us well, but you can take the junkyard mutt out of the junkyard . . . For instance, right now I wasn't quite sure if he was licking Ogilvie's spaniel or tasting it.

'There's something funny going on,' Ogilvie said, out of the corner of his mouth, staring straight ahead, like this was Gorky Park and not Kirkton Park.

'Not from where I'm standing, slap-bang in the middle of a murder charge, there isn't,' I replied.

'What do you know about Simon Keggie?' he asked. 'I mean *really* know.'

I didn't pay a lot of interest to local government, not until my Council Tax Bill came in every year – and then I tended to do a lot of shouting. All I really knew about Keggie was that he was a popular politician, not easy if you're a Tory in West Lothian, who'd risen through the ranks to become Provost, whatever that entailed. I also knew that he'd assaulted the man who'd broken into his house, had injured him badly in self-defence and then been acquitted due to a lack of evidence, or, as I preferred to see it, my own courtroom brilliance.

'There was no lack of evidence,' Ogilvie said.

'It was all down to my courtroom brilliance then?'

The PF didn't see it that way. 'There was more than enough evidence if MacDonald hadn't gone back on his police statement *and* if you hadn't pulled some spurious motion about self-incrimination. Then again, from my years of experience dealing with you, spurious motions are your *raison d'être*.'

I turned to face him. 'Why are we here?' I asked. 'Apart, obviously, from letting our kids play on the swings and our dogs sniff each other's backsides?'

'We're here because I think Keggie had something to do with the murder of Angus MacDonald,' he said bluntly.

I said nothing, not taken in by the idea that Ogilvie might be trying to help me in some way. This was the man, the procurator fiscal, who throughout my career in his jurisdiction had been the fragment of eggshell in my egg salad sandwich, and, lest we forget, the man who'd put me on a murder petition in the first place. Not only

172

that but he'd opposed bail. For all I knew, this meeting was a catch-and-kill attempt to find out my line of defence and abort it.

'Come on. You must have been thinking the same thing,' he said. 'While your past history would suggest you'll try to cobble together some cunning defence, I'd guess your final position has to be that you had nothing to do with MacDonald's death, and if that's correct, then somebody else must be responsible.'

'Hugh, why *are* we here?' I said, not sure if he expected me to marvel at his firm grasp on the bleeding obvious. 'You're the procurator fiscal who put me on a murder petition.'

'You're a solicitor, Robbie. I couldn't charge you with shoplifting without asking for Crown Office approval.' I'd always wondered why that was. Probably, to spread the enjoyment around Castle Grayskull that a defence lawyer was in the frame. 'The cops submitted a report in which you were the prime suspect. I didn't think it was enough to go on, but I couldn't ignore such a serious matter, which was why I sent it through to Edinburgh. I was surprised as you were – okay, maybe not *quite* so surprised – when word came back to prosecute and oppose bail.'

I took a step back, almost tripping over Bouncer. 'Are you trying to say that you think I'm innocent, Hugh?'

Ogilvie winced. 'I wouldn't go as far as to say that. I think you know something about it, unless your phone took itself out for a drive that night. But kill this man MacDonald? Why would you? Because he'd been pestering your wife? I know Joanna. She can handle herself very well without your help. No, think about it,' he said, as though perhaps my mind had been on other things since my arrest and during a week on remand. 'Who had previously assaulted and almost killed MacDonald?'

173

'Keggie? The motive for that was MacDonald breaking into his house at midnight,' I said.

Ogilvie's dog was on an extension lead and had gone off on a wander by itself to a nearby tree. He began to reel it in, but the dog squatted, and he stopped, reached into his pocket and brought out a purple disposable bag. Once he'd returned with a neatly parcelled package, he said, 'Would you stop thinking like Keggie's lawyer for two minutes? What housebreaking? There was not a scrap of evidence that MacDonald broke in. Do you think Keggie was actually in the habit of leaving his doors unlocked at night? Don't give me that. And let's not forget MacDonald's original statement to the police. The one you somehow managed to keep from the jury. In it he said he'd been invited to MacDonald's place.'

'As much as I'd like to believe there was something in that, I think housebreaking is the more likely scenario,' I said.

Ogilvie shook his head. 'I should have done the trial myself,' he muttered. 'I'd have found out why MacDonald was really there.'

He was talking nonsense. My wife was twice the trial lawyer Ogilvie could ever hope to be. 'I'm not sure the outcome would have been very different,' I said, in a diplomatic tone I seldom used when conversing with the PF. 'Joanna did her best. What chance did she have when the complainer wouldn't speak up?'

'That's not what I meant. Josh Wedderburn practically begged me for that case. I let him have it, and he proceeded to drag it out for a year. Two Crown adjournments because he said he wanted to nail down the medical and forensic evidence, then he doesn't call the trial in until the last day before the case time-barred, and promptly takes unwell. You saw how hard it was for me to get an extension. Even though Josh told me he'd be okay by Tuesday, I don't know why, but I had a feeling he'd come up with some other excuse. That's why I got onto Joanna straightaway, and I can tell you Josh wasn't very happy about it.'

I had presumed that any trial-dodging by Josh Wedderburn had been due to laziness, not wanting to take on what wasn't a particularly good Crown case. Now it seemed that both Ogilvie and Joanna were of the same mind, namely that Wedderburn had been trying to fabricate a way of having the case time-barred. What good that did me was less clear. Ogilvie had a theory which I had to admit showed a degree of imagination on his part.

'I don't believe there was any housebreaking. I believe MacDonald's original statement that he had been invited to Keggie's home.'

'Yeah, but a housebreaker would say that.'

Ogilvie tapped his temple. 'Assume for a moment he didn't break in. If he was invited, he was obviously there for a reason.'

'And what was that?' I said.

'That's what I'd like to find out.' Ogilvie bent down and patted his dog. Fed up with Bouncer's attentions, it was now sitting at its master's feet. 'I'm telling you, something very fishy was taking place that night and it led to that assault. Whatever business it was they were discussing, it was something neither of them wanted the world to know about.'

'MacDonald's a big, powerful man,' I said. 'Keggie's no weakling, but he's old and out of shape. I'd still fancy MacDonald in a square go even if Keggie had a heavy walking stick.'

Ogilvie shook his head. 'That was no fight. You've seen the medical evidence and the photographs. The injury was to the back of the head. Keggie kept the walking stick in an umbrella stand by the door. MacDonald was leaving. That's when he was struck. The first blow would have floored him. He must have only just managed to scramble his way out onto the street. It saved him from further attack. I think Keggie had lost it and was trying to kill him.'

Bouncer sauntered over and lay down, pretending that he could behave too.

'None of that gives Keggie a motive for killing MacDonald nearly a year later,' I said. 'Unless ...' Ogilvie nodded patronisingly at my attempts to piece things together. 'Unless he knew that if MacDonald was killed before the trial, not only would it look extremely dodgy ...'

Ogilvie picked up the threads. 'But, worse still, MacDonald's statement would replace his testimony in the box and there would be a much better chance that Keggie would be convicted of a serious assault and jailed, than if the case was simply time-barred or MacDonald was somehow persuaded not to speak up.' Ogilvie was becoming quite excited with all this theorising. A tide of crimson rose from the collar of his shirt and swept across his face. His left eye threatened to pop out.

'Hold on, though,' I said. 'Keggie might have taken him by surprise once, but he wouldn't be so lucky a second time.' I couldn't say anything, but I remembered how MacDonald had so easily dealt with me and Stan's two men.

'He wouldn't need to be lucky,' Ogilvie said. 'The first attempt, I believe, was spur-of-the-moment out of anger, and unpremeditated. But Keggie's an influential politician. On his say-so, a lot of things happen in West Lothian or, just as importantly, don't happen. Planning applications are passed or refused. Licences granted or not. Contracts are allocated to certain companies in preference to others. If you have someone like that on your side, then you don't want them drummed out of the Brownies. No, what you need to look for, Robbie, is Mr Big. Someone whose interests would be adversely affected if Keggie was sent to prison. The sort of person who'd have no qualms about putting pressure on one of my deputes to have Keggie acquitted. Once that was done, why not get rid of a nuisance like Angus MacDonald?'

There was only one Mr Big I knew, and he wasn't talking to me right now.

'Why are you trying to help me, Hugh?' I asked.

'I'm the procurator fiscal. I prosecute cases in the public interest and where I think there is sufficient evidence to convict an accused of a crime.'

'Thanks for reciting the home page of the Crown Office website,' I said, 'but, really, why are you helping me?'

Ogilvie called to his son. His name was Hugh junior. Somehow, I'd thought it might be. 'I'm helping you because I think there's a rotten apple in my office. I also think there are political shenanigans going on. Keggie only just lost out on being elected last year. He was running against Harvey Rudd, the Justice Secretary. Is it a coincidence that it was one week before the election that he was charged with assaulting MacDonald?'

'You think MacDonald had something on Keggie and was going to reveal it just before the election?'

Ogilvie shrugged. 'It happens.'

'Blackmail?'

'Who knows? All we have is an unexplained late-night

visit that led to one man sustaining a serious injury. I wanted to get to the bottom of it. You and your spurious objection at the trial put a stop to that, but I see you as a link to the truth of what happened that night.' I couldn't remember anyone having called me a link to the truth before. For professional reasons I usually preferred to avoid the truth if at all possible. I let Ogilvie continue. 'You were Keggie's lawyer. Now it's in your own interests to find out if what happened led to MacDonald's death and why. I assume you'll go about things in your own inimitable fashion, and when you find out, I want to be first to know.' His second call to Hugh junior met with as much success as had the first. 'I'll do what I can to help, of course, within reason,' he said.

At the third attempt, Tina and Ogilvie's son came charging over to us, and stood there looking up, breathlessly. My daughter was first to pipe up. 'This boy says that his dad puts the baddies in jail, but I told him my dad kills the baddies. That's right, isn't it, Dad?'

Ogilvie turned to me with a syrupy smile. 'I don't have to remind you of your right to remain silent, do I?'

29

In any criminal case in Scotland, the Crown is under an obligation to disclose to the defence all the evidence against the accused. Despite this information being in the hands of the prosecution from an early stage in proceedings, it is usually drip-fed over a period of months via an encrypted email system that occasionally works. The thing about the Crown Office and Procurator Fiscal Service is that it's staffed by civil servants who never want to take personal ownership of a case. It's like a never-ending game of pass the parcel, each depute hoping they'll not be the one holding the case papers when the music stops, and the case eventually comes to trial. Defence lawyers who send letters to the procurator fiscal are like children sending letters up the chimney to Father Christmas. It's strictly one-way traffic. PF deputes fear that to respond might imply an attachment to a particular case. Better to ignore all correspondence. That way, if things go wrong with the preparation, no one knows who to blame.

Normally, first to arrive is a provisional list of witnesses, giving names but no addresses and as such a fat lot of good. Then comes the schedule of non-sensitive documents comprising a list of all those items that are of little interest to anyone. Next, are the pro forma arrest forms, then the transcripts of the police interviews, followed by more weeks of nothing until, one day, the witness statements arrive, and much, much later, often on the eve of the trial itself, come late-breaking reports from forensic experts. That's what usually happens. Not in my case. Perhaps because I was a solicitor, perhaps because of Hugh Ogilvie's apparent willingness to assist my cause; whatever the reason, disclosure was made swiftly and without a hitch.

I was as pleased as I could be in the circumstances. The early arrival of the evidence would give me plenty of time to prepare my defence, and, following upon Ogilvie's advice, I'd asked Grace Mary to set up a visit for me to see Simon Keggie. As yet there had been no response despite repeated requests.

Grace Mary downloaded and printed the Crown disclosure around lunchtime on Wednesday, and I spent the rest of the day perusing the bundle of evidence. The witness list comprised mainly cops as well as my wife who had made it onto the list as one of the few civilian witnesses along with a handful of forensic experts. It was the experts' reports that I was most interested in. These contained few surprises. Analysis of the splodges of blood on the outbuilding floor had revealed nothing of interest, but, even though there was no body, when the DNA from the kitchen floorboards was compared with the blood samples taken in the Simon Keggie case, the forensic lab could give odds of one billion to one against it belonging to anyone other than Angus MacDonald.

As for the telecommunications data, the data from my mobile phone company had formed the basis of a detailed report, complete with coloured schedules and appendices containing the locations of various phone masts and GPS sources, all nicely pieced together on a map to show the route taken by my phone, from my house to the alleged murder scene and back again. Could I turn the fact that my phone was with me into a positive for the defence? First rule of murder club was no mobile phones. Everyone knew that, not least criminal defence lawyers. Thankfully, the one thing that wasn't contained in any of the reports was mention of the pickaxe handle. Without it, I felt the evidence was reassuringly weak. The only way to keep it like that was by another meeting with the two cops from the Specialist Crime Division. I was surprised they hadn't been back in touch.

Right at that moment Grace Mary came through to my room, looking like she'd just met Hamlet's dad.

'You're not going to believe it,' she said, in a way that made me think that while I might not believe it, I was going to like it even less. 'The indictment. It's being served tomorrow.'

The service of an indictment at a solicitor's office is a regular occurrence. From my secretary's tone of voice, she could only be referring to one particular indictment and an arrival that was around six months premature.

I couldn't speak. It felt like something had ruptured inside of me and was spreading coldly amongst my vital organs.

'Fiona Faye's on her way. She's managed to get a courtesy copy. I haven't told Joanna. I thought you would rather . . . You know . . . Anyway, I'll leave you to it,' Grace Mary said, withdrawing quietly from the room, closing the door behind her.

Ten minutes later she returned ushering in Fiona Faye QC. Black suit, white frilly blouse, pearl earrings and bouffant blonde hair that looked like it had been styled by a construction engineer. She lobbed a sheaf of papers stapled in one corner onto the desk in front of me.

'Take a look at the list of labels,' she said. 'The case against you was wafer-thin before. Now it seems to have put on a little weight.' So had Fiona but now wasn't the time to mention it. Never was the time to mention it.

I flicked through the sheets of the indictment, past the charge, past the list of witnesses and documentary productions, to the schedule of physical productions, otherwise known as labels. There was the usual array of forensic samples and computer disks, but at the foot of the page next to the heading 'label 26', the words 'pickaxe handle' screamed at me from the page.

'There's blood on it,' Fiona said. 'They've also found DNA on it. It's yours. Crown counsel tells me there's a forensic report on the way.'

I handed the indictment to Grace Mary and asked her to make me a copy.

'Well?' Fiona said, after my secretary had left the room. 'The DNA?' I sat down on the edge of the desk and looked at the floor. Fiona lifted my head with the help of one of my ears.

'It's a long story.'

'Then I don't want to hear it. Not yet. Not the first draft.'

'You know I didn't do it, don't you, Fiona?'

'I don't know anything, Robbie, and what's more I'm not interested. I'm only concerned with the evidence, and that shows blood on one end of a pickaxe handle and your DNA on the other. If you didn't do it, then there are lots of possible ways you didn't do it. Pick the one you want me to tell the jury and come back to me with the final version. Meantime, I'm going to contact the Crown and find out why on earth they've served this indictment so quickly.'

'Can't you have it put it off to give us more time to prepare?' I said.

Fiona shrugged. 'I could lodge a section 75A, but I have a feeling it will be a waste of time. I've worked in Crown Office. Nothing is done quickly. If your indictment has been served this fast, it's because the powers on high don't want to give us time to prepare, and anyway, what grounds would we have to postpone? You know what those preliminary hearing judges are like. Crown adjournment? Fine. Defence adjournment? Not so fine. All I'll get is an earful of justice delayed, justice denied and how it only took twenty-nine days to prepare Peter Manuel's defence.'

'Yeah, well, look where it got him,' I said.

'Robbie, you have to see that from the Crown's perspective, yours is not a difficult case to try. Why wait? They've got everything they need.'

'What do you mean – everything they need? They don't have a body. I'd have thought that a dead person might come in handy for a murder trial. As for this pickaxe handle, okay, there may be some blood on it, but how can they say anyone was killed with it?'

'Because Robbie, it has blood on it.'

'There's nothing in the report says it's MacDonald's blood,' I said.

'No, but there's clearly been a massive blood loss. MacDonald's kitchen was swimming in the stuff.'

'I was never in his kitchen. I was never in the house.'

'Robbie, have you even read the forensic reports?'

'Forensic scientists? You'll tear them a new one in court. Come on, Fiona. This isn't the telly. We all know there are plenty of mistakes in expert reports, mainly because it's hard to write while you're bending over backwards to help the prosecution.'

Fiona sighed. 'Robbie, stop kidding yourself. There is a pretty decent circumstantial case against you. Lots of threads to make a rope. MacDonald was annoying your wife. Your phone was at his home—'

'No, Fiona, my phone was in a two-hundred-yard radius of his home.'

'Yes, on the night he disappeared, presumed murdered, and on the night and at the time your wife says you went out to do some shopping and came back with nothing other than a sore elbow. *And*, Robbie,' she said, before I could protest further, 'there's MacDonald's blood in his kitchen, and there's the discarded pickaxe handle which also has traces of blood on it as well as your DNA. It would be a doddle to prosecute that. The witnesses are nearly all cops and forensic scientists. Talk about singing from the same hymn sheet: these witnesses should be on *Songs of Praise*. The Crown just needs to drop them into the witness box, wind them up and off they'll go, regurgitating their statements. Quick and easy? It would be hard to spin a trial like that out for more than a week.'

Grace Mary returned with two copies of the indictment. She gave one to me. Fiona took hers, folded it and tucked it inside her handbag. Together we walked down the stairs to the High Street where a red sports car was badly parked at the bus stop. Fiona opened the passenger door and laid her handbag on the seat before turning to me and pinching my cheek. 'We can beat this Robbie, but I'm going to need two things. I want to know where you were that night and I want an explanation – a believable explanation – as to how your DNA ended up on that pickaxe handle.'

30

To paraphrase the late, great Brian Clough, if blue flashing lights are not the worst thing to see in a rear-view mirror, they're definitely in the top one. I drove on for another hundred yards, just to make sure it was me they were interested in, and eventually took the hint when the headlights neared and flashed full beam. I parked at the side of the road at the entrance to Kingscavil cemetery. A familiar dark-coloured unmarked saloon car pulled in behind me. It had to be Dicker and Sandeman. They'd told me they'd wait a week. It had been six days. I got out and walked over to the car. DI Dicker, wedged behind the wheel, rolled down the driver side window. 'Get in,' he said, and I did.

'Smoke?' DCI Sandeman, facing front, held a cigarette up so I could see it in the back seat.

'No thanks.'

'Don't mind if I do, do you?' she asked, lighting up.

Dicker almost managed to turn his bulk around in his seat. 'We hear things are moving along pretty fast. You've got a court date.'

'Not for the trial, for the preliminary hearing.'

'Too bad about the pickaxe handle thing,' he said, in a manner that suggested he'd get over it. 'But you know how it is. We couldn't sit on important evidence like that forever. Not if you weren't playing ball.'

'You said I had a week to think things over.'

'That was before the Lord Advocate decided to stick a rocket under the prosecution,' Dicker said.

'So why am I here? You've handed over the pickaxe handle.' I tried the back door, but the security lock was engaged. 'What more is there to discuss?'

There was no answer at first. Sandeman rolled down her window and pinged ash. 'Do you actually believe he's dead?'

'What are you talking about?' I said.

'I'm talking about Angus MacDonald.' She took a casual draw on her cigarette and blew smoke out of the window. 'All a bit convenient don't you think?' Not for me it wasn't, but I let her continue. 'He does his best to get Keggie off with the assault and then he just disappears, leaving behind a pickaxe handle and some blood. The only thing missing is him. Now the Crown serve an indictment on you *tout de suite*. You'd think they'd at least wait for a body to show up. Bodies usually do, eventually. Makes the job a lot harder without one. Juries like to see a corpse in a murder case. The post-mortem photos are half the fun.'

'You're forgetting that in Scotland double jeopardy is more or less a thing of the past,' I said. 'If they try me without a body and I'm acquitted, they can have another bite at the cherry if one turns up. New evidence.'

Sandeman took another drag and a sideways glance at her partner.

'And what if that body was to turn up breathing?' Dicker asked. He took off his glasses, breathed on each lens and began to wipe them on his shirt.

I leaned forward, elbows pressed against the front seats. 'You really think MacDonald's alive?'

'Why not?' Dicker said. 'It's a great way to disappear. Better than leaving a pile of clothes on the beach. All you need is a sucker like you, a drop of blood here, a drop of blood there. Those cadaver dogs can find a dead flea at a hundred paces, and yet they've come up with nothing so far. And as for the forensics labs? Well, you know what I'm talking about. They'll express an opinion so long as Crown Office tells them what they want it to be.'

'Can I quote you on that?' I said, flopping back in the seat, too many questions racing through my head.

It was Sandeman's turn. They made a great double act. 'We gave you one chance and you didn't take it. Now that things are a lot worse, don't refuse the second, it could be your last.'

I waited to hear their offer.

'You know we didn't put your DNA on that pickaxe handle. That was you. You could try and explain it away by saying that we took you to the murder scene and had you contaminate the evidence, but what we'll say is that you asked to be taken there and, as you know, the seal on the production bag was never broken.'

'It was always your intention to lodge the pickaxe handle,' I said.

'Okay.' Sandeman held up her hands, almost scorching the roof lining with the tip of her cigarette. 'You've got us. We lied. But we're not lying now. We think MacDonald's alive. We think his disappearance has to do with Simon Keggie. We also know from High Street CCTV that on the night he disappeared your car wasn't seen heading in the direction of the locus, which means someone took you there. It also explains how you managed to overcome a tank of a man like MacDonald and come out of it with only a bruised elbow to show for it. Now, we could spend a lot of time checking the registrations of all those cars picked up on CCTV that night, but I've a feeling we might eventually come up with a false plate or a hired car. All we want from you is the name of the person or persons who took you to see MacDonald.'

Give them the name of Stan Blandy? Not likely. 'That's a lot of speculation on your part,' I said.

'No . . .' Sandeman took a couple more quick drags and dropped the cigarette stub out of the window. 'That's police work. It's what we do. Give us a name and let us do the rest.'

31

'They've served the indictment!'

Thursday morning, breakfast was running late at the Munros. I was making a cup of tea while Joanna furiously mashed Jamie a banana in a wee yellow bowl. He'd already eaten half my porridge. My son might only be ten months old, but he had the appetite of a plague of locusts at an all-you-can-eat salad bar. When he was born and the midwives had brought tea and buttered toast, he'd thought it was for him. Joanna stopped mashing. 'Why didn't you tell me last night?'

'I thought it would be better after a good night's sleep. I didn't want to keep you up worrying.'

'But it's way too early. The indictment shouldn't be out for months yet. What's so urgent? Someone must be pushing this. Who at Crown Office really hates you?' That was a list that would take someone a long time to compile. 'I mean, they don't have a body, they don't have a murder weapon . . .' Joanna had read the expression on my face, even though I was unaware it had changed. 'No, Robbie. Tell me they haven't got it.'

I took the spoon and bowl from her and gently lowered her onto a chair by the table. 'It's been lodged as a label,' I said.

'And?'

189

'And there's a forensic report showing blood on one end and my DNA on the other.'

Joanna gripped her brow with one hand and massaged it, gazing at the floor.

'I had a quick consultation with Fiona Faye yesterday. She's all set to take on the defence, but—'

'She wants to know why your DNA is on the pickaxe handle?'

I nodded.

'And where you were on the night in question?'

I nodded again.

'What did you tell her?'

'She knows my defence is a work in progress, and that she'll need to be patient.'

'Patient? How can she be patient if there's a preliminary hearing coming up in the next two weeks? If your defence is alibi it'll have to be lodged. And then there's your witness list. Have we got someone lined up to throw doubt on the DNA evidence?'

'Calm down,' I said, inserting a spoonful of mashed banana into Jamie. 'There is some good news.'

Joanna looked up, expectantly.

'I don't think he's dead.' I said.

She frowned. 'How can you possibly say that?'

Jamie was doing his imitation of a fledgling, head up, mouth open. 'I'm not the one saying it. The police are.' I tried to spoon in some more banana and only narrowly missed. I wiped my son's face with kitchen roll and tried again.

'I don't understand,' Joanna said.

'It's like this. The cops stopped me on the way home last night.'

'The ones from the SCD?'

'Yeah, they're not buying it.'

'Not buying what?'

'I said right from the start that it was strange that a nobody like Angus MacDonald goes missing for less than a day and somebody reports it. When does that ever happen for an adult male? And when the cops go searching for him, they are immediately so suspicious of foul play that they get the necessary authority to obtain information on the movements of my phone. How long do inquiries like that normally take? Weeks? Months? No, someone must have contacted the cops and said there'd been a murder. This wasn't a routine missing person's inquiry. And after all that, what do they find – no body, just some blood on a kitchen floor and a pickaxe handle—'

'With your DNA on one end and his blood on the other,' Joanna reminded me once more, as if I could forget.

'We won't know that for certain until the forensic report comes in, Jo, but, yes, probably. Even so, don't you think it's all very convenient? What easier way to make yourself disappear?'

'I can think of a few ways that wouldn't necessarily involve sloshing your own blood all over the floor,' Joanna said, relieving me of bowl and spoon. 'Anyway, why would he want to disappear?'

Jamie tried to grab the bowl from Joanna, but she pulled it out of the reach of his sticky little fingers.

'I had chat with Hugh Ogilvie,' I said.

'And?'

'He believes Simon Keggie and MacDonald were up to something. He doesn't believe there was a break-in.'

'I said all along MacDonald hadn't broken in,' Joanna said. Without taking her eye off me, she scored a bullseye on the moving target that was our son's mouth.

'Ogilvie thinks Keggie or MacDonald or both of them managed to nobble Josh Wedderburn, so he'd have the case time-barred.'

The kettle began to boil as Tina bundled her way into the kitchen, satchel upside down over her shoulders, looking for someone to put her hair into bunches.

'There's bands in the drawer. Give them to your dad,' Joanna said, her voice lighter, more relaxed. An air of optimism gathered like the steam from the kettle, filling the room.

'Not him, Mum. You. Dad's hopeless.'

Joanna handed me the bowl and spoon again. 'So, what else did the cops say? I take it they still want to know who it was abducted MacDonald in the first place? Why don't you tell them? What harm can it do if he's not dead? Doesn't make them murder suspects. The cops probably only want to find out if they were in on the plan to fake MacDonald's death, which they probably were.'

I didn't know what I thought about that. Was Stan in on it in some way? He'd certainly found MacDonald with supreme ease, but then, someone with an inside track to the DVLA or police national computer could have done that, and Stan certainly fitted the bill. I had to speak to Stan again, explain the situation and tell him I needed to give the cops names. It wouldn't have to be his driver and the other big clown. Two patsies would do. What was the worst that could happen? They'd be charged with wasting police time. It had all been a practical joke: Angus MacDonald trying to escape child maintenance payments or something. He'd put them up to it. There were countless ways they could spin it, just so long as they admitted that the man I was charged with murdering wasn't dead.

I placed the bowl on the highchair and let my son get

stuck in. I hugged my daughter, kissed my wife and went back to Jamie and the mashed banana before there was an environmental incident. I was thinking about another slice of toast when Joanna's phone buzzed.

'That was Grace Mary,' Joanna said. 'They've found MacDonald.'

I turned around, smiling. 'I knew it. Where?'

Joanna blinked a few times. Her bottom lip trembled. 'He was floating in the River Avon, downstream of Muiravonside Country Park.'

32

Jeff Freeman's trial came around sooner than I had anticipated. Sheriff Albert Brechin presiding, the weasel that was Josh Wedderburn prosecuting. Wedderburn smiled across the well of the court. It was two o'clock on a Monday afternoon and the procurator fiscal depute was keen to finish early.

'Shouldn't take more than half an hour, should it, Robbie?' he said with a smirk. Under legal aid rules, if a trial didn't last more than thirty minutes the solicitor wasn't paid. It was why a lot of us defence lawyers suffered from weak bladders and sought toilet breaks if the prosecution looked set to crumble before the half-hour mark. 'It was good of you to agree the police evidence by joint minute, but you might have shot yourself in the foot, don't you think?'

I gave him the best worried expression I could fake. 'What do you mean?'

He laughed. 'Well, you've agreed the Crown case. There's nothing I need to do other than put the joint minute up, show the video to Brechin and let him stick twelve months up your paedo film director. I mean, it's obviously obscene, filming two seventeen-year-old girls prancing about wearing nothing but thongs you could have cut a camembert with.'

He was still sniggering when the sheriff was led onto

the bench. Eleanor, the sheriff clerk, called my client's name and the bar officer showed him into the dock. Brechin opened the red cover of his immense hardback notebook, took the lid off his fountain pen and stared down at Wedderburn. 'Who's your first witness, Mr Fiscal?'

'M'Lord, my friend ...' by which he professionally, if erroneously, meant me, 'has kindly agreed a large part of the Crown case and a joint minute of admissions has been lodged.'

Brechin put his hand over the front of the bench and the sheriff clerk passed up to him two sheets of paper, stapled at the corner.

Sheriff Brechin studied the two-page document through the half-moon spectacles that sheriffs are born wearing. 'It says here the police attended the accused's home and took possession of Crown label 1. What is that, procurator fiscal depute?'

'It's the mobile phone belonging to the accused, M'Lord.'

'I see.' Brechin continued reading. 'It was in his pocket. And there was found on said mobile phone video footage which was later transferred onto Crown label 2—'

'A pen drive, M'Lord,' Wedderburn chirped, without being asked.

'And that this transfer was carried out by the High-Tech Unit of Police Scotland, and Crown production 1 is the certificated evidence of that?'

'That's correct, M'Lord. All your Lordship need do is view the material on label 2 and decide whether it comprises indecent images of Dani Quin and Layla McEwan, the children referred to in the charge.'

At this invitation the sheriff rose from the bench.

'I have viewed the material in chambers,' he said upon his return, some time later.

'He has,' Eleanor the clerk mouthed silently to me. 'Several times.'

Sheriff Brechin lifted the joint minute and continued reading. 'I see the accused was arrested and later, when questioned, following caution and charge, said, *I was making a movie. You've got to start somewhere.*'

The young PF depute smiled up at the bench and nodded. His naivety was like a breath of fresh air. Unfortunately for him, I was about to let go an enormous fart into that fresh air. I almost felt sorry for him. Josh Wedderburn was a recent recruit to the Procurator Fiscal's Office in Livingston. We hadn't crossed swords on more than half a dozen occasions, whereas Sheriff Albert Vincent Brechin and I had been going at it hammer and tongs for what seemed like forever.

The sheriff held up the joint minute of admissions by a corner, using finger and thumb. He didn't say anything at first, probably racking his brain for other occasions when I'd agreed any evidence at all, far less the entire Crown case. There weren't any. He turned over to the second page, most likely to check that I hadn't signed it 'Mickey Mouse'.

After a moment or two he waved the papers at me. 'And you've agreed this, Mr Munro? The whole Crown case?'

I stood. 'Indeed, M'Lord.' And sat down again.

'Well, procurator fiscal?' he said.

Wedderburn got to his feet. 'Your Lordship has viewed the video footage and it's been agreed in the joint minute that the footage was taken from the mobile phone belonging to the accused, and found in his possession. He also admitted under caution that he'd been making what he describes as a movie, so I'll lead no further evidence and close the Crown case.' With the elegant flourish of a concert pianist he tossed his black gown back and sat down again. Then he made a gun out of his two fingers, pointed them at me and stage-whispered, 'Over to you, Robbie.'

I rose to my feet. 'M'Lord, I'd like to make a submission that there is no case to answer due to insufficient evidence.'

Wedderburn was on his feet. 'M'Lord, this is nonsense, Mr Munro agreed the evidence, it's right there in the joint minute.'

'That's what worries me,' Brechin said. He looked down at me, literally as well as figuratively, and said, 'Before you start, Mr Munro, having viewed the video evidence I can tell you I'm left in no doubt as to its indecency.' Brechin's jowls wobbled at the memory.

'M'Lord,' I said. 'It's admitted that the video your Lordship has taken the trouble to view was made by my client and was indeed found in his possession. Although it's not stated in the joint minute, I'm even prepared to agree that it's indecent. However, what my friend has failed to prove is that either of the subjects of the video, Dani Quin or Layla McEwan, was under the age of eighteen at the time.'

The PF must have had springs on his feet. 'M'Lord, my friend knows that the age of a complainer is presumed to be the age set out in the charge, unless preliminary objection is taken at the outset of the case.'

Brechin's gaze slowly turned from me to Wedderburn. I thought I saw, perhaps for the first time, pity in his eyes. There is a scene at the start of one of my favourite films, *The Matrix*, where a squad of policemen are sent to apprehend a female character called Trinity. Agent Smith of the Secret Service tells the police lieutenant to have his men stand down for their own protection, to which the lieutenant says, 'I think we can handle one little girl.'

'No, Lieutenant,' says Agent Smith. 'Your officers are already dead.'

There was a look of Agent Smith about Sheriff Brechin as, seemingly resigned to the inevitable, he drooped an arm down from the bench to receive from the clerk a sheet of lined paper with my handwriting on it, and Jeff Freeman's signature at the bottom. 'It seems the accused handed in such an objection at the pleading diet,' he said.

Wedderburn demanded to see the written objection. 'This was never intimated to the Crown.'

From my case file I produced the copy of an email I'd sent to the Procurator Fiscal's Office the same day I'd met Jeff Freeman – the day before the pleading diet. I'd deliberately sent it to the general office and equally deliberately addressed it to no one, confident that it would receive no one's full and undivided attention.

'Never mind,' I said, as I handed the copy email across the table to Wedderburn. 'Looks like you're going to get that early finish right enough.'

33

The rest of the working week passed in a blur of court appearances, paperwork and late nights. The whole time my pending trial was hanging over me like a shroud thrown over the sun. Friday evening, I was sitting at my desk, staring at the wall. All the things I could have done with my life. All the things I didn't do and would probably never get the chance to. I didn't like to say anything to Joanna, but I was trying to put my affairs in order. If I was sent to prison what would she do? Would they give the wife of a convicted murderer her job back with the Crown Office and Procurator Fiscal Service? I didn't think so. In which case I had to make sure she had a business worth running after I'd left. Relationship-wise, I couldn't bear to think of Joanna wasting the best years of her life with a husband in prison, having to drag the kids back and forwards to visit their jailbird dad. Better for her to make a clean break. Better for me too. I could get my head down. Serve my time.

It was nearly nine o'clock when Joanna called.

'Do you know what time it is? When are you coming home?'

'Just finishing off a few things,' I said. 'I'll be back in half an hour.'

'Are you okay?'

Okay? Yeah, I was just dandy. I bit my tongue. 'I'm fine.'

'Well you don't sound it.'

'Joanna, what do you want? I'm busy.'

'Yes, you are – busy dodging me and the kids. What's up with you? You've hardly spoken to me all week, even though we're supposed to be sharing the same office, and the kids have hardly seen you.'

'I'm sorry, Jo, I'm just trying to . . . you know . . . sort things out for you. In case . . .'

'I can sort things out myself, thanks, Robbie, and there isn't going to be an *in case*. You need to snap out of it. Stop feeling sorry for yourself. What would you say if you were one of your clients? You'd tell them to get a grip. The Crown case has so many holes, you could spit peas through it. And Fiona Faye is the best in the business, she'll rip the prosecution to shreds. There's a way out of this. You need to focus. Try and stay positive.'

Easy for her to say, I thought as I cancelled the call. All I could think about was giving Sandeman and Dicker what they wanted. A name. Stan Blandy. It was that simple. Tell them it was Stan's men who had abducted and murdered MacDonald and let them take care of it from there. It was so tempting. So the right thing to do. And yet, so dangerous.

My phone wasn't back in my pocket before it buzzed again. The screen showed a withheld number. It was Stan. For a moment I thought his powers extended to mind-reading. He came straight to the point.

'Where's Maggie's phone?'

I didn't understand. It was just over a week since I'd returned the phone to Maggie. It was the reason I'd been permitted an audience with him.

'I gave it back to her,' I said.

'That wasn't her phone.'

'And it's taken her a week to find that out?'

'The one that got nicked was her old phone. The one you gave her had the same cover, but the phone's not hers. She didn't notice it until she tried to transfer some stuff from it to the new one.'

Having had the phone cracked, Stan had also made the sort of enquiries only he could make and discovered the phone I'd given to Maggie was in fact registered to an owner in Fife who'd reported it stolen months before when on a pub crawl in Linlithgow. Another of Meeko's victims, I assumed.

'Sorry about that, Stan, but I never said it was Maggie's phone. It was Maggie who said it was.'

'Where's Maggie's phone?' he repeated.

'I don't know.'

'But you know who stole it, don't you? One of your clients, you said? Stephanie somebody.' I reminded him of that night outside the Red Corner when he'd brushed aside my offer to try and get the phone back from Meeko, saying he'd buy the boy a new one. 'That was before I knew it was Maggie's phone he'd taken,' Stan said. 'I want it back.'

'Okay Stan, I'll try and get the phone back. Give me a few days, and I'll see what I can dig up. After all, I've nothing more important to do,' I grumbled, but only after he'd hung up.

Later, I was on the High Street, locking the door to the close that led to my office when someone tapped me on the shoulder.

'Hello handsome,' Joanna said. 'Fancy taking a girl out for a drink?'

In a pale blue cardigan over a cream blouse and jeans, dark hair tied back, she looked great. But then my wife always did.

'What about—'

'Your dad's watching the kids, and Malky will be making his usual Friday night appearance sometime, so he can help. I said we wouldn't be late.' She linked her arm through mine and steered me eastwards.

'Where are you taking me?' I asked as we approached the mini-roundabout at the end of the High Street.

'I thought you might like a drink and to listen to some music. It might take your mind off things for a while,' she said, and arm in arm we crossed the road at the foot of the station brae and headed towards the Star & Garter. A poster by the door advertised an open mic night. It was partially obscured by a large man, the sleeves of his white shirt rolled up over thick forearms. He had in a Bluetooth earpiece, and a microphone was pinned to his immense black waistcoat. He smiled at Joanna as we approached.

'Miss Jordan,' he said, and stood to the side to let us walk up the steps. Standing outside the premises as he was, I gathered the big man was either working the door, or - I thought, as we entered the bar to the sound of a male voice and a painful rendition of 'Wichita Lineman'- a music lover.

'I take it you know the bouncer,' I said.

'He's been a Crown witness at a few trials. He works at pubs and clubs all over the place. Doesn't take much snash from the punters.'

Inside the bar, I pointed up at the blackboard on the wall chalked with the latest cocktails. 'What'll it be?'

'I brought the car,' Joanna said. 'You have a beer. I'll just have a Diet Coke.'

I didn't put up a fight. I told her to look around for a seat and squeezed myself between the occupants of two wooden bar stools to get to the counter. By the time I'd been served with a pint from the hotel's adjacent micro-brewery and a Diet Coke, the singer had changed from a male country and western singer to a young female vocalist with a set of Scots folk songs and a voice as pure and clear as a Highland stream.

Joanna hadn't managed to find us somewhere to sit, and so we had to stand at the end of the bar furthest from the singers; the safest place to be if Linlithgow's answer to Glen Campbell was to make a comeback, but not the best location to hear a beautiful rendition of 'Mountain Thyme'.

'Good, isn't she?' Joanna said, tilting her drink, ice clinking, in the direction of the stage.

I took a long pull through the head of my pint, and then put my mouth to my wife's ear. 'Jo, I'm sorry if I've been—'

She pulled away from me and handed me her glass of Coke. 'Put your drink down,' she said.

'But—'

'Just do it and come with me.' Without waiting she pushed her way through the bar, and with a farewell gulp of beer, I set our drinks on the countertop and followed her into the lobby.

'You know who that was singing just now, don't you?' she said.

'The girl? No. Should I?'

'Not the girl. When we came in. That was Josh Wedderburn.'

Apparently, the singing cowboy with more keys than Florida was indeed the young fiscal depute who'd tried his best to have Simon Keggie's case tossed.

'The girls at work told me he's here for every open mic night.'

'And?'

Joanna pointed at the door of the gents' toilets. 'I think he's in there. Go check if he's alone.'

A shove in my back suggested I wasn't to ask further questions. I opened the door, stepped inside and saw the checked shirt of Wedderburn standing by one of the urinals with no one else in sight. He glanced over at me, gave me a tight smile and faced the wall again. I stepped out, and almost bumped into Joanna. 'He's there.'

'Good,' she said. 'You wait here and make sure no one else comes in. I'll not be long.'

She marched towards the toilet doors. I tried to grab her arm, but she twisted out of my reach. I don't know how long passed. Seemed like ages, but it was probably less than a minute later when I heard my wife scream. I burst through the door to find her standing by the sinks, her blouse front ripped open, one or two buttons rolling across the tiled floor, past the pointy toes of Josh Wedderburn's cowboy boots.

I tried to shout, but the words caught in my throat and emerged as a strangled roar. My eyes clouded over, the blood rushed from my face and seemed to run into my arms, clenching my fists. It was rage that had lain dormant for weeks now. Heating up as I'd stood in the dock of the Sheriff Court, simmering away every day of my week in prison, threatening to boil over whenever I looked at the yellow pages of the indictment on my desk and the charge that threatened to take me away from my family. Here, standing right in front of me in plaid shirt and Wrangler jeans, was the perfect opportunity to release it.

I took a step forward. Wedderburn backed away, stretching out his arms, showing me his palms. 'I . . . I never touched her, Robbie. This is a set-up. I can explain.'

Joanna took a grip on Wedderburn's bolo-tie and with the other hand drew a fingernail down the side of his face. He yelped and I pulled my wife away from him. 'What are you doing, Jo?'

Joanna screamed again.

'Stop doing that!' Wedderburn yelled, clutching his cheek, torn between stepping forward to silence Joanna and trying to keep me at a distance.

The door was thrown open and the doorman barged in. He looked from me to Joanna to Wedderburn and then back to Joanna again.

'Are you okay, Miss Jordan?'

'I'm fine,' Joanna said. 'Really. It's nothing.'

'Are you sure?'

Joanna smiled weakly and nodded. Pulling her cardigan tightly about her she took hold of my arm. 'Let's go, Robbie.'

There was only one place I wanted to go, and that was directly at Josh Wedderburn taking both my fists with me. Joanna tightened her grip. 'I said, let's go.' She put a hand on my chest and pushed me backwards. 'I mean it. We'll talk this over with Josh later.'

That was a major understatement.

'Right, you,' the doorman said, pointing a finger at Wedderburn. 'Take your stuff and get out.' An aggrieved expression on his face, Wedderburn sidled carefully past me, circumnavigated the door steward and left. The big man looked down at Joanna. 'Let me know if he bothers you again.'

Joanna put a hand on his arm. 'It's all right. I'm sure it was just a misunderstanding,' she said in a way that left little doubt it had been nothing of the sort.

I let her lead me back to the bar where we tracked down

our drinks. The young singer was still in the Highlands with the 'Massacre of Glencoe'.

'Jo, what was all that about?'

'Relax,' she said. 'I'll explain everything later.'

I really wanted everything explained there and then and was about to protest when I saw Wedderburn making an exit carrying a guitar case.

Joanna tugged at my arm. We were leaving.

'I want an explanation,' Wedderburn said, when he saw us walking down the steps towards him. 'He pointed to the scratch on his face. 'How am I supposed to explain that to people?'

'Tell them you fell off your horse,' I said.

Ignoring him, Joanna walked on. Wedderburn followed. The doorman looked like he might too, but I gestured that everything was under control, and the three of us continued a further ten metres or so until we were opposite Far From the Madding Crowd Bookshop, between the station brae and St Michael's Wynd. That was where Joanna stopped and turned to face her accuser.

Joanna had a lovely smile. She gave Wedderburn a different smile. One I didn't recognise and never wanted to be on the receiving end of. 'I'll give you an explanation, Josh,' she said. 'Just as soon as you give me one.'

'I don't know what you're talking about.' He looked at me, a pained expression on his face. 'Robbie, what is this? What's going on?'

I wished I could have told him. Joanna grabbed a hold of Wedderburn by the shoulders and squared him up. He reeled in his neck, leaning back, presumably in case my wife struck again with her nails.

'I want an explanation. Why did you deliberately try to have Simon Keggie's case thrown out?'

'Don't be ridiculous. Why would I—'

'You can tell me, or I can accuse you of dragging me into the toilets and sexually assaulting me,' Joanna said.

Wedderburn looked past Joanna to me. 'Are you hearing this, Robbie? Your wife's threatening to fit me up for—'

'For a crime you didn't do? You better believe it,' Joanna said. 'That way you can join my husband in prison for a crime *he* didn't commit either.'

I didn't know what to say or do. I'd never seen Joanna like this before. Out of the corner of my eye, I saw that the door steward had not lost interest in us. The eyes below the overhanging brow were fixed on our little party. He left his post at the foot of the steps and took a few slow paces in our direction.

'I'm not having this discussion,' Wedderburn said.

'One more step and I'll scream again,' Joanna said.

Wedderburn was going to walk away until he spied the ever-approaching figure of the doorman. Not sure what to do, he placed the guitar case on the ground and held up his hands in surrender. 'You're crazy,' he told Joanna. 'I've done nothing wrong.'

My wife disagreed. 'Here's how it's going to be, Josh. Either you tell me why you tried to ditch the Keggie case, or I'm going to scream again, get that bouncer over here, and then, after they've scraped what's left of you off the pavement, I'm going to make a report of sexual assault.'

Wedderburn tried his own little smile. It was fooling nobody. 'And I'll say you made the whole thing up. Which you did.'

'Why would I do that, Josh?' Joanna asked.

'Because . . . because . . .'

'Because I wanted you to tell me why you had tried to

have Simon Keggie's case time-barred? Is that going to be your defence? Any other ideas? I'd ask Robbie to think one up for you, he's unusually good at that type of thing, but unfortunately he's got a lot on his mind right now.' Joanna took a casual look over her shoulder. The door steward had stopped but was still watching. She turned back to Wedderburn and looked him in the eye. 'One scream and I can have that bouncer here in five seconds. I wonder what prison life is like for a convicted sex beast who's also a procurator fiscal.'

Was my wife bluffing? It was why I never played her at poker.

'What's it to be, Josh?' she said. 'Are you going to squeal or am I going to scream?'

Wedderburn looked like a cowboy whose horse has bolted just as a Comanche war party is riding into town. He tried to speak but could only stutter.

Joanna lifted her chin and took a very deep breath.

34

It wasn't until the following Thursday that the defence was allowed to view MacDonald's body. Apparently, even if you were a solicitor, attending the post-mortem examination of the person you're supposed to have murdered was considered bad form. It was exactly a week since the body had been found. Joanna had attended in my place and I'd been awaiting the result like a gambler with his shirt on the favourite.

'Well?' I asked upon my wife's return. 'How'd it go?'

She grimaced. 'Difficult to say. The final autopsy report isn't going to be available for a few weeks and they're still waiting for the toxicology results. They might have to put off the preliminary hearing. They might even desert the indictment pro loco and re-serve once they process all the new information.'

'Jo, just tell me. How did he die?'

Grace Mary came through into my office on hearing Joanna's voice. She saw the look on my wife's face. 'I'll make us a cup of tea,' she said, and left again.

Joanna placed her bag on my desk and dropped into the chair opposite. 'It definitely involved a blunt object. You didn't need to be a pathologist to work that out. The main cause, though, was two bullets to the chest. They've got the bullets and they've been sent to ballistics.'

'He was shot? Where do they think I'd get a gun from?'

'They'll say there are ways. A lot of your clients are criminal after all, and I suppose they don't have to prove you pulled the trigger, just that you were acting in concert with whoever did.'

'What else?' I asked.

It got worse. There were signs that MacDonald had been tied and beaten. I remembered the electrical ties, the blows he'd received from Stan's driver. Joanna continued. 'The marks on his wrists were obvious. In fact, the body was surprisingly intact. They said it was down to immersion in cold water. It's going to make an exact timing of death problematic.'

Grace Mary came back into the room, while the kettle boiled. 'I can't get hold of this Jessica Barrett QC at Crown Office. I've been trying all week. Each time I've been told she's busy and they'll have her call back, but she never does. I think that's because when they ask me what it's about, I don't know what to tell them. The first time I called I said it was to do with your case, Robbie, and they said Miss Barrett was head of sex crimes and I'd been put through to the wrong department. I've seen her name somewhere before. What's so important about her?'

'She's Scotland's youngest QC,' I said.

Joanna butted in. 'She's also the fiancée of the Justice Secretary.'

It came as news to me. What a coincidence. Politician's girlfriend gets rapid promotion.

'But most importantly,' I said, 'she's the Crown counsel that ordered the fiscal to drag out Simon Keggie's trial so that it would time-bar.'

'But I thought Joanna was the fiscal for the trial?'

'I was,' Joanna said, 'but only because I took it on very last-minute. The person at the PF's solemn unit

210

who was supposed to run the trial was a man called Josh Wedderburn. I bumped into him on Friday night. He confided in me . . .' That was a nice way of putting it, 'that he'd been asked by Jessica Barrett to find a way of ditching the case as a personal favour to her.'

'Why would she want him to do that?' Grace Mary asked. Which was precisely what I wanted to know. 'And why would he agree?' The answer to that was easier. Jessica Barrett had only recently been promoted to head of the Sexual Crimes Unit; nonetheless she was seen as a prime candidate for a future Lord Advocate. For career purposes, it wouldn't have done Wedderburn any harm to have someone that high up in Castle Grayskull in his debt.

'And what's it all got to do with the case against you, Robbie?'

Discussions were put on hold until Grace Mary came back with three mugs of tea. She placed them on the desk, using my mouse mat as a giant coaster, the contents of each a different shade, like a boring paint chart. I took the one that was darkest brown and took a sip. 'It's like this, Grace Mary. I had a meeting with Angus MacDonald.'

'The dead guy?'

'That's right, but before he was dead.' She rolled her eyes, but let me continue. 'I'm not saying any more about that, because I don't want you ending up on the Crown witness list, but I never laid a finger on him.'

'Or a pickaxe handle?' Grace Mary said. She held her hands up in mock surrender. 'Just making sure.'

'Not a finger, not a pickaxe handle or any other blunt object, and definitely no gun,' I assured her. While I took a breath and another sip of tea, Joanna picked up where I left off.

'I never believed that crap Robbie was putting forward

on Keggie's behalf,' Joanna said, and Grace Mary seemed to accept my wife's summation of the defence I'd put together for my client. 'Angus MacDonald wasn't a housebreaker. He was a freelance wildlife photographer with no previous convictions, for Pete's sake.'

'Then why would Simon Keggie assault him?' I said. 'At midnight in his own house?'

Joanna had no answer to that. 'I'll tell you what else I don't know,' she said. 'I don't know why someone would want to murder him and throw his body in the Avon. And yet, both happened, Robbie. If we can find out the reason, the *real* reason, why Keggie attacked him, I think it might help us find the motive for the murder. Josh Wedderburn is a patsy, but we now know that Jessica Barrett put the fix in, so she clearly had an interest in whatever was going on.'

'That's if this Wedderburn person is to be believed,' Grace Mary said.

'Oh, he's to be believed,' I said. 'Trust me, I saw the look on his face when . . . when he . . . confided in Joanna. That's why it's so important we speak to Jessica Barrett.'

My secretary picked up her mug from the desk. 'I'll give Crown Office another try.'

'Do that,' I said, 'and while you're at it, any joy getting hold of Simon Keggie?'

Grace Mary shook her head. Keggie was another one trying to dodge me like I was a bullet. As my secretary was leaving, she almost bumped into my dad who was coming into the room, change bag over one arm, Jamie cradled in the other.

'I'm just dropping the wean off,' he said. 'I promised Tina I'd take her to Sandy's for something to eat.'

'No more ice cream lunches, Alex,' Joanna said.

'Of course not,' my dad lied. He handed our son over

to Joanna. 'So, tell me. What's the news from the post-mortem? That's where you were this morning, wasn't it?'

Joanna looked at me.

'Bashed head, blunt object, shot twice in the chest,' I said. 'It looks like they'll have to put the trial off.'

'At least that's something,' he said. 'Give the pair of you more time to build up a defence. Maybe you'll remember where you were the night it happened.' He gave me no more than the twitch of an eyelid, but Joanna spotted the wink.

'There'll be no made-up alibis,' she said. 'There's no point—'

'Me and Dad both going to jail?' I said.

'I was going to say, there's no point in leading an *I was with my dad watching the football* alibi. Who's going to believe that?'

'But there's Malky too. And Brendan from the Red Corner said he'd—'

'Alex, will you listen? I don't care if you rope in Her Majesty the Queen. An alibi isn't going to explain Robbie's DNA on a pickaxe handle with the blood of a dead man on it who's later found floating in the River Avon!'

My mind raced back again to that night in the outbuilding, and the way MacDonald had taken me out of the equation with one sweeping leg kick before skittling Stan Blandy's two henchmen.

'You saw MacDonald, Joanna. He was a big guy, and fit looking. What age was he?'

'Early forties.'

'How could he let himself be beaten up by a sixty-odd-year-old out-of-shape politician, and then again by someone else just a few weeks later? Don't they teach them hand-to-hand combat any more?'

213

'Don't who teach them?' Joanna asked.

'The Army.'

'I don't think MacDonald was ever in the Army,' Joanna said. 'According to his witness statement—'

'The one he wouldn't speak to in the witness box?' I said.

'Doesn't matter. He'd hardly have lied to the police about his work history. What would be the point of that? He lived and worked in the Highlands most of his life as a freelance photographer. He only moved down to the central belt a couple of years back when his wife died. He bought the place near Muiravonside as work in progress and has been employed part time in the country park. It might have been someone there who reported him missing the next day when he didn't turn up for work.'

By this time, I'd finished my tea. Joanna had scarcely touched hers. I could tell she was still doubtful about the MacDonald/Army connection.

'Trust me, Jo, he was ex-Army,' I said. 'He had an Army tattoo. You must have seen it at the post-mortem.'

Jamie was reaching out and tugging at Joanna's hair. Gently she shook her head free of his grasping little fingers. 'There was no tattoo, Robbie.'

'There must have been,' I said. 'A big one on his left forearm. An Argyll and Sutherland Highlanders motif.' I laughed. 'You're not telling me it dissolved in the water?' I glanced over at my dad who was listening intently. 'Sans Peur.' The only French words I knew growing up, though never quite sure why a Scottish regiment had a French motto. 'You remember Uncle Jim's tattoo, Dad. Well, this one was like that, only bigger and in colour.'

It was my dad's turn to laugh. 'I remember Jim's tattoo

all right, but I'm with Joanna on this one. You must have been seeing things.'

What was he talking about? Yes, I'd seen it. It was one of the last things I had seen before being dumped unceremoniously on my arse. I might have bumped my elbow, but not my head.

My dad put a hand on my shoulder. 'You've been through a lot, son. It's understandable if—'

I shrugged free and looked at each of them in turn. 'Stop it. I know what I saw. You weren't there. I was.'

'And you saw an Argylls tattoo on a MacDonald. Is that right? Robbie, the Argylls were a Campbell regiment. There's more chance of the Pope joining the Orange Lodge than a MacDonald getting his arm inked with an Argylls tattoo. I mean to say, there's still pubs near Glencoe where a Campbell can't buy a drink. Did they not teach you about The Massacre at school? There's even a song about it.'

Joanna looked at me. I looked at her. We knew the song well. In fact, we'd heard someone singing it last Friday night. My dad started in on the opening line. 'Oh, cruel is the snow . . .' when Grace Mary came through and mercifully saved us from any more.

'Jessica Barrett. I remember where I've seen that name before.' She handed me the indictment, flipped over the citation sheet and pointed to the foot of the page. 'She signed your indictment.'

35

I made the call and arranged to meet the cops from the SCD. I still didn't trust them, so I wanted somewhere there'd be plenty of witnesses. Around five o'clock that same Friday afternoon I arrived at the Falkirk Wheel, the world's biggest – the world's only – rotating boat lift. I parked in the high car park situated on a level with the Union Canal and waited by the maquette of the Kelpies. The hundred-foot equine sculptures of Baron and Duke were four miles further down the Forth and Clyde canal, though it was quicker to walk than navigate a barge through the many intervening locks. My phone buzzed. Private number. It was Stan Blandy calling exactly one week since he'd last been in touch, no doubt demanding Maggie Sinclair's phone. I bumped the call as soon as I heard his voice. Two could play at being uncontactable.

I'd been hanging about for about twenty minutes, watching the Wheel transport tourist-filled barges between the two canals, and trying not to get run over by students whizzing around on Segways, when the big black car drew up and parked alongside mine. DCI Sandeman alighted. She was more casually dressed than normal and minus her fat companion. She removed a packet of cigarettes from the handbag slung over her shoulder and shook one loose as she sauntered over to me. 'Thought they were a lot bigger than that,' she said, looking at the miniature Kelpies.

'They are. These are scale models,' I said.

'I'm joking. I passed the real ones on the motorway.' She lit her cigarette, took a leisurely draw and blew smoke out of the side of her mouth. 'Left it a bit late to get in touch, haven't you? I wasn't going to come. I'm off duty. Not sure there's all that much I can do to help at this stage. Not now that we've got the body.'

'But you don't have the weapon,' I said.

Sandeman disagreed. 'No, we have one of the weapons. The gun's probably at the bottom of the river.'

We walked down the path from the car park. 'I don't know where the real murder weapon is,' I said, when we'd reached the visitor centre. 'But I do know what you have is the wrong body.'

Sandeman snorted jets of smoke down her nostrils in amusement.

'It's true. The man they pulled out of the Avon – he's not MacDonald, or, if he is, he's not the MacDonald who was stalking my wife, and he's not the MacDonald who gave evidence at the trial of Simon Keggie.'

We walked on in silence, around the café to the esplanade by the basin where a few boats were moored and tourists queued for a spin on the wheel. There were some metal tables and a few chairs scattered around them. Sandeman pulled one out and sat down. I joined her.

'That's ridiculous,' she said at last. 'The DNA from the blood on the kitchen floor matched MacDonald's. There's also blood in the outbuilding and on the pickaxe handle.'

'But the blood in the outbuilding and on the pickaxe handle isn't MacDonald's,' I said.

I'd read over the forensic reports a hundred times. it

wasn't until I'd learned of the dead man's missing tattoo that I'd read them again, this time properly. Sandeman was right, the blood in the kitchen was indeed MacDonald's, but the report had gone on to say it was not possible to positively identify MacDonald's DNA from the few drops of blood on the filthy stone floor or from the streaks on the pickaxe handle. Naturally I'd assumed there'd been insufficient material for a clean sample. The outbuilding floor was filthy, and there were only traces of blood on the pickaxe handle. The samples would have dried out or might otherwise have been contaminated. The reasonable inference to be drawn was that, if there was blood in the kitchen and blood in the outbuilding, they both came from the same source. When I'd mentioned it to Joanna, she'd phoned the forensic lab and dragged the truth out of them. Not that Police forensic scientists were prone to untruths – they were just trained to be as unhelpful to the defence as possible, but in a truthful sort of a way. The truth was that DNA had been extracted from the blood swabs taken from the floor of the outbuilding and also the pickaxe handle. It was also true that it hadn't been possible to identify the DNA as MacDonald's – because it wasn't his. The report was perfectly true. Perfectly true and perfectly misleading.

The truth was that the blood belonged to someone, and that someone had a dirty great big Argylls tattoo on his forearm.

'Whose is it, then, the blood in the outbuilding?' Sandeman said, the cigarette between her lips waggling up and down as she spoke.

'I don't know his name. Maybe you could try and find a match on the DNA database.'

There was an ashtray on the table, but Sandeman didn't use it. She let her arm drop to her side, flicked ash off her cigarette and let the wind take it away. 'I could,' she said. 'If you'll tell me who else was there with you in that outbuilding.'

Had she been listening to me? 'I've just told you. The man in the outbuilding wasn't MacDonald. I've never met the real MacDonald. Not even when he was supposed to be giving evidence at Simon Keggie's trial. He was a plant, making sure Keggie wasn't convicted.'

The DCI shrugged. 'It's still your DNA on one end of the pickaxe handle and MacDonald's blood nearby. Maybe you killed him so that this other MacDonald could take his place at the trial. You were Keggie's lawyer after all. What better way to secure an acquittal? I'll bet those politicians pay well. Legal aid solicitor like yourself, wife and a couple of kids . . .'

This wasn't at all how I'd imagined things going. 'The person you should be looking for is the person who took MacDonald's place in court,' I said. 'A good place to start asking questions would be with Keggie. He must have known that wasn't MacDonald in the witness box.' I remembered our lunchtime consultation at Mr Singh's and how confident Keggie and his wife had been that I, the lawyer dropped in at the last minute on a recommendation from slip-and-trip Sammy Veitch, would secure an acquittal.

Sandeman shrugged noncommittally. 'Or I could start with the procurator fiscal depute who prosecuted the case and didn't recognise that the chief witness was the wrong person. Your wife, wasn't it?' She stubbed the cigarette out in the ashtray and wafted a hand at the spirals of smoke that rose from the dying butt. 'You know? The more I think about it, the more I think we should be bringing your old lady in for a spot of questioning.'

'That's not happening,' I said.

'Oh, it'll happen all right,' Sandeman said. 'I'm back on duty in forty-eight hours. If by then you don't have the names of whoever was with you in that outbuilding . . .' She planted the palms of her hands on the table and leaned across at me. 'Your missus is coming in for a chat.'

36

A husband shouldn't try to keep secrets from his wife, mainly because she'll find them out anyway; however, desperate times called for desperate measures and there was no way I was going to break the news to Joanna that she was a couple of days away from being handcuffed, marched into a police station and interviewed on suspicion of conspiracy to murder.

To quote Samuel Johnson, when a man knows he is to be hanged in a fortnight, it concentrates his mind wonderfully. I wasn't to be hanged, but the prospect of life imprisonment had me keenly focused on the issues at hand. I knew what I needed to do, and to do it I needed a van and two people crazy enough to help me.

'*What* kind of van?' Jake Turpie asked.

'One that's easy to throw someone into,' I said.

'I thought that's what you said.' Jake turned on a steel toecapped boot and set off down an alley of wrecked cars, stacked high either side. I followed in his wake, dodging the oil-skinned puddles that were a feature of Jake's scrapyard whatever the time of year or weather. This do you?' he asked, slapping the front panel of a Ford Transit that was a series of rust spots travelling in close formation.

'Nah, I'm looking for something with a side door,' I said. 'Something you could bundle someone into without too much hassle.'

Jake raked the sole of a boot along the shale path. After he'd finished shaking his head, he looked up at me. 'Bawheid, you couldnae bundle firewood. Are you sure you've thought this through?'

I had, and I hadn't intended being the one doing the bundling. 'What's Deek up to tomorrow?' I asked, strongly suspecting that Jake's colossal sidekick would be doing what he normally did: collecting money from late payers to Jake's informal payday loan scheme. Credit control was something Deek managed to do without threats of litigation. Just threats.

Jake sniffed. 'I could make him available I suppose.' He booted a front tyre. 'What are you going to do with it afterwards?'

'I don't know. Bring it back here, I suppose.'

Jake rubbed his jaw. 'Well now. If you're talking about me giving you a loan of Deek and this van and me having to start up the crusher . . . It's not going to be cheap. Then there's getting rid of the body, that'll cost you too. You're best with a Mini or one of they wee Fiats if we're going to sail it out into the Forth and dump it.'

It seemed we were talking at cross purposes.

'Jake, I just want to stuff someone in a van and have a word with them.'

'And after that . . .?'

'There's no after that. After that I let them go again.'

'What about the cops? What about Deek?'

'Deek can wear a mask. But it won't matter. After I've spoken to him, this person will be going nowhere near the cops, trust me.'

Fully concentrated as my mind was, I'd concluded that there were two people who definitely knew that the Angus MacDonald who'd given evidence at the councillor's trial wasn't the real Angus MacDonald. One of them was the imposter with the Argylls tattoo, the other was Simon Keggie, and while I had no idea how to track down the former, I knew exactly where to find the latter. There was a good reason Simon Keggie had seemed so confident during the pre-trial consultation at Mr Singh's. He knew he was taking a walk. Eddie 'The Fixer' Frew must have orchestrated the whole thing. Eddie got to Jessica Barrett QC, who in turn had pressurised Josh Wedderburn. The reason why Keggie hadn't been quite so cool at his actual trial was because the plan looked like it had failed. That suggested the decision to bring in the fake MacDonald had been done in an emergency. But by whom? Eddie was dead and buried by then. I needed to know everything Keggie knew, and since he was point-blank refusing to speak to me, I'd have to give him a little encouragement.

Jake booted a stone down the rutted avenue. 'You can have the van for five hundred. I'll leave it on the track with the keys in it. After that, you're on your own. And don't bring it back here. Dump it somewhere.'

'Come on, Jake. I can't do it myself. I just need a wee hand to chuck this guy into a van so I can drive him somewhere isolated, have a chat and then boot him out the door. I guarantee there'll be no comeback.'

Jake did some more jaw rubbing. 'A grand for the van and Deek. One hour. Understand?'

I understood all right. Everything apart from me paying £1,000 per hour for the services of a clapped-out van and a big eejit like Deek Pudney. 'I'll give you two hundred for Deek *and* the van.'

'Seven-fifty. Take it or leave it,' Jake said.

I wasn't for taking it, but neither was I leaving it. 'One hundred for the van, and I'll do the next court case for

223

Deek or one of your boys, whoever gets in bother first.'
Jake hesitated. 'You know it's just a matter of time,' I
said.

'Two-fifty *and* the next case for free,' Jake said.

I pulled out five folded twenties. 'I've only got a hundred.
Come on, Jake. If you don't help me out on this, you'll not
have a lawyer because I'll be in jail.'

Jake snatched the money from me with an oily hand.
'No one better end up dead. If they do, I'll be needing a
lot more than this,' he said, scrunching the money in my
face before stuffing it into the pocket of his boiler suit.

So far so good. I had the van, but only one person crazy
enough to help. I needed one more.

37

'It just does, that's all,' Malky said. 'End of. Full stop. Finito.'

On the way home, I called in at my dad's house to collect Tina. She'd gone there straight from school, and I found her in the kitchen deep in conversation with my brother on the subject of after-school snacks: the most important meal of the day.

'But, Uncle Malky, I like them cut into wee triangles, like Mum does.'

Discussions with persons more intelligent than yourself are never easy; still, my brother was doing his best. He'd had lots of practice.

Malky smiled patiently at his niece's naivety. 'Listen, princess. Who's the adult here?' I would have interrupted, but I wanted to know the answer. He stroked Tina under the chin. 'I don't make the rules, darling. It's just a fact. Accept it. A jam sandwich tastes better if you put it on a single slice of bread and fold it over – strictly no cutting. Don't ask me why. I'm not a scientist,' he said, lest there be any confusion on that score, then presented my daughter with the palm of his hand to indicate he was taking no further questions.

'It's only June, we're a bit early for the Royal Institution Christmas lecture,' I said, as Tina, noticing my arrival, came over and threw herself at me.

'Kids,' Malky said. 'What do they teach them at school these days?'

To the best of my knowledge they taught today's children the same sort of things they'd tried and largely failed to teach my brother thirty-odd years ago.

'We went to the Crying of the Marches today, Dad,' Tina said, swinging from my neck and kissing my cheek. 'The teacher took us down the street, and this fat man came out and he was all dressed up and was ringing a bell and shouting stuff.'

The Riding of the Marches is an annual event in Linlithgow that takes place on the first Tuesday after the second Thursday in June. The town crier makes an announcement the Friday before, telling the townsfolk, also known as Black Bitches, that they must attend in their best *carriage and equipage, apparel and array* or be fined one hundred pounds Scots. Nobody knows why the event is held at that time of the year, just as most don't know the purpose is to check the town boundaries, or march stones. Nowadays this is done by a procession of local dignitaries, townsfolk, bands and decorated floats that head west from the Cross Well to the River Avon at Linlithgow Bridge, then east to Blackness for lunch and 'Blackness Milk', a mixture of whisky and milk, before returning to circle the Cross Well three times. In days of yore it had been less of a celebration and more of a requirement to make sure nobody encroached on the Royal Burgh's land. The only leisure activity in those bygone days was the custom of thrashing any small boys the marchers found en route, just for sport. Nowadays the beatings had been replaced by two days' school holidays, which the children enjoyed almost as much as the adults liked the pubs opening at the crack of dawn – and dawn comes early to Scotland in June.

I put together a quick PB and J, sliced it the way Tina liked it and sent her to watch TV while I spoke with Malky.

'Where's Dad?' I said.

'He's gone up to the golf club to put his name down for Saturday's medal.'

'Good,' I said. 'I need to talk to you about something.'

'Something you don't want to talk about when Dad's here?'

'You know what next Tuesday is, don't you?' I said.

'The Marches.'

'That's right. What are your plans?'

'Same as usual, I suppose.'

'Go down the High Street to watch the parade at eleven o'clock, and then visit as many boozers as you can between then and the parade coming back from Blackness at five?'

Malky shrugged. 'Pretty much.'

'What are you doing at six o'clock?'

'Probably taking Tina to the shows and then coming back here to crash out.'

'I'm talking about six o'clock in the morning. I need your help with something.'

'The morning?' Malky looked at me as though I was asking him to step through a rip in the space/time continuum.

'You know I'm in big trouble, don't you Malky?'

'And some.'

'And that you're my brother.'

'So they keep telling me.'

'Well, I need you to do the brotherly thing, get out your scratcher for once before noon, and help me out.'

'And this helping involves me getting up at six in the morning?'

'No, Malky,' I said. 'It involves you getting up at five in the morning because we have a van to pick up at six.'

38

Marches Day is a long day. It starts at 5am when the town is wakened by fife and drums playing Linlithgow's very own anthem, 'The Roke and the Row'. An hour later the town piper reawakens all those who had the cheek to go back to sleep. An hour after that, the Linlithgow Reed Band, playing the 23rd Psalm, marches from the West Port in search of liquid refreshment, which they find at the home of the incumbent Provost of the Town Council of the Royal and Ancient Burgh of Linlithgow: an honorary title and not to be confused with Simon Keggie's official role as Provost of West Lothian Council.

Deek was waiting for us in an allegedly white Mercedes Sprinter that didn't so much need washing as ploughing. It came complete with sliding door and dodgy number plates, all as previously arranged. At half past six in the morning, dawn had broken over three hours ago. With me driving, and Malky and Deek squashed in the front passenger seats, we avoided the High Street, and headed up Manse Road. When we were about half a mile or so out of town and on a narrow country road, I pulled into the triangular turning point outside the Cauldhame Estate and parked the van at a forty-five-degree angle to the road.

Simon Keggie's home was situated a hundred yards further south, in a private complex of new-build bungalows on what had formerly been green belt. The fact that Keggie, chair of the Local Authority's planning sub-committee, had secured one of these sought-after plots, hadn't come as a huge surprise to anyone. Most Council planning committee members saw more brown envelopes than the Post Office.

'What are we supposed to be doing now?' Malky asked. He'd been moaning all morning, and I'd formed the distinct impression that his heart wasn't really in the whole abduction thing.

'Waiting,' I said. 'Keggie will be going into town for fraternisation at the Provost's house at seven and then onto the Burgh Halls for breakfast with the Deacons' Court. When we see him heading this way, I'll pull out in front of his car. He'll have to stop. We sit tight until he gets out of his car, and that's when you and Deek jump out and chuck him in the back. Deek will sit on him, I'll drive on and you'll follow in Keggie's car.'

'What!'

I might have omitted to mention the need to take Keggie's car without the owner's consent.

'It's only for a very short distance,' I said. 'About halfway between here and Dechmont there's a track on the right that goes into a forest. It's less than a mile away. We'll take Keggie there and I'll have a word with him about a few things.'

'What things?' Malky asked. I didn't think Malky needed to know that what I wanted from Keggie was the identity of the fake Angus MacDonald. If I could find the man who'd given evidence at Keggie's trial, I could prove it was his blood on the outbuilding floor as well as on the pickaxe handle and that he was very much alive. Murder cases didn't last long when the body was still breathing.

'Why can't you just phone Keggie or go and see him normally?' Malky asked.

'Because he won't take my calls, and I know that if I pitch up on his doorstep, he'll refuse to let me in or phone the cops or both.'

'Send him a letter, then. That's what real lawyers do.'

I'd thought about writing, but Keggie would get himself a lawyer, and I'd end up in a train of correspondence going nowhere. Time was of the essence and a more direct approach was required.

'Malky, let me do the thinking. Just put on your mask and stop asking daft questions. It won't be much longer.'

The fabric of Malky's ski mask stifled his mutters. After a few seconds he pulled the mask off again. 'What if his wife's driving him or if he's getting picked up or he's ordered a taxi? Let's face it. He's not going to the Provost's house at seven in the morning for boiled eggs and soldiers. There'll be trays of whisky and the Deacons' breakfast is the biggest piss-up this side of Hogmanay. Why would he be driving?'

The fact that my brother had been complaining all morning was bad enough, but that he was starting to make sense was worrying. I'd assumed Keggie would simply drive down Manse Road, over the canal, take a right and park somewhere at the Low Port where he could collect his car the next day.

'Or he could be walking, in which case he's probably left by now and we've missed him,' Malky said. He began to put his mask back on, then ripped it off. 'Ach, I can't breathe in this thing, and Deek squashing into me doesn't help. I'm going out for some fresh air. Let me know if anything happens. He stretched across Deek, opened the door and the two of them got out. Deek returned by

230

himself and closed the door. If Deek had any concerns about the plan, he hadn't voiced them. For him it was just another Tuesday.

Ten minutes later, eyes trained on the road ahead, I saw the nose of a car appear from between the sandstone pillars that guarded the entrance to Keggie's exclusive estate. Deek donned his ski mask with practised ease. I lowered the passenger side window and yelled to Malky to get ready. Turning the key in the ignition the engine caught first time. I released the handbrake. Foot poised over the accelerator like a guillotine over a French aristocrat's neck, I waited for the vehicle to emerge onto the road and come this way. It didn't. It turned the other way and headed off at speed. It wasn't Keggie's car. I knew that, partly because I knew Keggie's car was blue not white, partly because Keggie's car was a Jaguar XF not a Volvo C90, but mainly because Keggie's car didn't have yellow stripes on the side, nor flashing blue lights on the roof.

'Polis,' Deek said, tearing off his ski-mask and shoving it under his seat. The Volvo was followed by an ambulance, and then by another two marked police cars. A horn peeped loudly behind us and a car skidded to a halt on the gravel of the turning point. There were no rear windows, so I checked the side mirror just in time to see Joanna approaching on foot and at speed. She wrenched open the door and hauled me out. 'What do you think you're playing at?'

Malky appeared from around the back of the transit, looking sheepish.

'Did you call her?' I shouted at him over Joanna's head.

'Yes, he did,' Joanna said, 'and just as well.' With the assistance of my shirt collar she escorted me to her car.

Malky was already getting into the back beside Tina who was half asleep and wrapped in a blue fluffy dressing gown. Jamie was strapped into a child seat, and from the smell needed a nappy change. I had a feeling it would be my turn.

Deek lumbered over to us as Joanna got in and started the engine. 'What do I tell Jake?'

I climbed into the front passenger seat. Joanna revved the engine and the rear wheels spat gravel.

I dropped the window, stuck my head out and shouted. 'Tell him I want my hundred quid back!'

39

For obvious reasons, Joanna wasn't best pleased with me; nonetheless, she did agree we should get Marches Day out of the way before we talked things over. Just after ten o'clock, clan Munro gathered at my dad's house. My old man and Malky kitted out in suits, Joanna, a non-Black Bitch who couldn't see what all the fuss was about, in jeans and T-shirt, and Tina in her best summer frock and sandals. Jamie was asleep in a pushchair, the handles of which were festooned with small plastic saltires and lions rampant, courtesy of his granddad.

We were all set to start the long walk to find a good spot on the High Street to watch the procession at eleven, when my phone buzzed. It was DI Dicker.

'Time's up,' he said. 'Tell your wife we can come for her now or she can make her way voluntarily to—'

'My wife's going nowhere,' I said. 'I need more time.'

'There isn't any more time,' Dicker said. 'You either tell us who was with you when you abducted MacDonald or—'

'I've already told your boss. It wasn't MacDonald,' I said. The others had already started walking. Tina turned and shouted to me to hurry up, and I waved to indicate I'd be right there. 'Hello?' There was silence on the other end. 'Do you hear me?' I said. 'It wasn't MacDonald. It was somebody else. I need to speak to Simon Keggie.' More silence and then I heard another voice in the background. Dicker came back on. 'We'll be at your place in half an hour,' he said, and hung up.

I put my phone away, cupped my hands and yelled after my departing family to tell them that I had to go back to the house for something and would catch them up. Ignoring the protests, I jumped in my car and drove home. Right on time a dark BMW 7 series pulled up outside the house. The two SCD officers alighted and I went out to meet them.

DCI Sandeman gave Dicker a short sideways glance. The fat cop shoved me against the car and started to pat me down. Then he lifted the front of my shirt and shoved his hand under, groping the front of my chest.

I pushed him away. 'What is this?'

'He's clean,' Dicker said, taking a step back so that his boss could stand face to face with me.

'Okay,' she said, 'let me explain a few things to you. Simon Keggie is dead. He was murdered this morning at his home. I want to know more about this other man. The one you say gave evidence at Keggie's trial in place of MacDonald.'

'You believe me now?' I said, tucking my shirt back into my trousers.

'Just answer the question,' Sandeman said. 'This person you say you met in the outbuilding at MacDonald's place? Was he carrying something? A bag or a holdall?' She cast her colleague another sideways glance. 'Or a rucksack? Something like that?'

'What's that got to do with anything?' I said.

Sandeman squeezed her eyes closed and rubbed them with a thumb and forefinger. 'Mr Munro, you seem to think we're here to tell you things, when in fact it works the other way around. For the last time. And I do mean the last time—'

'Okay, he didn't have anything with him. Satisfied?'

'Good. Now we're getting somewhere,' Sandeman said. 'Maybe you can answer this too – who was it abducted him?'

'I've told you. I don't know.'

Dicker coughed a laugh. 'So, some people you don't know drew up in a car one evening and took you away from the bosom of your family to meet some other man you don't know, in an outbuilding full of horse shit and spiders. Is that it?'

All I had to do was give them the name of Stan Blandy and they'd get off my back. Why was I putting myself and my family through this for something I didn't do? I thought about it long and hard and came to the conclusion that, no matter what, I still couldn't give them Stan's name.

Sandeman exhaled loudly. 'Tell your wife we'll be in touch.'

She reached for the handle of the door. I bumped my hip against it and kept it there. 'My wife knows nothing, and she'll say nothing during any interview.'

'Looks fishy though, doesn't it?' Dicker butted in. 'The two of you working the same case, the main witness replaced by a fake and neither of you bats an eyelid.'

'We were both brought into the case at the last minute. Joanna had no say in it. She was only given the papers on the Friday afternoon before the trial was due to start on the Tuesday. Face it. The case against my wife is non-existent and what have you actually got against me? A pickaxe handle with my DNA on it and the blood of some person I'm not charged with murdering. There won't be a scrap of my DNA at the actual murder scene because I was never there.'

'We can make the blood on the pickaxe handle anybody's we like,' Dicker sneered. 'Our lab, our rules.'

The Scottish Crime and Drug Enforcement Agency had been notorious for fabricating evidence. Why should their successors be any different?

'Take me to see Keggie's wife and I'll see what I can find out,' I said.

Sandeman shook her head. 'Her husband was murdered a few hours ago. She'll be in no fit state to talk to anyone.'

Upon hearing voices, Bouncer hurdled the fence at the side of the house and came around the front in order to see what was going on. He jumped up at the two cops, tongue lolling, tail wagging, while they tried in vain to fend him off. I'd have brought him to heel, but nobody in my household paid much attention to what I had to say.

'I don't care what sort of state she's in, I want to speak to her,' I said. Keggie's wife knew something. I was certain of it. I thought back to the pre-trial consultation at Mr Singh's. Keggie's wife had been there. Why? For moral support? He didn't seem the type to need it. I remembered her squeezing my arm, telling me that, not asking me if, her husband would be acquitted. Keggie's defence had been a reasonably good one, but it hadn't been a guaranteed winner, not if the jury had been allowed to hear the real MacDonald's evidence as per his police statement. Why had Keggie assaulted MacDonald? The dead man wasn't a housebreaker. Just because I'd been going to lead that defence, didn't mean I believed it. No, MacDonald had gone to see Keggie for a particular reason and that reason eventually got him killed. For me, Mrs Keggie's foregone conclusion that her husband would be acquitted, meant she knew something, and if she was shocked, vulnerable and weak, as she must be with her husband on his way to the morgue, what better time to squeeze the truth from her?

'If you want any information from me, you're going to have to get me in to see Mrs Keggie,' I said.

Sandeman folded her arms. 'And if we don't?'

'Then by all means arrest my wife, and we'll not need to meet again, not until I cite you as defence witnesses at my trial and accuse you of taking me to the murder scene and trying to fit me up.'

'Yeah, you do that,' Dicker said. 'See how far it gets you.'

He climbed into the front seat. His senior officer stayed where she was, staring at me. After a moment or two, she shoved me aside and opened the back door of the big black Beamer. Leaving Bouncer in charge of things, I got inside.

40

The Keggies, or, to bring things right up to date, the remaining Keggie, had a lovely house – that is once you'd ignored the temporary inconvenience of all the police tape and the tent-like structure that had been erected across the front of the building. No one told me how Keggie had died, only that he'd been murdered, but from the comings and goings of the people in paper suits and breathing apparatus, I gathered it must have been right on his doorstep, and the presence of a couple of firearms officers snooping about suggested use of a gun.

As the SOCOs went backwards and forwards, I sat in the car with Dicker, watching the back of the fat cop's neck sweat in the rays of a midday sun that had turned the car into a greenhouse on wheels. Eventually, Sandeman returned with a young WPC who told me I could have ten minutes, no more, with Mrs Keggie.

The uniformed cop led me down the side of the house, through a door into a large kitchen, and from there via a dining room to a conservatory built onto the back of the house where the recently widowed Mrs K was sitting in a wicker armchair. Without a word, I sat down. There was a wooden coffee table between us, on it a glass of something dark and, next to that, a cardboard cube of tissues. Mrs Keggie didn't acknowledge my entry, just sat staring out though the conservatory door, over a south-facing expanse of lawn that was neatly bordered by a shrubbery in full bloom and a row of evergreens standing to attention in front of a high sandstone wall.

'Patricia doesn't want any medication,' the policewoman said, 'so we thought a little brandy might be just the thing.' Just the thing? Your husband has been murdered in cold blood on your doorstep, still, never mind, what's it to be, Rémy Martin or Hennessy? 'The doctor's been, and her sister is on her way down from Bridge of Earn to take her up there for a few days until … Well, I'll leave you to it,' she said, throwing Mrs Keggie a weak smile and sliding the glass door. It closed behind her with a click.

I didn't know where to start, but I'd have to, and quickly, because I'd only a few minutes. 'Mrs Keggie—'

'What do you want?'

'Mrs Keggie, I'm so sorry. I know this is the worst possible time, but—'

'Why are you here?' She lifted the glass of brandy and took a sip. 'Do you know who killed my husband?'

I looked at my shoes and shook my head. 'No, I don't. But I thought you might know something that would help me find them.'

'And why would you want to do that?'

'I was your husband's lawyer.'

She set down the glass. 'You were my husband's stand-in lawyer. I think I'd rather let the police handle things.'

'Your husband and Angus MacDonald were mixed up in something. MacDonald was murdered.'

'Well, if anyone, you should know that,' she said.

'Another thing I know is that Angus MacDonald wasn't a housebreaker,' I said. 'Your husband assaulted him for a reason. I'd like to know what that was.'

I thought she might answer, but instead she tugged a tissue from the box and dabbed at her eyes. I didn't notice any tears. 'I think you should go now,' she said.

'I'm sorry, I know how distressing this must be for you,' I said, 'and I don't want to drag this out any longer than I have to . . .' I could see her look over my right shoulder at the glass door I'd come through earlier, and assumed the WPC was hovering somewhere in the background, ready to come in at a pre-arranged signal. Perhaps it was the tissue being pulled from the box; whatever, I heard a click behind me and the glass door sliding along its runners.

'I believe if your husband hadn't assaulted Angus MacDonald the night he came to your house, he wouldn't be dead and neither would Angus MacDonald, and I wouldn't be in the frame for his murder.'

'I think that's enough, Mr Munro,' the policewoman said from behind me.

I didn't acknowledge her presence. 'Mrs Keggie, when we met at the restaurant, you seemed very certain your husband would be acquitted, and when his trial did eventually go ahead, he surely must have known that the man who gave evidence at his trial was an imposter. Did you?'

The widow stared into the depths of her brandy glass. A firm hand took a hold of my shoulder.

'Mrs Keggie, I can go, but the truth is going to come out sooner or later. There are fifteen jurors and a sheriff who will all swear that the man in court was not the man your husband was charged with assaulting and he wasn't the man I'm charged with murdering. Your husband knew that, and I think you did too. Your husband's dead, don't make things worse for yourself.'

'I said that's enough.' The cop's grip on my right

shoulder tightened, while her other hand took my left elbow and tried to prise me from my chair.

'Leave him,' Mrs Keggie said. 'No. Really. I'm fine.'

The cop had to be persuaded some more before she left, muttering that she'd be back in five minutes, making it clear I would be leaving then no matter what.

The glass door clicked shut again, but I could see through the smoked glass the outline of the policewoman standing inside the next room watching us.

When I turned to Mrs Keggie, the eyes beneath the fringe of dark hair were like rivets in plate steel. 'If I speak to you, you'll find out who did this to Simon? Promise me.'

'I'll do my very best,' I assured her.

She turned to stare out at the garden again. 'I knew Simon had put things in place so he wouldn't be convicted. I didn't know what exactly. I was in the witness room most of the day, and he told me what had happened later. Of course, I was surprised, but that's why you lawyers get paid so much, isn't it? Are you trying to tell me you weren't in on it? That's not the impression Eddie Frew's partner gave us.'

I let that slide. 'Why did Angus MacDonald come to your house that night?'

'He had photographs for sale.'

'What kind of photographs?'

'Not really photographs. It was a video. Of Harvey Rudd.'

'*The* Harvey Rudd?' With a name like that there couldn't have been that many others. The Harvey Rudd I knew was Cabinet Secretary for Justice, though what he knew about the justice system other than from watching TV crime dramas, I had no idea. Rudd was mid-thirties and a career politician. From private school, he'd gone to St Andrews University to study the history of chocolate biscuits or something, then a job as a parliamentary assistant before being awarded a safe seat.

Mrs Keggie took another sip of brandy before continuing. 'MacDonald told Simon that if the video was revealed, the public wouldn't just not vote for Rudd, they'd want him strung up.' She lifted the brandy glass and wet her lips. 'Simon wasn't that far behind in the polls. MacDonald wanted twenty thousand for the video. The night he came to the house we had the money ready, but he said he'd changed his mind and wanted more. A lot more.' Mrs Keggie looked about her. 'We'd just bought this place. We didn't have that kind of money on tap. The election was the following week. There was an argument. I heard it all from my bedroom. I went into the hallway. When MacDonald made to leave ….. There was a walking stick by the door … His back was turned … Simon tried to stop me.' She took a moment to gather herself. 'When the police came, Simon told me to say I'd been asleep and never heard a thing. They took him to the police station. He asked for Eddie Frew; they'd known each other for years. He said Eddie could fix anything. When he came back from his appointment, he said Eddie was going to sort it and the case wouldn't even go to trial. We gave him the twenty thousand. When Eddie died, we went to see his business partner who said not to worry, that he'd find Simon a new lawyer. You know the rest.'

But, I didn't. I knew some of the rest. What I didn't know was who had replaced MacDonald in the witness box or who had arranged it. Had it been Eddie 'The Fixer' Frew's Plan B, should the time-bar scheme collapse – just like he had in the bar at Queensbury House? If Sammy's former business partner really had put a contingency plan in place, all I could say was that the man was worth every penny of the exorbitant fees he charged.

Mrs Keggie pulled another tissue from the box. Immediately, the glass door behind me clicked.

'Mrs Keggie, where is the video?'

She delicately prodded the corner of each eye. 'I don't know. We wondered if MacDonald had been trying to scam us all along, but the election was past, Harvey Rudd had won, and we'd given all our money to Eddie Frew to get Simon off the assault charge.'

She put her nose in the tissue. The door to the conservatory slid open and the policewoman stepped into the room. This time I needed no encouragement to leave. I stood up, thanked Mrs Keggie once more, and before I could be led back the way I'd originally come, I said, 'Would you mind if I used this other door?'

41

I scraped my knee climbing the sandstone wall but was over it and onto the grass verge of Manse Road before Mrs Keggie's uniformed minder knew what was happening. I'd have to cover a straight kilometre of tarmac before I'd hit the outskirts of town, and the Specialist Crime Division officers would have no problem catching up with me before I'd gone any distance at all. So, instead, I headed off in the other direction, and, after fifty metres or so, jumped a hedge into a field where I lay low beneath a galvanised feeding trough.

'What do you want?' Jake growled when I called him. 'If you think you're getting your money back—'

'I don't want it back,' I said, 'but I've not had my money's worth yet, so I need you to send Deek for me.'

'Deek's busy. Call a taxi.'

'Come on, Jake, this is urgent.'

'Where are you?'

'In a field up by—'

'A field?'

'Just tell Deek it's a bit further on from where he was this morning. Tell him to drive slowly, and I'll see him coming.'

'I'll call you back,' he said.

My phone buzzed immediately after he'd hung up. It was Stan Blandy. 'Have you found that phone yet?'

'Stan, this is really not a good time,' I said.

'Where are you?'

'Right now, Stan, I'm lying in a pile of crap in a field, hiding from the cops.'

I thought that answer might have piqued his interest. It didn't. 'I'll phone tonight and that better be a good time,' he said, and the phone went dead.

Jake called back five minutes later, having located Deek. It was going to cost me another hundred and I was in no position to haggle. I waited, watching through the gaps in the hedge. When I saw the filthy Merc Sprinter coming along the road at about ten miles an hour, I jumped out, waving my arms. Once in, we took the long road back to Linlithgow. The High Street was closed to traffic, so Deek dropped me off on Royal Terrace and from there I crossed the railway bridge and jogged down Lion Well Wynd.

I doubted if the death of Simon Keggie would have been formally announced yet, although I was sure rumours would be spreading. Even then, Marches Day would continue as normal. It would take more than the assassination of the Provost to stop a tradition that previously only The Great War had managed to postpone.

I arrived on the High Street shortly before one. The procession had long since passed by and would be taking refreshments at Linlithgow Bridge before retracing its steps, then heading east to Blackness for even more refreshments. For the people of Linlithgow, the first Tuesday after the second Thursday in June was always a highly refreshing day. Indeed, so refreshed did some townsfolk become that they had to be carried home at the end of it.

I joined the street crowds that were now drifting in all directions. Those with kids were going home or to the fairground or just hanging around chatting to pass the time until the procession returned on its way east. Those without kids were making a beeline for the nearest pub, and on Linlithgow High Street one is never far away.

The nearest boozer to me was the Red Corner Bar, which was handy because that was my intended destination. It was heaving with customers. Marches Day for publicans was like the New Year sales: a huge volume of customers all wanting to spend their money. The difference being that on Marches Day the prices went up instead of down. I pushed my way to the bar, lifted the flap in the counter and walked behind it to where Brendan and a flustered looking Mickey the barman were pouring pints like the rain pours in Paisley.

'Where do you think you're going?' Brendan shouted at me over the racket.

'Your office,' I said, pushing open the door at the back of the bar and entering a small room, three walls of which were haphazardly stacked with crates of beer bottles, aluminium kegs and boxes of crisps. In one corner a group of mops, brushes and pails had congregated, in another the mortal remains of an industrial-size deep-fat fryer gently corroded. Brendan came in after me, wiping his hands on a grimy tea towel. 'Make it quick, whatever it is,' he said. He closed the door, went over to a small roll-top desk overflowing with paperwork, tipped a grey cat from the only chair in the room and sat down.

I leaned my back against a filing cabinet, on top of which a pile of boxing magazines supported a precariously balanced portable TV with a coat-hanger aerial. 'Have you seen Sammy Veitch?' I said.

'Sammy? No. Why? Look at the state of you. Where have you been?'

I wiped a hand across the mud-caked knees of my

246

jeans, dislodging a few lumps on to the threadbare rug that covered some of the bare floorboards.

'Whoa! Stop that. I've just tidied this place,' Brendan said. 'What's going on?'

'It's complicated,' I said. 'The cops are looking for me. I need to find Sammy and I can't go looking for him in case I'm spotted.' Brendan's blank look suggested none of that explained the necessity of me depositing mud on his office floor. 'I need you to find him and bring him here.'

'Robbie, do I need to remind you it's my busiest day of the year?'

'No, Brendan, you don't,' I said. 'Do I need to remind *you* that without me you'd be standing outside at a lemonade stall because you wouldn't have a licence?'

'Come on, Robbie. The place has been going like a lavvy door when the plague's in town, ever since six o'clock this morning. Hide out here as long as you like, but I've no time to start hunting every pub in Lithgae for a wee teuchtar in a kilt. It's The Marches. The town's full of them.'

From under a pile of invoices on the desk, I retrieved a phone and handed it to Brendan. 'Call around a few of Sammy's locals. Tell them it's urgent, just don't mention my name.'

'What am I going to say is so urgent?'

'I don't know. Use your imagination. Just get him here.'

And get him here he did, though it was nearly an hour later that, with the help of Brendan's hand in his back, Sammy staggered into the room under the weight of many whiskies.

'Robbie!' he beamed; arms outstretched. He came over and gave me a hug. 'Happy Marches Day!' He turned to stare at the door that had closed behind him. 'Where did

Brendan go? He said he had a bottle of whisky for me.'

I took hold of Sammy by the shoulders, steered him towards the chair and pressed him down into it, almost squashing the cat.

'Simon Keggie is dead,' I said. 'Somebody shot him at his home this morning. Any ideas who might have done it?'

'What? No. Of course not. That's terrible, Robbie.' Sammy looked around, caught sight of the crates of beer and raised himself from the seat. 'Do you think Brendan would mind awful much if I cracked open one of—'

I tried to shove him back into his seat, but missed and he stumbled, knocking the chair over. It clattered onto the floor. Sammy stepped backwards, tripped over an upturned chair leg, stepped in a plastic bucket, and careered off into the corner. Eventually a combination of drink and gravity brought him to rest amidst a nest of brushes and mops. I took a grip on the front of his tweed jacket, lifted him to his feet and pulled his face towards mine. 'Listen, I'm in trouble and you put me there. I don't care if it's Marches Day or Christmas Day and I don't care how much you've had to drink. You'd better sober up and start talking or else—'

'Or else what?' Brendan said. Having flung the door open he marched into the room. 'What're you doing, Robbie? Leave the man alone.' He tried to loosen my hold on the lapels of the tweed jacket, but I wasn't going to leave the man alone. Not until he'd told me what I wanted to know. I gave Sammy a shake. This time Brendan caught hold of my wrists and was successful in separating me from the man in the kilt.

'What is all this?' he said to Sammy.

'I don't know, Brendan,' Sammy whined. 'I just came in and Robbie started going mental.'

'You want to know what's happening?' I said, reaching over Brendan's shoulder and poking a finger into Sammy's face. 'This lowlife helped fit me up on a murder charge.'

Brendan recoiled at the very idea.

'It's true,' I said. 'Ask him.'

The door opened and my dad came in, holding a half-eaten scotch pie in a greasy, white paper bag. 'Ah, Sammy. I heard you were here,' he said, taking a bite. 'What you doing? You and Robbie trying to keep that bottle of whisky you won in the raffle all to yourself?' The bottle of whisky he was referring to being the figment of Brendan's fertile imagination that had lured Sammy to the Red Corner Bar. Sammy must have been pretty drunk to believe he'd won a raffle he'd never entered. My dad looked around, his initially cheery expression making a slow retreat. 'Is something the matter?'

'It's okay, Dad. I'm just talking to Sammy about my case. There's nothing wrong. You head off and we'll catch up later.'

But my old man wasn't for leaving. He looked from me, to Brendan, to Sammy and back to me again. I could sense the years of police training kicking in. I half expected him to whip out a notebook and start jotting down our particulars. 'If there's nothing wrong,' he said, 'how come Sammy's got a face that could haunt a house . . .' He came closer and sniffed the air around me a few times. 'And you're smelling like a cow's arse?'

Brendan, no doubt acutely aware of the throngs of drouthy customers on the other side of the door, anxious to be parted from their cash, piped up. 'Robbie thinks Sammy fitted him up for that charge he's on. You know. The murder one,' he added for the sake of clarification.

My dad absorbed the information for a moment or

two, then picked up the fallen chair, righted it and pressed Sammy down onto the seat. Something that passed for a smile broke beneath his moustache. It was a smile I felt sure many suspects in years gone by had witnessed shortly before being bounced off the walls of a police cell.

'That's not right is it, Sammy?' he said softly, his bulk casting a sobering shadow over the man in the chair. 'You'd never do a thing like that. Would you?'

Sammy had the look of someone whose post-Marches Day hangover had come early. 'It's . . . It's . . . Listen, Alex, I can explain . . .'

My dad handed me the half-eaten pie and began to roll up the sleeves of his shirt. 'Good,' he said. 'I'm all ears.'

42

Even the strongest men break under many hours of intense interrogation. Sammy Veitch cracked faster than a Humpty Dumpty suicide bid; holding out barely long enough for Brendan to return to the bar, or for me to eat the rest of my dad's scotch pie.

Back home, Joanna was waiting for me in the living room, like death awaits us all. Jamie was down for his afternoon nap, and Tina and her Uncle Malky had gone off to the fair.

'Did you know about this, Alex?' Joanna asked my dad accusingly. 'Did you know your youngest son was hatching a plan to kidnap a politician this morning?'

'It wasn't a kidnapping,' I said, forcing a light little laugh into the proceedings. 'I wasn't asking for a ransom or anything.'

'Just an abduction, then?' Joanna said. 'Oh, well, that's fine. You're out on bail for murder and if breaking into houses isn't bad enough—'

'Keggie's dead,' I said. 'He was murdered this morning before I got there. I don't know the details, but I've spoken to his wife.'

Joanna took time to take in this information, process the data and formulate her next question. 'Eh?'

'Keggie's dead. It looks as though somebody shot him

on his doorstep. With the help of the police, I managed to speak to his wife.'

'The police are helping *you*?' my dad said. 'Why?'

'It's a long story. I've got two cops from the SCD—'

'The what?'

'The Specialist Crime Division.' My dad's face still drew a blank. 'They're like the old Scottish Crime and Drug Enforcement Agency,' I said, 'but, hopefully, not quite so bent. They're helping me . . . sort of. Well, we're supposed to be helping each other.'

'And what have you done so far to help them?' Joanna said.

Nothing was the answer to that. Not yet. I sat my wife down and told her and my dad about my discussion with the recently widowed Patricia Keggie. When I'd finished, my dad began to fill Joanna in on Sammy's confession, something he thought better done with a glass of whisky in his hand. By the time I'd retrieved the bottle of Springbank 21 that Brendan had given me, and brought it through with a couple of glasses, he'd already summed up the gist of things for my wife.

'Just to recap, Robbie,' she said. 'This morning, after a failed abduction attempt, you gatecrashed a murder scene to speak to the victim's widow, then interrogated a fellow solicitor in the back room of a pub?'

'Well, yes, it sounds bad if you put it like that . . .' I said.

Once again, my wife insisted on countering my protests using accuracy and logic. 'What other way is there to put it?'

'Not like you're the prosecutor and I'm the accused in the witness box who you're trying to tear a strip off,' I said. 'Try and see things from my point of view.'

252

She laughed, if you could call it a laugh. 'Robbie, sometimes I think you live in a cartoon world. I love you for it, but, if not me, who else is going to give you the version of life without the unicorns and pot of gold at the end of the rainbow? I'm trying to help build you a defence, meantime you're charging around like a loose cannon!'

'I don't think loose cannons charge around,' my dad said. 'I think that's more to do with . . . You know . . . bulls and . . . maybe china shops . . .'

Springbank 21 is bottled at 46 per cent alcohol by volume. On receipt of a look from Joanna, the old man thought his drink might be helped by a drop of water and made a tactical retreat to the kitchen.

I continued in his absence. 'Jo, you've got to see there are certain inquiries that can't be made through the proper channels. I can't write polite letters to people asking them to speak to me when I know there's no chance of them replying. You know how hard I tried to speak to Simon Keggie, and where did it get me – or him? And don't you think it's a bit rich you blaming me for going off like a loose cannon, when you were the one forcing Josh Wedderburn to cough up his guts on pain of either having his face pounded by a bouncer or facing a trumped-up sexual assault charge, or both?'

'That was different,' Joanna said. 'If Josh had called my bluff, I wouldn't have done anything. There's a difference between saying something and actually doing it.'

'And there's a difference between being a lawyer and being the person who's actually facing prison.' I manoeuvred myself over to the couch and sat down facing my wife. 'I need you to take the pieces I'm giving you and build me a defence. A proper one. Starting with the fact that we now know Simon Keggie tried to buy an incriminatory video of Harvey Rudd from the *real* MacDonald in order to win the election. When he asked for more money, Mrs Keggie whacked him over the back of the head with the blackthorn walking stick.'

'I can't believe she'd do that,' Joanna said.

'You know what they say, Jo. Behind every good man—'

'There's a woman with a bloody big lump of wood ready to bring it down on someone else's head?' She reached for my glass, had a sip, grimaced and handed it back to me.

'I'm only telling you what she told me,' I said. 'And she's got no reason to lie. MacDonald's dead, and so is her husband. She hit MacDonald, Keggie told her to tell the police she'd been in bed at the time, then he went to see Eddie Frew, who promised to sort things out.'

Joanna was still somewhat dubious. 'Okay. Let's assume Mrs Keggie is telling the truth and that there was a salacious video of Harvey Rudd. Did she say what it showed?' She hadn't, but as Joanna observed, it would have to have been somewhat sensational to threaten the career of a politician. Long gone were the days when adultery, a visit to a prostitute, drug-taking or even dodgy expenses claims were seen as resignation matters. 'And where does Sammy Veitch come into it all?'

According to Sammy, he hadn't come into it very much at all. He knew about the plan to time-bar the case, but only because Eddie had told him he had someone at Crown Office in his pocket. 'I was sent in blind, Jo. I was just there to make up the numbers, and because Sammy knew that if there was an attempt to extend the time-limit, I'd oppose it because—'

'Because you object to everything in court?' Joanna sniffed. 'Time-bar. I suppose it was quite a good idea really. I mean if you're going to chuck a prosecution and don't want to take too much flak. Especially with a case like Keggie's.'

I agreed. It might look slightly fishy – a technicality leading to the acquittal of a local politician – but it wouldn't be the first time the prosecution had run out of time and a case had to be deserted. It could easily be shrugged off. There were more cockups than conspiracies in the Scottish justice system. The Crown wouldn't even have had to admit to a blunder, just blame the underfunding and pressure of court business. These things happened. The law fixed the time limits and the prosecution had to prioritise their caseload. And anyway, who was going to complain about a burglar-basher not being prosecuted?

'It all comes back to Jessica Barrett,' Joanna said. 'She's the one who told Josh Wedderburn to drag the case out. She's also the Crown counsel who marked your indictment in record time.' She thought for a moment. 'What else did Sammy know?'

'Not much. He didn't know the plan had failed until I met him in the pub that Friday night. After that he called Keggie who was spitting nails. He'd paid Eddie a lot of money. Money Sammy now sees as part of his retirement plan—'

'Do you think it was Sammy who arranged for the fake MacDonald to threaten me?' Joanna said, jumping to the same conclusion I had.

My dad returned from the kitchen with a glass of water and a teaspoon. 'Trust me, pet. It wasn't Sammy,' he said.

Sammy had been quite adamant about that, even under duress from my dad. According to him, he'd simply reassured Keggie, told him there was nothing to worry about, that I was a miracle-worker and that everything would be fine. His faith in me was quite touching, really.

'Then who?' Joanna asked. 'Josh Wedderburn? He knew his plan had failed and that Hugh Ogilvie had passed the case to me.'

'But after all that, substituting the fake MacDonald for the real one? That's way too risky if you ask me. Someone would notice.'

I didn't agree. Not in this case. MacDonald was a nobody – the alleged victim of an assault a year before and a man who lived in a village ten miles from the court and had only recently moved down from the Highlands. There had been a day when prosecutors met with complainers to take precognitions, usually to ensure that they'd be sticking to the script, but financial cutbacks, or maybe it was just laziness, had put an end to that practice except in the most serious of cases. The photos of MacDonald showed the image of a man with a bushy beard. The rest were of the back of his head and torso. As for the cop who'd taken the real MacDonald's statement, after a year he might possibly have recognised him again, but the cops had their own separate witness room at court and quite often they remained at the police station until they were called in. The police photographer had testified and left before the fake MacDonald had been called to the stand, and no witnesses yet to give evidence would be allowed into court during the imposter's testimony. Who would be in the actual courtroom to notice it was the wrong person? I'd no idea what he looked like, neither did Joanna or any of the other court officials. Furthermore, witnesses were never asked to produce ID before they gave evidence; neither were accused persons for that matter. It was just assumed that unless compelled to do so, nobody would come to court voluntarily to appear in the dock or the witness box.

'We still don't know why someone would want to replace MacDonald,' I said.

My dad knocked back his drink and held the empty glass out to me for a refill. 'Because the real MacDonald was dead?'

'That has to be it,' I said. 'With MacDonald dead, the Crown would have used his witness statement against Keggie, with a much higher chance of a conviction.'

Joanna shook her head. 'I know Josh Wedderburn's an idiot, but I can't see him getting himself involved in something as serious as that. Allowing an awkward case to time-bar as a favour to Crown counsel? Sure. But not attempting to defeat the ends of justice or conspiring to commit murder.'

She was right. Wedderburn was only following orders. The first person he'd have told about the problems with the time-bar plan would have been the person who'd asked him to arrange it in the first place.

'Robbie,' Joanna said. Eyes wide, face flushed, she shifted to the edge of the couch. 'Think about it.'

To be fair, I had been. So much so that my brain was starting to hurt. Fortunately, I had the perfect solution, and at the moment the perfect solution was forty-six per cent alcohol. Following my dad's example, I carefully added no more than half a teaspoonful to the Campbeltown whisky. You can add water to a dram, but if you ruin it you can't take it out again.

Joanna continued. 'Jessica Barrett is engaged to Harvey Rudd, the person whose video the real MacDonald tried to sell to Keggie.' She looked like she might try another sip of my whisky, then thought better of it. 'Okay, here's how I see it having happened. Imagine if you were Angus MacDonald and had a blackmail video of Rudd. You'd need to be Billy Big Bollocks to blackmail Scotland's Justice Secretary. So, what do you do? You go to his rival and offer him the golden ticket: Local Councillor to Member of the Scottish Parliament in one swift *Sun* newspaper headline. I'll bet Mrs K would have loved that. A wee flat down Holyrood, courtesy of the taxpayer, accompanying her husband on all sorts of foreign junkets. No wonder when she saw the dream walking out of the door, she went berserk with the walking stick.'

It seemed plausible enough. Because of Mrs K's fit of temper, MacDonald was hospitalised, her husband was charged, the video never saw the light of day and Harvey Rudd won the election.

'You've totally lost me,' my dad said. 'Rewind a bit. Who's Jessica Barrett?'

I poured my dad another dram. 'I'll fill you in later. Just sit back for now and watch a great mind at work.' I looked to my wife. She was thinking again. It was what she was good at. She took some time. I could almost hear the pieces clicking together.

'After MacDonald was assaulted, someone got word to the Justice Secretary about the video. Only four people knew about it.'

'MacDonald, Keggie and his wife. Who's the fourth?' I said.

Joanna smiled. 'Eddie Frew, of course.'

Yes. That was it. I could see it now. That was why Eddie had been at Parliament House a couple of weeks before his death. For a little chat with the Justice Secretary. I could imagine the discussion between them. Eddie would never have tried blackmail. He was too smart for that. But he'd have told Rudd that the topic of the video was likely to come up during Keggie's trial. MacDonald wasn't a housebreaker. He was at Keggie's house for a reason, and that reason was to sell him the evidence of some misdemeanour by Rudd. If Keggie's trial had gone ahead and MacDonald testified, not only could Keggie have been convicted, but the real reason for MacDonald's late-night visit would have been revealed. Worst case scenario, it would have meant prison for Keggie and disgrace and loss of office for Rudd. Eddie was in the perfect position to solve the problem for both men. And at a hefty price from each, no doubt. He'd already taken twenty grand off Simon Keggie. All it needed was for Rudd to have someone high up in Crown Office put pressure on a lowly PF depute like Josh Wedderburn. No trial, no conviction for Keggie and no mention of Harvey Rudd's embarrassing video. And who better to provide that pressure than your own fiancée?

'It was a nice plan,' Joanna said, 'but it fell apart when I took over the case. If the trial was to proceed, there needed to be some fast thinking about what to do with MacDonald.'

My dad's hand reached for the whisky bottle again. 'Wait a minute. Are you two suggesting that Scotland's Justice Secretary is a murderer?'

'He has to be behind it,' I said. 'MacDonald was killed before he could give evidence and mention the video in court.'

'But Keggie must have known that the MacDonald in the witness box wasn't the man his wife battered,' my dad said.

Undoubtedly, but Keggie wouldn't have alerted anyone to the fact. He'd have assumed it had all been fixed to secure his acquittal. That's why you paid Eddie Frew the big bucks. It was perfect.

'What's even more perfect, Robbie,' Joanna said, 'is that when your mysterious client thought he was abducting the person who was stalking me, he was right enough, but we all believed that person to be Angus MacDonald, who by that time might already have been dead. When the fake MacDonald was abducted and escaped, you'd unwittingly fitted yourself up for the murder that he committed.'

'Then I'm in the clear,' I said.

Joanna shook her head. The colour had gone out of her face. 'No, Robbie. You're not. No video, no proof, and we're pretty much back where we started, with only a wild conspiracy theory involving a senior politician.'

There were three loud raps at the front door.

My heart sank. 'I think that could be the cops, Jo. Quick. I'll go see them and tell them you're not in. You hide upstairs.'

'What are you talking about, Robbie? Hide? Why?'

'Because,' I said, climbing to my feet. 'If it's the cops, they're not here for me. They're here for you.'

43

Joanna refused to hide. We argued about if for a while until the knocking on the front door stopped and there was louder knocking at the back. When eventually I opened it, I fully expected to be greeted by the fat florid face of his royal smugness, DI Dicker. Instead it was the angry wee face of her royal bamishness, Stephanie 'Meeko' Meek, in T-shirt and jeans and in an abnormal state of near sobriety for Marches Day, or for any day with a 'Y' in it. She wasn't for opening pleasantries. 'Did you break into my house?'

I glanced back at the clock on the cooker. It was only just after three. It's a long day when you get up at five in the morning to do a spot of abducting, especially if you haven't managed a wink of sleep the night before. I stepped outside. For a change it hadn't rained on Marches Day. The sun was still shining defiantly down on the Royal Burgh, and the golden crown atop St Michael's Church glinted in the hazy distance. I invited Meeko over the doorstep, but she refused, staying fixed where she was, hands on hips.

'Someone broke in and trashed my flat,' she said.

The state of the place, how could she possibly have noticed?

'Okay, listen, Stephanie,' I said. 'I may have been in

your flat a week or so ago, looking for something. I'm sorry about the damage to your door, but—'

'I'm not talking about that time you and that wee shite Bop broke my windae. I'm talking about last night. Someone smashed the door in. Came breenging in late on. I thought it was the polis and climbed out the bog windae. Hurt my ankle when I landed.'

There was no reason for anyone to break in to Meeko's house. Well, obviously, *I'd* had a reason, but ...

'Stephanie, do you remember a Friday night a few weeks back, outside the Red Corner Bar? You stole a mobile off a wee guy. Brendan from the Red Corner was there. You had an orange hoodie on. You fell in the street.'

My recounting of events didn't seem to be ringing any bells. 'I want compensation or I'm going to the cops,' she said.

'Do that,' I said, 'but all you'll get is another visit followed by a hurl in an ambulance, and a few broken bones to go with your sore ankle.'

She took a step back, fists clenched by her sides at the ready. 'That right?'

'Cool your jets, Stephanie. I had nothing to do with what happened last night, but I think I know who did it. That boy you stole the phone from is connected to some serious people. The folk who trashed your house will be back. Have you still got the phone you took?'

Meeko sniffed and shrugged. After some gentle persuasion she grudgingly dug into the pocket of her jeans and brought out a mobile phone. 'This isn't mine,' she said. I can't get into it. And mine has got my initials scratched on the back.'

'Did yours have a sparkly pink cover?' I asked.

Apparently it had, but only after she'd taken the cover

off the phone she'd stolen from Maggie's stepson. I thought back to the break-in. I'd been in such a rush and so pleased to find a phone in my client's orange hoodie, that I'd never checked to see if there was one in the other pocket.

'Give me that phone, and I'll get yours back,' I said.

'Then I'll not have a phone,' she pointed out.

'If you can't get into this one, you've not got a phone now.' Meeko couldn't argue with my infallible logic. 'And that other phone wasn't yours anyway. You stole it from some girl on a pub crawl.'

She put out a hand. 'Thirty quid.'

To buy the phone she stole so I could give it back to its owner? I didn't think so. And yet, I did need that mobile. I put my hand in my pocket and held out a ten-pound note.

'Fifty and you can keep them both,' Meeko said.

'Ten,' I said, slapping the money in her hand while relieving her of the phone. 'And I'll tell the person whose phone this is not to go near you again.'

Grudgingly, she stuffed the tenner in her pocket and began to walk away.

'It might be best if you stayed away from your place for a wee while,' I called after her. 'Just until I return this phone.'

She turned, looked at the ground for a moment and then up at me, a slight grin on her face. 'Did you really kill that guy?'

'What do you think?'

She stared hard at me for a moment. 'Probably. Maybe. Dunno ...'

'That's what I'm hoping the jury's going to say,' I said, and closed the door.

44

The newly charged mobile phone was in the centre of the kitchen table, my dad, Malky, Joanna and me surrounding it. The contents of the phone were absolutely none of our business, which was why we were so keen to delve into them. Malky picked it up with an air of confidence. 'When's her birthday?'

I recalled it from my time at Caldwell & Craig. I was sure Maggie expected that one day it would be declared a national holiday, and she insisted no one forget the date or remember her age.

'What about her son,' Joanna said. 'She might use his date of birth. What age is he?'

'She's got a stepson,' I said. 'Don't know what age he is. Maybe thirteen or fourteen? Something like that.'

Malky tossed the phone back into the middle again and got to his feet. 'Give me a shout when you're finished.'

'Why do you need to open it, anyway?' my dad said. 'Just give her the thing back.'

Part of me was just sheer nosy. The other part of me, the part that disliked extreme physical violence, especially towards myself, wanted to make absolutely sure it was the right phone before Stan next called. I couldn't see him taking kindly to me giving him the good news only to discover that what I had was yet another entry in Meeko's stolen mobile phone catalogue. I needed that phone as a lever to speak to Stan again about the night the fake MacDonald was abducted. The SCD had asked if he had been carrying anything at the time. Why that mattered I didn't know, but it was obviously important. I hadn't seen him with anything. Stan's men would know for certain. If I could find out from them, there'd be no need for me to mention Stan's name, and if I could give the SCD the information they wanted and help them, maybe they'd help me. The problem I foresaw was having Stan agree to another meeting. The last one had been arranged on the pretext of me returning Maggie's phone to her. By Stan's way of thinking, that first meeting had been on a false pretext. If I handed the correct phone over now, I would simply be settling my debt. What I was relying on was Stan's obvious keenness to have the phone returned. Why all the fuss? Maggie had a new one. She could collate her contacts again using the firm's IT system. What was so important about this phone?

It was Joanna's turn to pick it up. 'Caldwell & Craig is one of the oldest law firms in Scotland isn't it, Robbie? You said Maggie was always very proud of that. What date was the partnership formed?'

That I did know. It was the day slavery was abolished in Britain, which was ironic given the hours the firm expected its employees to be chained to their desks.

A quick Internet search revealed that the Slavery Abolition Act took effect on 1st August 1834, so my wife tapped in 181834, and when that didn't work, 010834. After some Googling, she even tried the date the Bill received royal assent. Still the screen remained frozen.

'What are you doing?' Tina jumped up on my lap, chewing on the pink ball of candyfloss she'd brought back from the shows.

'We're trying to guess six numbers so we can get into this phone,' I said, putting her down on the ground again, the better for me to tease out the candy floss from my hair.

'I know Mum's,' she said, proudly. 'I guessed it.' She tore off a piece of candyfloss and stretched over the table to give it to my dad. 'Mum's is easy. It's 1,1,1,1,1,1.'

'Seriously, Joanna?' I said. 'Not even your birthday or mine or one of the kids' or . . .' I looked across at my wife. She was staring intently at the phone. 'You don't think . . .'

The answer was, yes, she did think.

'It's pathetic isn't it,' I said, taking the now live phone from Joanna. 'A security code with hundreds of thousands of possible combinations and the best the legal brains of Joanna and Maggie Sinclair can come up with is six ones.'

'My phone only needs four numbers,' Malky said, 'so I've gone for—'

'1872 like every other Rangers supporter?' I said. 'What about you, dad. What's your code? 1314 like every SNP voter?'

He cleared his throat. 'Never mind that, just have a look for whatever you think's going to be in there.'

So I did, swiping through recent calls, contacts, texts, and basically breaching every General Data Protection Regulation and privacy law it was possible to breach, until I came to the gallery where Maggie's photos were stored.

Malky had returned and leaned in for a better look as I flicked through them. 'She's very bendy for someone . . . When was she born? That makes her . . .' Arithmetic had never been my brother's strong point. You didn't need to be good at sums to head a ball out of the penalty box or bring down a striker through on goal. 'Well . . .' he said, 'you know what they say. There's many a tune played on an old flute.'

'It's fiddle,' I said.

'Well she's doing plenty of fiddling in that shot,' my dad said. He got up, went around the table and whisked Tina off her feet. 'Come on, pet. This isn't for wee girls. Me, you and Uncle Malky will have a game of dominos.'

Malky didn't look like he was going anywhere. 'Go back to the one with the judge's wig and the black latex leggings. I still don't know how she got herself into those.'

I switched off the phone and powered it down before my eyes began to bleed. That was why Maggie wanted the phone back so urgently. She'd been sexting Stan Blandy like some randy adolescent.

There was a call logged on Maggie's phone to a contact that was saved simply as 'SB'. I pressed the screen. Stan answered straightaway.

'I've got it,' I told him.

He awarded me with a satisfied grunt.

'What do you want me to do with it?' I asked.

'I'll send somebody through for it. Where are you?'

'First of all, I want to talk about my case,' I said.

'I've done all the talking I'm going to about that.' The quietness of Stan's voice was worrying, but so what? Worry was all I did these days. 'I'm going to ask you again. Where are you calling from?'

'I don't have to talk to *you*,' I said. 'It's your driver I want to speak to. Just a quick word. Send him through for your phone and we can kill two birds.'

'No, I've a better idea. Speak to him now and then drop the phone off at Maggie's home first thing tomorrow. Do you know where she stays?' I did, roughly. Stan gave me the address and I wrote it down on the back of an envelope.

After a minute or two a gravelly voice came on the line. 'Yeah?'

'The night you brought MacDonald to my house, where did you find him?'

Another pause, presumably while the driver took instructions from Stan. 'He was coming out of his house.'

'Did he have anything with him?'

'Like what?'

'I don't know. A holdall or a rucksack. Something like that.'

'He had a wee red rucksack,' the driver said. 'Dunno what was in it. Clothes, I think. Big Harry chucked it out the window when we were on our way for you. We took a phone off him an' all. We smashed it and got rid of that as well. After that we came and got you.'

'Was that all?'

'There was some money. We kept it.'

Stan came on the line. 'That's it.'

'Come on, Stan. Maggie'll get her phone back. Just let me ask your man one more question,' I said.

A few seconds later the driver grunted down the phone at me. 'Can you remember whereabout you chucked the stuff?' I asked.

He could, more or less. I hung up.

'Where do you think you're going?' my dad asked, when he saw me reaching for my jacket.

'Out,' I said, 'and you and Bouncer are coming with me.'

45

According to Stan's driver, the rucksack had been thrown out of the car window on a bend not far from MacDonald's home. I wished I'd paid more attention on the journey, because the road had more bad turns than amateur night at a working man's club. I took 'not far' to mean somewhere within a couple of hundred yards from his house, and parked the car on the verge of the narrow roadway at what was a particularly sharp bend. There was a drystane dyke bounding woodland on the left and, on the right, a stob and wire fence running the length of the road, skirting open fields and scrubland leading down to the river Avon.

'You and Bouncer walk a hundred yards that way, I'll go this way,' I said to my dad. 'Search the other side of the wall and work your way back here to the car. It'll be just like looking for a golf ball. You're used to that. The only difference is you can't throw another rucksack down and say you've found it.'

My dad deemed my remark unworthy of a laugh and set off down the road while I walked up the hill in the other direction. How far could someone throw a rucksack from a car window? It would depend on how strong the person was and how heavy the rucksack; still, it couldn't have landed more than a few yards the other side of the wall.

The dyke was only around four feet high and climbed without difficulty. The problem was what lay beyond, for between it and the trees the grass was long and lush with clumps of gorse in full yellow bloom and eruptions of bracken everywhere. After half an hour of wading knee-deep through the greenery, scratching my hands on gorse bushes and bramble briars, I couldn't have covered more than a quarter of the distance back to the car. I yelled to see how my dad was getting on, received no yell in response and assumed he was having the same problem. There was a moment when I thought I'd struck gold. A dark shape sitting in a clump of nettles. When I reached for it, I stung my hands, and after all that it turned out to be nothing more than an old bin-liner full of hardened mortar. I looked around and saw some docken plants growing near the foot of a tree. I'd never been sure if rubbing the leaves on nettle stings did help or whether it was purely the placebo effect, but my dad had sworn by them when I was a boy on the basis that why else would God always grow docken wherever there were nettles? I'd always thought it would have been better if God had just given up on the nettles as a bad idea and saved everyone a lot of bother. I was wondering whether I should trudge over and pick a few leaves, when I saw something dark at the base of a tree a few metres further on. At first, I thought it just a shadow. It wasn't. It was clearly something man-made, and the closer I got to it, the redder it became. It had to be the rucksack Stan's driver had told me about. If so, it must have been quite some throw. Jumping through the undergrowth, like I was jumping through waves at the beach, I emerged onto the pine needle-strewn forest floor and ran over to the object, a rucksack, sure enough, red with navy-blue and white flashes. I knelt down, and as I began carefully to unzip it, I heard a rustle behind me and the soft crunch of pine needles underfoot. Still hunched over the bag, I thought I was turning to tell my dad the good news, when two arms shot out, seizing me, wrenching me to my feet. A forearm clamped around my throat. I felt a knee in my back. The trunk of the pine tree went into soft focus then slowly started to dissolve. I struck out behind me, using my elbows and fists. I might as well have been using a balloon on a stick. I let my legs give way, hoping my dead weight would send us both to the ground, but the steel bar across my throat held me upright. I tried jerking my head back into my attacker's face, but such was the vice around my neck it barely moved. Backheels to the shins were puny and ineffective. Blood thundered in my ears, then gradually everything went very still and someone switched the daylight off.

There was no sound, then far away I heard the rumble of a voice like distant thunder. My hands felt the sharpness of pine needles and something wet wiped itself across my face. I opened my eyes and the face before me was enormous and shadowy, a wide grin in the middle of it and a lolling tongue. Slowly the world came back into focus. I sat up.

'Take it easy and breathe,' my dad said, shoving Bouncer aside with his knee. He was holding a gnarled piece of wood in an equally gnarled hand. 'Get up nice and slowly. You'll be fine. You've only been out a few seconds. Just watch where you're standing.' Rubbing my throat, I looked to my side. Lying face down was the body of a large man, dressed for summer in a white short-sleeved shirt and khaki shorts.

'I was lucky,' my dad said. 'Bouncer had a go at him. He never heard me coming.'

I stood up and gave the body a prod with the toe of my shoe. 'Is he . . .?'

'No, he's still breathing,' my dad said.

I checked the pockets of the man's shorts. There were pouches either side. In one of them there was a mobile phone in a flip-open black wallet. Tucked inside that was a bank card and a driver's licence.

'William Hendry,' I said. 'Bishopbriggs address.'

I lifted one of his arms and pointed to the tattoo.

My dad pulled out his own phone. 'We need to bring some law into this,' he said.

'No, wait,' I said. 'We need to think how to play it.'

'Play what? This guy attacked you.'

'Yeah, that's what we'll say. What the evidence will show is that you clunked him over the head with half a tree. If this is the guy who killed MacDonald, then what's in this bag might prove my innocence. I need time to decide what to do with him and it. We'll have to put him somewhere or else he'll be up and away as soon as he comes to.'

'Putting him in jail would be a good start,' my dad said, starting to punch numbers into his phone.

I took it from him and switched it off. Then I reached down and took Hendry under the armpits, telling my dad to take hold of his legs. 'Not jail,' I said. 'Not yet. But somewhere very much like it.'

46

The Royal Burgh of Linlithgow might be partying, but for the rest of West Lothian it was auld claes and parritch. I called Hugh Ogilvie shortly before five. The procurator fiscal was finishing up for the day and suggested I take Bouncer for another walk in Kirkton Park and he'd take a detour on his way home. He came by himself this time. No dog, no Hugh junior. We met at the stone archway. On a pleasant summer evening the park was busy; too busy, I said, for the procurator fiscal to be seen with a bailed murder accused. He wouldn't want anyone to think we were colluding.

I led him across the road, through a black iron gate into a churchyard. There was no one else there apart from a woman in jeans and a hoody, threading her way slowly amongst the gravestones as she studied the inscriptions. We walked in the opposite direction, towards the ruins of Old Bathgate Parish Church.

The church was said to date as far back as the reign of Malcolm IV in around 1160, and having entered via a gap in the north face, we found ourselves between long high walls that bounded a narrow interior with grass for a floor. The only way out was the way we'd come in, the only other break in the structure, a small lancet window. On the walls were various ancient memorial plaques. The oldest I could see was dedicated to the memory of Andreas

Crichton of Drumcorse, Chamberlain of the Lordship of Linlithgowshire, who, according to his headstone, had died in 1514. It was true what they said. You're dead a lot longer than you're alive. Which is why I wanted to make the most of my time and not unwind my mortal coil sewing mailbags in Saughton Prison.

'You have something for me?' Ogilvie said, when satisfied we were hidden from public view.

I unslung the red rucksack from my shoulder and set it on the ground between us. 'In there you will find the property of one William Hendry, a former soldier in the Argyll and Sutherland Highlanders, murderer of Angus MacDonald, and, most likely, Provost Simon Keggie.'

'Where did you get it?'

'It's a long story.'

'Give me the Ladybird book version.'

'You were right to suspect Josh Wedderburn of trying to ditch the Keggie trial. What you don't know was that the instructions came from Crown Office: Jessica Barrett QC.'

'How can you possibly know this?'

'Wedderburn confessed to Joanna. I was there when he did. And when the attempt to time-bar the case didn't go as planned, this Hendry guy was sent to threaten Joanna into dropping the case.'

'Why didn't she say anything?'

'You know what she's like. It only made her more determined to go ahead.'

'She must have been threatened after I had the time-bar extended.'

'The same evening.'

'But why would Jessica Barrett want Keggie's case binned?'

He wanted the shortened version, so I gave it to him.

'He did it because MacDonald and Keggie were bartering over an embarrassing video of the Justice Secretary.'

Ogilvie looked down at the rucksack. 'Is your tinfoil helmet in there too?' he said.

'It's not a conspiracy theory, Hugh. Mrs Keggie told me about the video.'

'Okay, then. Let's say I believe you. What does it show?'

'I don't know, but it was bad enough for Harvey Rudd not to want it to leak. That's why he had his fiancée put the gentle squeeze on Wedderburn. When that didn't work, I believe he sanctioned the murder of MacDonald, and Hendry took his place as the complainer at the trial. I think he also authorised the murder of Keggie too, just to make sure.'

While I was talking, Ogilvie's head was swivelling from side to side, like he was watching Wimbledon on fast-forward, looking to make sure there was no one else around. 'You can't say things like that about the Justice Secretary,' he hissed.

'I can, I said, 'and if my case ever comes to trial, I will.'

Ogilvie thought about it. 'Okay, I'll buy it for now. How did you find this Hendry?'

'I didn't know who he was, but I had some people I know track him down. They found him and we met at MacDonald's place the night Keggie was acquitted.'

'In the outbuilding?' Ogilvie asked, eyebrows raised.

'It wasn't the introduction I'd been expecting,' I said. 'Hendry, who I thought at the time was MacDonald, ran off.'

'And how is it you came by this?' Ogilvie nudged the rucksack with the side of a shoe.

'When I was . . . introduced to him by the people I know—'

'You mean when they'd abducted him?'

'Whatever, he was outside MacDonald's place. He had the rucksack with him. They took his phone and smashed it before they came to collect me.'

'Sound like professionals. Pity you didn't leave your own phone at home. Careless of you.'

'It's what innocent people do,' I said. 'But getting back to these people—'

'The ones you know but won't say who they are?'

'They threw the rucksack away. I found it tonight.'

Ogilvie picked up the rucksack by a strap, using only his thumb and index finger. 'Have you touched anything inside here?'

I'd only opened the top of the rucksack for a quick look. It had been enough.

Ogilvie unzipped the rucksack. Using a pen, he gently teased out the sleeve of a pair of white paper overalls. It was spattered dark red. The PF pushed the sleeve back inside and zipped the rucksack closed.

'No weapon?' he said.

'No, but if those overalls turn out to contain Hendry's DNA and are splattered with MacDonald's blood, I take it I'm in the clear.'

The procurator fiscal grimaced in unconvincing sympathy. 'It's not quite so easy as that, Robbie. Don't think I'm not terribly grateful, but are you forgetting a certain phone trail and a pickaxe handle? All the contents of this rucksack give me is a solid case against two people for murdering Angus MacDonald, when before I had only one.'

'Angus MacDonald was shot,' I said. 'So was Simon Keggie.'

Ogilvie smiled. 'If you had the pickaxe handle, maybe it

276

was this mysterious Hendry person who had the gun. So it doesn't matter. Not if you were acting art and part. When you flee with the craws . . .' He hung the rucksack from his wrist, looked set to turn and go, then stopped. 'Of course, you could always call as witnesses those people, the ones who abducted Hendry. No doubt they'd be happy to vouch for you. Fine upstanding chaps, are they?'

This time he did start to walk away. I pulled him back by the shoulder. 'The pickaxe handle might have my DNA on it, but it's Hendry's blood, not MacDonald's.'

'So you tried to stop him shooting MacDonald. Good on you. Lodge a defence of incrimination. Fiona Faye can be extremely persuasive in front of the right jury.'

Ogilvie shrugged free of my grip and marched off at speed. I went after him, but when he'd reached the main road there wasn't much I could do. I stood and watched as he climbed into his car and drove off. Then with Bouncer at my heels, together we crossed the Edinburgh Road and walked into the park.

47

The woman in the jeans and grey hoodie was waiting for me in her car, which we'd left on Puir Wife's Brae on the other side of Kirkton Park.

I was about to jump in and had to stop myself from landing on my laptop which was on the front passenger seat. When I was seated, I laid the laptop on my knee and Bouncer climbed on top.

'Are you okay?' I asked, shoving the dog off my lap and into the back of the car.

Joanna showed me the graze along the side of her arm she'd sustained while, with the assistance of an adjacent memorial stone, she'd clambered, mobile phone in hand, to look through the lancet window in the side of Old Bathgate Parish Church. She gave me her phone. The images were clear side-on views of me and Hugh Ogilvie, the latter looking at a white article of clothing inside a small red rucksack. I gave her back the phone and kissed her.

'What do you think he'll do with it?' she said.

I was hoping he'd have it analysed and logged as evidence so I could use it at my trial, but it was my job to be suspicious of procurators fiscal, and Hugh Ogilvie in particular. Ogilvie could easily have agreed to the handover taking place at his office. It had been his suggestion that we meet secretly. His reason for that was that he didn't want to be seen with me in case there were allegations that he was assisting the defence. I didn't like that as an excuse, which was why I'd wanted a record made.

I put my hand in my pocket and pulled out the memory stick I'd extracted from the front pouch of the rucksack earlier.

'This is what it's all about, I'm sure of it,' I said, holding the fluorescent green object in one hand, while trying my best to stop Bouncer from chewing it with the other. 'What's on here is why MacDonald and Keggie were killed.'

'If only we could get into it,' Joanna said. Neither of us was particularly technologically minded. Grace Mary had insisted I buy a laptop a while back so as to keep in touch with the office when at court. It did have its uses, though the Sheriff Court internet worked about as often as a member of the Royal Family. I'd brought my laptop along with me on the journey to Bathgate, using the full extent of my IT expertise to access the memory stick, but even switching the laptop off and on, and wiggling the memory stick around a lot, nothing seemed to work. I needed to know what was on it, and quickly.

'You should have given it to Hugh Ogilvie,' Joanna said. 'The Crown have people who could get into that in two seconds. Why didn't you?'

'They also have people like Jessica Barrett, who's not only prosecuting me, but doesn't want what's on this pen drive or memory stick or—'

'Most people under forty just call it a USB,' Joanna said.

'Whatever, she doesn't want the contents coming to light. It could easily go missing.'

'So could the rucksack.'

'No,' I said, 'I trust Hugh Ogilvie more. Not much more, which is why we now have photographic evidence of it being handed over.'

'If you ask me the rucksack is of a lot more importance to your case than the USB. You don't even know what's on it.'

'No, but I have a feeling it could come in handy if things start to go badly with my case—'

'They're not going so great now.' Joanna started the engine. 'Where to? Home?'

I couldn't leave William Hendry locked up for ever. I racked my brains. Who did I know at seven o'clock on a Tuesday evening who had the tech skill to crack this memory stick? Tina was only an outside bet and it would soon be past her bedtime.

'They never have this trouble in the movies,' Joanna said, as she carried out a three-point turn.

'Movies!' I slapped the dashboard, giving Bouncer a fright. 'How long from here to the old Mains Distillery?'

'About twenty minutes. Fifteen if I drive like an absolute maniac,' Joanna said.

A quarter of an hour later we pulled up outside Jeff Freeman's flat.

'Now we're talking, Robbie,' Jeff said, throwing the door wide. Milky white legs stuck out from below the hem of a brightly patterned silk kimono. He gave Joanna a thorough up/down like he was applying a coat of paint with his tongue. 'And who is this lovely lady?'

'I'm not a lady. I'm his wife,' Joanna said, pushing Freeman aside in order to allow the three Munros entry.

'I'm calling in the debt you owe me,' I said.

'You don't hang about, do you?' Freeman said, trotting along beside us into the living room where a new, wall-mounted TV was playing a *Star Trek* rerun. Captain James T. Kirk was trying to talk sense to an amorphous space alien, which, fortunately for all humankind, spoke perfect English, though with an American accent. 'What do you want?'

I handed him the fluorescent green memory stick. 'I want to know what's on this.'

He stared at me as though I'd just asked him to spell IQ. 'Is that all? Have you tried sticking the shiny end into a computer?'

I explained our efforts and he gave me a patronising smile in exchange. 'Wait here.' He left the room to return with what looked like a brand-new laptop. 'The cops still haven't given me back any of the stuff they took when they searched this place. I've had to buy everything new,' he said.

The way Police Scotland operated, by the time his items of electronic equipment were returned to him, they'd only be of interest to archaeologists.

He sat down and powered up the machine. Like all new computers it was still in the honeymoon period and booted up immediately. He typed in a six-digit security code. I watched, interested to see if he used the same imaginative code as my wife. He didn't: 235711. He saw me watching. 'I only use prime numbers for the Lottery as well,' he said, slotting the memory stick into a USB port on the side of the laptop. Immediately, he identified the problem that Joanna and I hadn't noticed, or, even if we had, wouldn't have understood.

'This a Linux OS,' he said.

'Oh, is it?' I said, in a silly-me kind of a way, trying not to sound like in my spare time I enjoyed banging an antelope thigh bone against a lump of rock.

Freeman switched off the laptop and switched it on again, which, to be fair, Joanna and I had done several times before exhausting our IT knowledge, but this time as Freeman's laptop booted up he pressed F12 and a series of white letters and numbers appeared on a black screen. For me, that was usually a strong indication that something was terribly wrong. Not so for the man in the kimono, the hem of which Bouncer was sniffing. His hands ran across the keyboard and soon we were into a coloured desktop with an arrangement that looked more familiar.

'Great, isn't it, Linux,' Freeman said. 'A whole PC on a thirty-two-gig pen drive.'

'We think there's a video on it, Jeff,' I said, leaning over the back of the armchair, staring over his shoulder at the screen.

'Is that right?' he said. 'Nothing illegal, I hope. You know how I like to steer clear of that sort of thing.'

'Just find it,' Joanna said.

Freeman ran a finger across the touchpad, sending the cursor up to an icon in the top right corner of the screen, and double-tapped, producing a list of items. 'There's forty-three JPEGs and one MP4.'

I reached over and lifted the laptop from Freeman's knee. 'I'm afraid these are private,' I said.

Slightly disgruntled, Freeman, his silk kimono and Bouncer, still sniffing, shifted to the far-away armchair, while Joanna and I viewed the still images in turn, all forty-three of them, each one showing the variety of birdlife in the Highlands. There were black grouse, red grouse, all sorts of colours of grouse, several owls, a white-tailed sea eagle – scourge of the sheep farmer – even a capercaillie. Every type of bird except the kind I thought there might be. All beautifully framed and all absolutely of no use. Didn't

282

matter. MacDonald was a wildlife photographer. What did we expect? It was the video file we were interested in. We had to call Freeman over to help play it. He opened a programme called VLC player. The quality was high definition and the bar at the foot of the screen showed the clip to be nine minutes long. After five of those minutes, during which a deer darted into a clearing and then darted off again, I was ready to throw the laptop against the wall. Joanna laid a hand on my arm. 'Watch it all,' she said, and we did. The camera position never moved, and I guessed it was unattended with a motion detector. It was six minutes after Bambi had done a cameo that two black Labradors came into shot. Just behind them were two figures striding through the heather, both carrying shotguns and clad in tweed jackets and plus fours. One wore a flat cap, the other a deerstalker, the flaps tied up in a bow on the top of his head. At first, I had no idea who they were. The people I knew who carried shotguns seldom dressed in tweed, and if they wore hats at all, they were generally pulled down over their faces. As the two walked towards the camera, their identities became clearer. Harvey Rudd was the person in the checked bunnet. By his side, under the Sherlock Holmes hat, was the man I'd last seen presiding at the trial of the late Simon Keggie. Unlike his companion's shotgun, his was safely broken over his arm.

'Sheriff Sibbald. I knew it,' Joanna said, leaning closer to the screen. There was no sound, but Sibbald pointed and must have said something, because the nearest Labrador ran off out of the picture. The other, an older animal, started to run after it, crossing Rudd's path, misjudging the angle. Rudd stumbled, almost falling, a puff of smoke escaped the barrels of his shotgun and the undergrowth in front of him exploded. Was that it? A near accident when out shooting? Not exactly motive for murder. Joanna gave me a tight smile and squeezed my arm.

Forty-five seconds remained on the video clip when Rudd, having regained his balance, shouted to the dog. It slunk over to him, head bowed. And then it happened. Rudd drew back a heavy brown brogue and unleashed it, kicking the Labrador viciously in the ribs. Then, as the dog crawled away, he brought the butt of the shotgun down heavily on the animal's head. It slumped to the forest floor and didn't look like it would ever get up again. I was glad Bouncer wasn't there to see it. He was too busy smelling Freeman's kimono and wondering, as we all were, what that strange scent was.

The clip ended a few seconds later, the final fate of the Labrador unknown.

'In a way it's worse than I thought it would be,' Joanna said. 'No wonder Rudd wouldn't want this to come out.'

People kill for many things: money, hate, revenge. It was clear what Rudd's motive had been. These days politicians were Teflon-coated. Xenophobia, even anti-Semitism didn't register. Some people regarded them positively. Mike Watson, the Labour Party politician, had been jailed for setting fire to hotel curtains. It should have been curtains for his political career, but instead he'd been made Baron Watson of Invergowrie. A four-year perjury sentence for Jeffrey Archer had only resulted in a seat on the red benches for him too. A politician like Harvey Rudd could easily have ridden out the storm of a sex scandal, putting it down to an indiscretion. Drink or drugs problems, providing they were spun the right way, would have seen him as the brave victim of substance abuse, taking one day at a time and being a shining example to others. But this was different. The British public could forgive a lot of things. But not this. Not beating a dog to death. If Harvey Rudd was ever convicted, he'd forever be demonised, not as the politician who'd arranged the murder of two men, but as the politician who'd killed man's best friend.

I called Freeman back over and asked him to email me a copy of the video clip. He did it quickly, while on TV the end titles rolled and the Starship Enterprise boldly went.

'Let's go, Jo,' I said, and snapped my fingers at Bouncer.

'Are we quits now?' Freeman asked. I stopped him from ejecting the memory stick otherwise I'd never be able to remember how he'd managed to get into it.

'No,' I said, relieving him of his portable PC. 'I'm taking this too.'

48

Back home my dad had put Jamie to bed, and, full of Marches Day excess, was dozing in an armchair. The day after the Marches is a school holiday. Tina was up late, playing poker with her uncle Malky in the kitchen – and winning, if the heap of peanut M&Ms in front of her was anything to go by.

'And you'll go directly to see Fiona?' Joanna ordered rather than asked me. She put Jeff Freeman's laptop in my hand. 'Show her the clip of Harvey Rudd and the dog. Tell her everything. Understand? *Everything*, Robbie. If anyone knows what we should do next, it's her.'

I woke up my dad, told him he'd been relieved of command and drove him home.

'What is it, then?' he asked on the way. 'Rent boys, hookers, drugs or all three?'

'Worse,' I said. 'Harvey Rudd is a dog-killer.'

'He killed some mutt? How's that worse?' My dad had never been an animal lover.

'Thanks for all your help today,' I said.

He ruffled my hair and laughed. 'What's a dad for if he can't interrogate suspects and hit folk over the head with sticks for his son? Seriously, though, what are you going to do with him? You can't leave that man locked up much longer. He could be badly injured. I gave him a right good crack with that tree branch. It could easily have caused a skull fracture. What if he's suffered a brain haemorrhage? He could be dead or dying.'

I really hoped not. Life imprisonment was bad enough, but the thought of sharing a cell with my dad only made me long for the reintroduction of capital punishment.

'Don't worry. It's all going to be taken care of,' I told him as we pulled up outside his house, hoping I sounded confident. 'We'll talk about it in the morning. Meantime, get a good night's sleep.'

He got out, and as I was about to drive away, opened the door again and poked his head in. 'Get the police involved,' he said. 'Give Dougie Fleming a call. Tell him what happened. I'll speak to him if you like. He wouldn't dare not believe me.'

It was true. Dougie Fleming would believe my dad if he told him he'd just had tea with Nessie at Bigfoot's house. But he'd still find a way to nail me if he was given the slightest opportunity.

I smiled and gave him a thumbs up. 'Let me think about it. I'm going to speak to the QC, see what she says. On you go and watch some telly or have an early night.'

On the way back home, I pulled into a lay-by and called Fiona Faye. 'I really need to consult with you, urgently,' I said.

'Hmm, not easy this week, Robbie,' she replied, 'I'm in a trial that's likely to—'

'I mean now, Fiona.'

'Now? Are you crazy? It's half seven on a school night, and I've still got to—'

'I have video footage of the Cabinet Secretary for Justice killing a dog,' I said.

There was silence on the other end, and then, 'Say again?'

'Angus MacDonald, the man who I'm charged with murdering. He had a video of Harvey Rudd killing a dog. A black Labrador, to be precise. When Rudd found out about it, he arranged for an ex-soldier called William Hendry to steal the video clip. MacDonald was killed in the process. MacDonald was trying to sell the video to Simon Keggie, the Provost of West Lothian. Rudd had him killed too.'

'I see . . .' Fiona said. 'No, actually, I don't. Not at all. What does Joanna say about all this? Is she there now? Put her on.' From the tone of Fiona's voice, she had already fitted me up for a straitjacket.

'Joanna's not here, but it was her idea I meet with you. I've got a couple of SCD cops who I think are prepared to back me up.'

'Really?' Fiona said, slowly. 'The Specialist Crime Division would like to help *you*? And apart from this video clip and the assistance of the constabulary, what else do you have?'

'I've also got a bag of clothes worn by Hendry that's full of his DNA and spattered with MacDonald's blood.'

'All right,' she said, lightly. 'Where is this stuff?' I could sense my explanation so far had only heightened Fiona's concerns for my mental health.

'I gave the bag to Hugh Ogilvie, the PF.'

'Very trusting of you. When did this happen?'

'This evening. I've got photos of us meeting in a ruined church—'

I was interrupted by sounds of exasperation from the other end of the line. 'What evidence do you have *exactly* that you think is going to amount to a defence to the charge against you?' Fiona said sternly.

'I've got the real killer locked up in an outbuilding.'

There was another pause. 'Oh, Robbie. You've been under a huge amount of pressure lately. What you need to do is find Joanna, talk things over with her and then give me a call tomorrow. How about lunchtime? I'll be out of court by one o'clock. Now, I've got to go. Sorry.' The line went dead. What was I supposed to do now? I was leaving the lay-by when my phoned buzzed. It was Joanna. I thought at first Fiona had called her, but she was phoning for another reason.

'There are two police officers here,' she said in a stilted voice that made it clear they were listening in. 'They'd like to speak to you.'

'One fat man, one tall woman with a face like the north face of the Eiger?'

'That's right,' Joanna said. 'They say they want to help you. When shall I tell them you'll be back?'

Before I could answer there was a new voice: Dicker's. 'You'll get back here right now or your wife's coming with us for questioning.'

My whole predicament had come about when I'd tried to protect my wife, who was perfectly capable of looking after herself. I could leave her to take care of the two SCD officers. Couldn't I?

'My wife will tell you nothing,' I said.

Dicker laughed like cloth tearing. 'We'll see about that once she's under arrest and the kids are in care.'

Cold fear and hot temper ran over me like a shower in a two-star hotel.

'Please—'

'Understand, we don't want to do this, Mr Munro.' It was Sandeman's turn, her normal grating tones tonight more of a purr. 'I've given you chance after chance, tried to help you in every way possible. I put my neck on the line to have that housebreaking charge dropped. You say you're innocent, but for some reason don't want to prove it. If I can't make you see sense by being nice, then what am I to do?'

I took several deep breaths. 'He did have something with him,' I said. 'The person who killed Angus MacDonald. He had a small rucksack with him. The men who grabbed him – they threw it out of a car. I found it today.'

'Where is it?'

'I gave the rucksack to the PF.'

'What was in it?'

'Some clothes. I didn't take a good look.'

'Are you sure there was nothing else?'

Should I tell them?

'Now is not the time to hold anything back,' Sandeman said. 'Not when we're so close to proving your innocence. What else was in the bag? It had something to do with Harvey Rudd, the MSP, didn't it?'

'What makes you think that?' I said.

'You're not the only one who's been investigating this case. We've been looking into this for over a year. When are you going to believe that we're trying to help?'

My years as a defence lawyer had instilled in me a healthy distrust of the police. Still, I would have been prepared to trust DCI Sandeman, had it not been for my earlier encounter with Hugh Ogilvie in the ruins of Old Bathgate Parish Church. What if I presented my evidence to the SCD officers and they shared the same view of the evidence as the procurator fiscal: that it only showed that, whoever had killed Angus MacDonald, I'd been an accomplice? I needed to let them have the full package.

'I have a memory stick with a video on it of Harvey Rudd killing a dog. The video was taken by Angus

MacDonald. The forensics on the rucksack will nail a man called William Hendry for MacDonald's murder,' I said. 'All you need to do is find a link between Rudd and this Hendry person. To back it up, I can take you to Hendry and also give you the men who abducted him by mistake. They'll confirm they grabbed Hendry at MacDonald's place. They'll also confirm that I wasn't involved.'

'Suddenly, you know who they are?' Sandeman said.

I put her right on that. 'No, I still don't know their names, but I can arrange it via someone who does.'

'And they'll come forward and testify?'

'Providing they're given immunity.'

Sandeman sniffed. 'That's doable.'

Of course it was doable. What had Stan's men actually done? A spot of abduction, and a minor assault. What was that compared to convicting a double murderer?

'Anything else?' Sandeman asked.

'I want my prosecution deserted.'

'You know I don't have the power to do that,' she said.

'Then you'd better find someone who does, or I'll take my chances at trial.'

Muffled voices conferred on the other end of the phone, until Sandeman came back with, 'Where and when can we meet?'

I looked at my watch. It was nearly eight.

'Angus MacDonald's place, ten o'clock,' I said, and the line went dead.

It was time to call in the debt owed to me by Stan Blandy.

49

'I'm fed up telling you, I'm not having my boys speak to the police.' Stan seemed quite certain about that.

'But the cops aren't going to charge them,' I said. 'They'll be granted immunity if they give evidence, and your name need never be mentioned.'

Stan was unmoved. It was time to apply some leverage.

'I don't want to do it this way,' I said, 'but I still have Maggie's phone.' Stan didn't respond, so I ratcheted things up. 'I called you on it, so you must know I managed to hack into it. I found a lot of interesting pictures she'd been sending you. What do you think will happen if her husband, Lord Bantaskine, ever finds out about them?'

Stan failed to stifle a yawn. 'I'm not interested in the phone. Not any more.'

What was he talking about, not interested in it any more? He'd been pestering me for weeks for return of Maggie's phone. Earlier that same evening he'd insisted I return it to her straightaway. Now he wasn't interested? He had to be bluffing. 'All right, Stan, if that's your last word on the matter. You don't hand over the witnesses and I won't hand over the phone – at least not to you or Maggie. Maybe to her husband.'

I waited for him to crack. The seconds went past like elephants in diver's boots.

'Was there anything else?' Stan asked.

'No, I'm still waiting for you to tell me what's to happen with the phone.'

'Oh, I see,' he said. 'Well, since that woman and I are no longer seeing eye to eye on certain matters, I'm happy for you to keep it or give it to whoever you like. That do you?'

It would have to, because, with that, he hung up.

I drove home, making sure that there was no BMW 7 series in the vicinity before I parked, and went in to find Joanna looking worried in the living room. Tina was in the kitchen eating her poker winnings while her uncle Malky amazed her with a box of matches and his legendary fire-eating trick that he'd just invented.

'A fat lot of good that's going to do me,' I said, tossing Maggie Sinclair's phone onto the sofa. 'To think of all the bother I went through trying to get that back. The only person who wants that phone is Maggie, and what good is she to me?'

'I don't trust them,' Joanna said. 'Those two cops. The way they're going about things . . . it's not right. In fact, it's *really* not right.'

I tried to explain to my wife that Sandeman had told me she'd been on the case for over a year. Given that it involved a scandal with the Justice Secretary, of course there would have to be the utmost secrecy. She still didn't agree.

'No, there was something about the pair of them . . .' she said.

It was something of a role reversal for us. I was professionally sceptical of police, but my wife had been a procurator fiscal depute. Fiscals loved cops: trained witnesses, who came into the witness box stamped with the court's seal of approval before they'd said a word.

'I don't care, Robbie. You can't go and meet them by

yourself. Ogilvie's already got the rucksack. What if that never sees the light of day?'

'That's why you took the photograph,' I reminded her.

'Hardly conclusive.'

'Maybe, but how's he going to explain a secret rendez-vous with a man he's busy prosecuting for murder, or what's in the bag being handed over?'

Joanna shook her head. 'He could still squirm out of it one way or another. Are you telling me you trust him? That'll be a first.'

I put my hands on her shoulders. 'What are you like? I've never got on with Hugh Ogilvie, but even I wouldn't accuse him of conspiracy to murder. Not even after the fact.'

'Anyone who's worked with Ogilvie would tell you he'd do just about anything to further his career.'

'But, Jo, he can't make the evidence disappear. We've got your photos, how could he—'

Joanna pulled away from me. 'He doesn't have to make them disappear. All he needs to do is contaminate the contents of the rucksack and make them forensically useless, and he might do that for a promise of promotion. He's always wanted to be a sheriff and I'm sure Harvey Rudd could see to that. If you hand over that USB to the SCD, the one bargaining chip you've got, and it later goes missing—'

'There's still Hendry,' I said. 'He's going nowhere.'

Joanna sighed. 'Robbie, you don't even know if the man's alive. That's all you need, another dead body. They'll have you down as a serial killer before you know it. Wait until tomorrow. Talk to Fiona. Give her the USB. She'll know what to do.'

'I've already told Fiona about it,' I said. 'She thinks I'm one UFO short of an alien abduction. And I can't leave Hendry in that outbuilding overnight. What if he's seriously injured? He never so much as moved a muscle the whole time we carried him there and dumped him.'

'Robbie, you need to take a witness with you,' Joanna said. 'Someone reliable.' I knew from experience that my wife was an excellent judge of character, the day I proposed marriage being the exception that proved the rule. However, she'd had only one brief encounter with the SCD officers. Maybe they wanted promotion too, and what a scalp this would be for them. Yes, Dicker was an ignorant blimp, but there was something about the tall female Detective Chief Inspector that I trusted. Joanna didn't care. 'Promise me you won't go alone or I'm coming with you.'

'How can I take someone with me?' I said. 'The cops frisked me for wires the last time I met with them. They'd never let me bring along a pal.'

'Not a pal,' Joanna said. 'They can't complain if you take your solicitor along. Not if this is truly official police business. With a lawyer it would remain confidential. Phone your dad and see if he'll come back to stay with the kids and I'll—'

'No, Jo, I don't want you getting involved, and Dad will only call Dougie Fleming who wouldn't believe me if I told him it was hot in Hawaii. Not only that, but the SCD are already threatening to make you an accomplice. They say you must have known that wasn't the real MacDonald at Keggie's trial.'

Clouds were gathering at the end of what had been a beautifully sunny day. Drops of rain spat against the window. There was a saying locally that if it was sunny for The Marches, it always rained on the Bo'ness Fair. Not that guessing it might rain in Scotland on any given day was something the bookies would give you odds on.

I grabbed my coat. 'I'll be fine. I've got someone in mind who I think will help me out, and he's a lawyer.'

'And reliable?' Joanna said.

I kissed her. 'Two out of three ain't bad.'

She pulled me back by the collar. 'No, Robbie. Not Sammy Veitch.'

'He's a lawyer, isn't he?'

'Sort of,' Joanna conceded.

'Look, Jo, I only need someone to come with me so that I've got a witness to corroborate me handing over Hendry and the memory stick to the SCD. I wouldn't bother if you weren't being so sceptical.' What was wrong with my wife? Not that long ago she was practically begging me to cooperate with the cops. Now, after only a few of weeks out of the Fiscal Service, she'd gone full-blown defence lawyer and suspicious of everything in blue serge.

'He's better than nothing, I suppose,' Joanna said. 'What makes you think he'll go after the grilling your dad gave him this afternoon?'

I waved a hand. 'What's he got to complain about? I'm the one charged with murder thanks to his business partner's cunning plan.'

'I still think I should come with you. Malky's here. He can babysit.'

My brother chose that moment to burn his lip on a lighted match. It fell inside the neck of his shirt and he ran to the sink to throw water over himself, while his niece fell off her chair giggling.

'I don't like it, Robbie,' Joanna said. 'I mean, I *really* don't like it.'

'You stay here and make sure Malky doesn't burn the house down,' I said, putting on my jacket. 'Sammy owes me. This is the very least he can do.'

50

If there was one thing reliable about Sammy Veitch, it was that on a Marches Day evening he'd be propping up the bar at the Red Corner. I found him sitting alone. The bar was a lot quieter now. Marches Day is an early start and for most an early finish. Brendan brought over a mug of coffee and set it down in front of him. Brendan usually frowned on the consumption of non-alcoholic drinks on the premises, but after the earlier events of the day, he must have been feeling sorry for wee Sammy.

I went over and sat on a bar stool beside him. 'I've come to offer you the chance of settling your debt to me,' I said.

'Debt? To you?' Sammy didn't look up from the murky depths of the coffee mug. 'You should take that neck of yours down the scrappie's. It's two grand a ton for brass,' he said.

'How are you feeling?' I asked.

He turned, pointing his beard at me accusingly. 'How would you feel after being put through the wringer by your old man?'

'Come off it. He asked you a few questions. Big deal. Okay he might have been a tad angry, but he never shoved any bamboo shoots up your fingernails. What I meant was, are you sober?'

'Ish,' he said, giving the mug a nudge. 'I've had nothing

but coffee to drink since the medicinal dram Brendan gave me after my terrible ordeal.'

'Good, because I need your help.' I pushed the mug to one side, pulled him off his stool and led him over to the dartboard where there was no one who could listen in. 'I've got the real murderer locked in an outbuilding at Angus MacDonald's place.'

'What murderer is that, then?' he said.

I grabbed him by the front of his shirt. 'The murderer of Angus MacDonald,' I hissed. 'The same Angus MacDonald that I'm accused of murdering. Remember?'

He pulled away from me, removed the three darts that were stuck in the dartboard and walked to the three-foot strip of wooden beading nailed to the floor that served as the oche. It was a tripping hazard over which many a pint had been spilt. 'I remember you sacking me,' he said, going for the treble twenty and hitting the five.

'You weren't sacked, Sammy. You're still part of the team. It's just that Joanna's taken the lead. You said it yourself, you've done no criminal court work for ages. Joanna's been a defence lawyer and a PF. She practically lives in court.'

He didn't reply. His next throw was more accurate, and he hit a single twenty.

'I'm meeting the cops from the Specialist Crime Division at MacDonald's place to hand over the real murderer. He's a guy called William Hendry. My dad hit him over the head—'

'Why doesn't that surprise me,' Sammy said, embedding an arrow firmly into the treble one.

When he went to collect the darts, I blocked his path and pulled them from the board before he could get to them. 'If anyone has got a brass neck, it's you,' I said.

'You owe me. If you hadn't begged me to take on Keggie's trial, I wouldn't be in the mess I am. You and Eddie with your plan to time-bar the case. Landing me right in it.'

'It wasn't my plan, it was Eddie's,' Sammy hit back. 'And if you're going to see the cops, what do you want me for? You always say it's best to tell the cops no comment.'

Which was true enough, except, on this occasion, I was going to tell them everything and let them bring down Harvey Rudd in order to set me free.

'I want a witness to me giving them Hendry,' I said. 'Joanna thinks it's wise in case something goes wrong later. And I've other evidence to hand over too.'

'What's that?'

'A video clip on a memory stick that . . . Why am I telling you this if you're not going to help?'

He shrugged, and, without another word, showed me his back and sauntered over to the bar.

'It's good to know who your friends are,' I said, chucking all three darts at the board and nearly hitting it. 'Are you coming with me or not?'

Brendan lifted the mug from the counter. 'You want me to give this a blast for you in the micro?' he asked Sammy.

The wee man shook his head. 'No more caffeine for me,' he said. 'I've had enough excitement for one day.'

'Anything I can do, Robbie?' Brendan asked after Sammy had gone. 'If you need some backup, I can spare Mickey, things are not so busy now.'

Mickey the barman seemed willing enough and had been to court more than most lawyers. Unfortunately, I needed someone credible and reliable in case I ever had to call them as a witness. A jury would take one look at Mickey's schedule of previous convictions and feel sorry for the tree they'd cut down to print it.

It was nine o'clock. I was meeting Sandeman and Dicker at ten. I looked into the mirror behind the bar and a tired face stared back at me. I'd been running on adrenaline all day and it was fast running out. I stayed to drink Sammy's coffee and to bemoan the fact that I'd been let down by the two people who owed me the biggest debt. The two people who'd landed me in the predicament I now found myself. Who needed enemies when you had friends like that?

51

I could see a light on in Angus MacDonald's cottage when I drove up the bumpy track later than intended. DCI Sandeman was standing outside the front door, leaning against the wall, one foot resting on an ancient, cast iron boot-scraper. The rain was falling more steadily now, and she was sheltered by the overhang of the roof. When she saw me alight, she took a final drag on her cigarette, and pinged the stub into the courtyard.

'Have you got it?' she asked.

I held up Jeff Freeman's laptop, the green fluorescent memory stick protruding from the side. Sandeman smiled, opened the front door and made to usher me through. I hesitated. This was the house where Angus MacDonald had been killed. My DNA might be in the outbuilding, but not in the house itself.

'It's okay. Scene of Crime have been and done their thing,' Sandeman assured me. 'The cleaners will be coming in to give the place a scrub out later this week.'

I still wasn't sure.

Sandeman looked up at a darkening sky and turned the palms of her hands upwards to catch raindrops. 'Go in. You'll get soaked out here,' she said. And I allowed her to steer me through the front door and into what was a large kitchen for such a small house, the thick stone walls of which had kept the place cool, like a morgue. I looked around and saw dark stains outlined in marker pen on the linoleum floor: reminders that Angus MacDonald had been killed here. Struck over the head, possibly tortured and then shot twice in the chest. Individual splashes on the walls, on a large dresser and on the legs of some chairs were also circled. Swabs would have been taken and the blood identified as being that of the man Simon Keggie had been charged with assaulting. The trial seemed like an age ago.

Dicker was sitting at the table with his back to me. When he heard me come in, he raised his immense bulk from the chair. Before I could stop him, he'd walked over and pulled the memory stick from the laptop. 'This it?' I put the laptop on the table. 'Have you watched it?' he asked.

'It's not one for an animal lover,' I replied.

Sandeman hadn't moved from the door and was still holding it open. 'Anyone else seen it?'

'Does it matter?' I said. Very soon everyone would be seeing it.

'It matters,' Sandeman said, and, with that, walked out again.

I looked over my shoulder to see the door closing behind her. Where was she going?

When I turned to face Dicker again, the green memory stick had gone from one hand to another and been replaced by something square and black. He pointed it at me. I wasn't an expert in firearms but I knew a standard police-issue Glock 17 when I saw one – and this wasn't one of those. It was something older, a revolver with chips in the paintwork. Joanna had told me not to trust them, and as proof of that I now had a gun in my face.

'Who else has seen it?' His voice seemed to come at

me from a distance. How could I have been so stupid as to trust them? Me of all people. I knew the Scottish Crime and Drug Enforcement Agency were a law unto themselves, and for all intents and purposes the Scottish Parliament's secret police force. Why had I thought their successors would be any different? Of course they'd be investigating a scandal involving the Justice Secretary. But not expose it: to cover it up.

'Just me,' I said, eventually.

'Yeah?' Dicker said, sarcastically. 'Who else have you shown it to?'

'No one. I watched it on this laptop right before I arranged to meet you. It's not even my laptop. The video is in a special format. I didn't know how to view it. The person who showed me how, didn't see it.'

The fat cop grunted. 'How many copies did you make?'

'None. There's just the one,' I said, still dazed.

He cocked the revolver. 'How many?'

I set the laptop down on the table. 'The one on the stick and I had one emailed to me.'

'From where?'

'From this laptop to mine.'

'Where's yours?'

I'd left it in Joanna's car.

'In my office somewhere,' I said.

'Sit.' He pointed the gun from me to the laptop. 'Delete what's on that. Then delete the sent email, log onto your own email and delete it from there too. Make sure it's gone.'

It's funny how you run out of things to say when you're staring down the barrel of a gun. I opened the lid, booted up the laptop and, when prompted, typed in the first five prime numbers that were Jeff Freeman's security code.

I picked up the memory stick and took my time trying to insert it into the USB slot. I needed to stall, time to think. If I showed the video clip to Dicker and deleted the emails, then what? MacDonald and Keggie had both been shot in order to silence them. But I was different. There was no need to kill me. What could I say that anyone would believe? If I came up with a story about the Justice Secretary killing a dog as my defence to the murder charge, the jury would think I was a comedy act.

Dicker drew out the chair next to mine and pushed it to the side, giving him space to stand next to me, staring down.

I pushed the memory stick in and then realised I didn't know what to do after that. The usual Windows display appeared. How did I bring up the Linux operating system? Freeman had pressed one of the F buttons. I tried F1. Nothing. I tried F2. Still nothing. I was working my way up the Fs and had reached F7 when Dicker elbowed me in the side of the face. 'Hurry up.' He started to say something else when the door flew open and a dishevelled-looking William Hendry marched into the room, Sammy Veitch not far behind. Dicker shifted his fat frame and turned the gun on them. I had absolutely no idea what was going on. I only knew that there was one gun in the room and that presented the biggest danger to me. I jumped out of the chair and hurled myself at Dicker, hitting him side on. It was like trying to rugby tackle a giant marshmallow – a twenty-stone marshmallow – and the force was barely enough to stagger him. As I clung on, he brought the handle of the gun down onto the top of my head. Sparks erupted behind my eyes. The pain was immense. Through it I managed to brace my legs and keep shoving. Dicker stepped backwards. Stumbling over the chair behind him, he put his arms out to steady himself. Letting go, I grabbed the arm holding the gun. There was a loud bang and a bullet embedded itself in the ceiling. Dicker wrenched his arm free. Before he could bring the gun to bear, Hendry was on him, slamming a fist into his face. The fat cop's legs gave way. His glasses spun across the room. The handgun clattered to the floor and he slowly slumped to the ground beside it.

Sammy pushed his way past Hendry. 'Are you okay, Robbie?'

I could barely hear him. Bees buzzed in my brain. A trickle of blood ran down the side of my head and into my ear.

'What's going on?' I yelled at him.

'Long story.' He reached down for the gun. I intercepted him. 'It's okay, Robbie,' he said. 'We're all on the same side here.'

'Leave it,' I said. 'If that's the gun used to kill MacDonald and Keggie, it's got Dicker's fingerprints all over it.'

Sammy backed away, righted the fallen chair and tried to push me into it. 'Sit down 'til you catch your breath. Everything's okay.'

But I didn't want to catch my breath. I wanted to know what was going on. 'What's he doing here?'

'Calm down, Robbie. You might not like what I have to say.' He retreated a few paces until he was level with Hendry. 'This is Wullie. He's Eddie Frew's nephew. He's . . . helped Eddie out before on a few wee jobs. Look, I really think you should sit down.'

'No, I'm fine,' I told him.

'You might not be so fine in a minute or two,' he said, and I sat.

'It's like this. Eddie was working both ends of the

Simon Keggie case. He promised Keggie he'd get him off and promised Harvey Rudd there'd be no mention made of the blackmail video at the trial. He took big money from them both. All he needed to do was make sure the trial didn't go ahead, and Rudd was in a position to make sure it didn't.'

'Through his fiancée, Jessica Barrett?'

'I don't know the details.'

'But you knew what was going on?' I said.

Sammy shrugged. 'Me and Eddie . . . we were business partners, Robbie. I'm set to retire soon and . . . well, you've got to admit it was a good set-up. Eddie was quite pleased about the whole thing. After the trial I'm sure he would have been into Harvey Rudd for more money to make the video clip disappear. He was probably teeing that up when he had his heart attack in the Parliament bar.'

'And when the time-bar plan didn't work?' I said.

'I'll admit I panicked a wee bit. I sent Wullie to have a word with your wife . . .'

Hendry stepped forward and put a hand against my chest to keep me in the chair.

'There was no intention to harm her, Robbie. Wullie's just not all that good with words and can be a tad scary at times.'

The fat man on the floor groaned and showed signs of regaining consciousness. Sammy hurried on with his explanation. 'Last ditch, I sent Wullie up here that same Friday night to explain to MacDonald how he might have to give evidence after all, and what to say. Eddie had already given him money and no doubt told him there'd be more when he'd got Keggie off the hook and the Justice Secretary on it. He refused to cooperate. He wanted more money or he was going to court to tell everything. I told

306

Wullie to tell him to stay home, let us sort out the trial and I'd square him up later.'

It had been Sammy's idea to put Hendry in the witness box. I'd have been impressed if I hadn't been so angry.

'Wullie came up here on the night of the trial with money for him as arranged and to find out how much he wanted for the video clip. MacDonald was tied to one of these chairs. He'd been shot through the chest. There was a rucksack on the table.' Sammy jerked his head at Dicker. 'It was that guy, wasn't it Wullie, who appeared from nowhere, yelling Polis at you?' The big man confirmed with a nod. Sammy continued. 'Wullie hit him and left, taking the rucksack. That's when he bumped into your pals at the front door.'

There was more groaning from Dicker as he began to come round and started fumbling about for his glasses.

'Keep an eye on him,' Sammy said, and Hendry went over and put a foot on the fat cop's chest.

'Why didn't you tell me this before, Sammy?'

'I didn't know what you were up to. Who were those people who attacked Wullie? Were you in on it? I had to protect Wullie. I told him to keep a close eye on you.'

'When I got lifted and you came to the police station? My dad never asked you to go, did he?'

Sammy grimaced his answer.

I turned to the big man. 'Why did you attack me in the woods?'

But Sammy was doing the talking for him. 'Wullie was following you. He saw you with the rucksack and thought whatever was in it would help him if he ended up getting the blame.'

Out of the corner of my eye I saw something flit past the small window by the door.

'What did you do with Sandeman?' I asked.

'Who?' said Sammy.

'The other cop who was outside keeping watch.'

Sammy's face told me all I needed to know. I jumped to my feet, just as the door opened and the tall figure of DCI Sandeman walked in, a Glock 17 pointed at me.

'Sit down,' she said, and turned the gun on Sammy and Hendry who were standing over Dicker. 'You two. Get away from him.' She gestured with the gun. 'Over there and down on your knees.' They both obeyed, but only after she'd repeated the order. Slowly she edged her way to where Dicker was now sitting up, back against the wall. He'd located his glasses, but they were twisted and smashed beyond use. Sandeman kicked the revolver to him. 'Keep those two covered.' She came over to me. 'Give me the USB.'

I pulled it out of the side of the laptop. She snatched it from me, dropped it on the floor and stamped on it, grinding it under the sole of a sturdy shoe. 'There's a copy on the laptop,' Dicker said, dazed, but struggling to his feet. He joined his colleague, standing behind me, the revolver directed at Sammy and Hendry at the far end of the table.

'Delete it,' Sandeman said. I hesitated for a second. Sandeman put the gun to my head. 'Now.'

I opened Jeff Freeman's email, found the one addressed to me in the sent messages folder and deleted it.

'He's got one on his own email too,' Dicker said to Sandeman.

'Log on to your account and delete it,' Sandeman said, jabbing the muzzle of the pistol into the side of my head by way of encouragement.

'I need Wi-Fi,' I said. 'I don't have the password for this place.'

Sandeman jabbed me again. Harder. 'It's an LTE laptop. It doesn't need Wi-Fi. It'll work over the mobile phone system.' Trust Jeff to have the latest gear. 'Get on with it,' she said.

I brought up my own email account. While I was doing this, Dicker looked over at me, distracted by what I was doing.

Hendry, kneeling only a yard or so away from the fat cop, began rising slowly to his feet. Sandeman noticed and directed the gun at him. 'Down!' she yelled.

This was my chance. I had to make a move on Sandeman while the gun was aimed somewhere other than at my head, and hope Hendry would do likewise with Dicker. But the fat cop was wise to me. He sidestepped away from Sammy and Hendry, and, his gun steadily pointed at me, joined his partner. The two of them stood either side of me, a good twelve feet or so from the other two prisoners, giving them plenty of time to react if Hendry had any more ideas.

'You keep your eye on them, I'll keep my eye on what he's doing,' Sandeman barked at her colleague, ending her sentence with another jab to my head.

I clicked on my inbox and didn't have to scroll far down to see the email from Jeff with the paperclip icon beside it. One glide of the cursor, one press of the delete button and the motive for Angus MacDonald's murder disappeared into the ether.

I was about to close the laptop lid when a Skype box popped up asking if I would accept a video call from Robbie Munro. I clicked accept and onto the screen appeared the image of three people. Two of them were standing either side of my wife who was sitting at a desk, behind them a large bookcase. The one on Joanna's right was Maggie

Sinclair. The other was a man I didn't instantly recognise. That was because I was used to seeing him dressed in red silk and with a horsehair wig on his head.

'Robbie?' Joanna said. 'Is everything all right?'

Frozen for a moment, Sandeman slowly lowered the hand holding the gun. The pistol thudded off the floorboards. Dicker spun around; his revolver levelled at my temple. He looked at the startled face of his colleague, then down at me and, finally, squinting myopically at the screen, he looked into the horn-rimmed lenses on the face of Lord Bantaskine, just as the High Court judge leaned closer for a better look at the fat man holding a gun to my head.

52

Lord Bantaskine never got to see those photographs of his wife in provocative poses. Joanna had always insisted that my meeting with the SCD officers be witnessed by a lawyer, and my wife can be highly persuasive at times. Sufficiently so to persuade Maggie Sinclair that she should cooperate if she wanted her mobile phone back and to save her marriage.

In the end there were three lawyers watching as two senior police officers pointed guns at my head: a High Court judge, an ex-senior partner of one of Scotland's top law firms, and a former procurator fiscal depute. As witnesses went, it was hard to imagine a trio a High Court jury would find more credible and reliable.

It was some months later that I saw Sammy Veitch, kilt swinging, heading along Linlithgow High Street from the direction of the train station. He saw me at my office window and waved for me to join him. Late Friday afternoon, I knew there was only one place he'd be headed.

The last time I'd encountered Sammy was in a witness room of the High Court in Edinburgh, for it was to there we'd been cited as witnesses in the case of Her Majesty's Advocate -v- Rachel Sandeman and George Brian Dicker, along with Joanna, William Hendry, Maggie Sinclair and Lord Bantaskine.

Maggie and her husband hadn't joined us on that occasion, and thus missed out on the plastic chairs, sticky carpet, dog-eared celebrity magazines and lack of refreshments. Instead the Bantaskines had remained on standby over at Parliament House in the Judge's chambers, quaffing claret and snacking on roast peacock, or whatever it was High Court judges did when they weren't sending people off to Her Majesty for safekeeping.

As so often is the case at the High Court, those cited to give evidence were subsequently not required; a last-minute deal having been struck between Crown and Defence.

When looked at objectively, which is never easy to do when you're the subject, the evidence against me for the murder of Angus MacDonald had been sufficient in law, but on the slim side. On the other hand, the case against Detective Inspector George Dicker was so fat you couldn't have squeezed it into a pair of his trousers. The clothing in the red rucksack was littered with Dicker's DNA and spattered with Angus MacDonald's blood. Ballistics showed the revolver he'd placed at my head, as witnessed by Lord Bantaskine, his wife and my wife, was the gun used to shoot both the unfortunate wildlife photographer and the Provost of West Lothian.

On the morning of the trial, Dicker pled guilty. Fiona Faye QC, representing him, explained to the court, in her own inimitable way, that it had all been a terrible tragedy. Her client had become too involved in trying to resolve a nasty blackmail scheme between the two deceased. That coupled with his longstanding gambling addiction and recent divorce, had driven Dicker over the edge. She'd pled his excellent service record and the timing of his guilty plea, which had avoided the

312

unpleasantness of a trial. The only thing missing was a gypsy violinist.

There was a lot said, but also a lot left unsaid, for although Fiona mentioned in her plea in mitigation 'a blackmail scheme', she did not go into detail, and the judge seemed happily disinclined to inquire further on the subject. There having been no trial, neither I nor anyone else gave evidence, and no mention was ever made of Josh Wedderburn, Jessica Barrett QC or Harvey Rudd.

When senior counsel sat down again, the judge had no option but to impose the only sentence available: life imprisonment. For such grave crimes, a punishment element of twenty-five years was deemed appropriate before Dicker could be eligible for parole; however, in the light of all that had been said, that period was reduced to eighteen. It was ridiculously lenient for double murder. The Crown did not appeal sentence.

As part of the arrangement whereby her colleague fell on his sword, DCI Sandeman's plea of not guilty was accepted. She'd been unaware her partner had gone rogue, or so she claimed. She was suspended for a time and later retired with full pension on health grounds.

Closer to home, despite being hit over the head by my dad, William Hendry refused to discuss with the police why his blood and my DNA were on a pickaxe handle found in MacDonald's outbuilding, and, in return, I didn't think it necessary to mention any more about his taking up the role of Angus MacDonald at Simon Keggie's trial.

Jeff Freeman's laptop and mine were seized by the police as possible productions and later lost by the police custodier. After repeated complaints, we eventually received letters of apology and cheques for half their value.

Joanna was once more welcomed into the COPFS, and

Josh Wedderburn was relocated to the Procurator Fiscal's Office in Wick. Learned counsel, Jessica Barrett, took leave of absence to prepare for her imminent marriage to Harvey Rudd, still Cabinet Secretary for Justice and a shoo-in for First Minister when the incumbent retired.

Sammy was sitting on his usual stool, glass in hand and chatting to Brendan when he saw me walk into the bar. He waved me over. 'The man himself,' he said. 'What'll you have?'

'If it's all the same to you, I'd quite like my fee for the Simon Keggie case,' I said. 'It was nine months ago. You could have produced a baby by now, far less a cheque.'

Sammy winced as he took a sip of whisky. 'It's not that easy, Robbie.'

'What? Writing a cheque? Have you sprained your wrist?'

He reached up and put an arm around me. 'It's like this. Keggie paid Eddie in cash, and for me to pay you . . . well, there'd be certain tax implications.'

'You mean like you having to pay tax?' I said.

'Good, you can see the problem I've got, Robbie.'

'No, Sammy. I see the problem *I've* got. I'm not the one who's retired—'

'Semi-retired.'

'I'm the one with a wife, two kids and a dog the Justice Secretary hasn't killed yet.'

He smiled through his daft wee beard at me. 'If I pay you . . .' he pointed at himself and me in turn, in case I didn't understand who he was talking about, 'a fee, then I'd have to show where that money came from. It's all accountancy stuff, but what it means is that I'd need to open a ledger in Keggie's name and put some money in it so I could then give it to you. You know what that lot at the Law Society are like with their inspections. They'd only start asking awkward questions about why some dead guy is suddenly giving me money.'

Brendan mulled over Sammy's financial conundrum. 'What's wrong with cash?' he said. 'Lots of Robbie's clients pay with—'

'Yes, thanks Brendan,' I said. 'I'll do my own negotiations if you don't mind.' I turned to Sammy. 'What's wrong with cash?'

There was a lot wrong with it, apparently. 'I'm getting too old for this law game, Robbie. The years have taken their toll. The cash Eddie got from Keggie, I had to—'

'Give to Eddie's family?' I said.

Sammy finished his drink, smacked his lips and nodded a few times. 'Yes, yes, I suppose I maybe should have done that.'

'But you didn't.'

'No, I spent it.' He gave the bottom of his glass a rattle on the countertop. Brendan took it from him and went over to the optics.

'So that's it,' I said. 'You beg me to do a trial that gets me landed with a murder charge, I spend a week in jail, nearly get shot and you expect me to write off that fee as a bad debt?'

'Robbie, son. Money's not everything,' Sammy said. 'You'll realise that when you get older.'

'Is that right? Well, if *you* want to get any older, there'd better be cash or a cheque on my desk first thing on Monday morning,' I told him, as Brendan set up another round.

I went to walk away, but Sammy pulled me back. 'Don't be like that, Robbie. As a matter of fact, I do have something for you.' He reached into his sporran and removed a wad of tissue. He unwrapped it to reveal a rectangular piece of shiny metal. There were still a few shards of green fluorescent plastic adhering to it. 'A bit bashed, but it still works. Use it wisely,' he said, placing the memory stick in my hand and closing my fingers around it. 'Sometimes, having someone owe you a debt *can* be a good thing.'

AUTHOR'S NOTE

It may be thought that in this book I've been a little harsh on those fine men and women who make up the Scottish Police Authority's Forensic Services. The views expressed are, of course, not mine (despite what my wife might think), but those of the fictional Robbie Munro, who is, like a lot of us Scots lawyers, a well-balanced individual, having a chip on both shoulders.

Over the years I have witnessed a few major errors from various Crown experts, usually explained away as cock-up and not conspiracy. What I have learned is that you can never take a forensic report at face value. Lawyers owe it to their clients to investigate the findings of trained forensic scientists, which juries often find so compelling – probably because they've watched too much *CSI*. Often, I've found, what is left out of a forensic expert report can be of as much interest as what's in it.

Although I was in a much more recent case which had several glaring examples of cock-up or conspiracy, I intend to use that as the basis of another book – so no spoiler. One case that sticks in my mind dates from 1997, when a client of mine, his male co-accused and another man were charged with murder. The background was that one evening there had been an argument outside my client's front door. It had developed into a fight involving all three men on a garden path. At the time of the fight, the victim had been wearing a short-sleeved yellow T-shirt, a fact that later became important.

The fight stopped, but hostilities recommenced shortly afterwards, spilling into the street, across the road and into somebody else's garden. This second incident did not involve my client, and before re-engaging with my client's co-accused, the victim pulled off the aforementioned T-shirt.

When this second fight ended, the victim went back to his house where he discovered he'd been stabbed in the left armpit. Although there was no external bleeding, the blade had cut a major blood vessel, causing massive internal haemorrhaging. He'd gone into hypovolaemic shock and later died on the operating table.

Both accused were charged with murder. There were witnesses to both incidents, but no one had seen the actual stabbing. The big question was, when had the stabbing taken place? Was it during the incident involving both accused? Or the second, after my client had disassociated himself?

It seemed to me that the answer lay with the yellow T-shirt. If there was a cut in the cloth under the left sleeve, then it must have occurred during the first fight. If there was no cut, it must have taken place during the second incident, and therefore did not concern my client.

When asked, the Crown sent the T-shirt for analysis and the forensic report came back to say that there was indeed a tear under the left armpit, which matched the location of the fatal wound. Based on this forensic report, it seemed like a classic art and part situation, with the victim having been stabbed while wearing the T-shirt and while fighting with my client and his co-accused.

It was because he had not seen the knife wielded at any stage that my client reluctantly felt he had to accept the report's finding; nonetheless, it was felt important that the T-shirt be examined, and as there were two forensic pathologists on the witness list, we asked that they be summoned. I remember the various legal representatives waiting in the robing room at Falkirk Sheriff Court, where the High Court was sitting at the time. As I recall there were present, as well as myself, the solicitor for the co-accused, George Wood, Edgar Prais QC, Edward Targowski QC and, his junior Craig Caldwell, later to return to Falkirk as sheriff (and inspiration for the name of Robbie Munro's former law firm Caldwell & Craig).

At lunchtime two forensic pathologists arrived: Marie Theresa Cassidy, formerly of Glasgow University and later to become the first woman to hold the position of State Pathologist of Ireland, and also the famous Professor Anthony Busuttil, then Regius Professor of Forensic Medicine at Edinburgh University. The production bag containing the T-shirt was duly brought through by a court officer with permission from the Crown to open the security seal for the purposes of examination, and the T-shirt spread out on the table for inspection.

Sure enough, there was a small gap in the cloth at the left armpit where the stitches in the seam had separated; however, this 'tear' as described in the Forensic report, was clearly not something that had been caused by a knife. There followed debate as to whether the gap in the stitching would have been wide enough for a blade to have gone through cleanly. The expert opinion was that it was just about possible, if the point of the blade had hit the split in the seam dead centre and penetrated on from there.

Things weren't looking too good at this point, and the trial judge was waiting to get things started. That was when somebody – I'd like to think it was me, but am fairly sure it was another solicitor, one not involved in the case and who had been eating their lunch and looking on with interest – piped up, 'Why is the T-shirt inside out?'

The answer to that being, conspiracy: it was turned that way to match the wound, cock-up: that's what happened when the victim pulled it over his head before the fight with my client's co-accused. Whichever, once the T-shirt was the right way round, the gap in the stitching was now under the right armpit where there had been no wound.

In the world of police forensics, the report was entirely accurate, it just happened also to be entirely misleading. There was indeed a tear – of sorts – under the left sleeve of the T-shirt and the victim had been stabbed in the left armpit. What the forensic scientists had thought it unnecessary to mention was that the T-shirt was inside out when they'd examined it and the difference it would have made to their findings if it had not been.

On the basis of this new evidence, my client's plea of not guilty was accepted, though his co-accused was later convicted.

ACKNOWLEDGEMENTS

With thanks to former ex-Corporal Adam Steven, formerly of the Argyll & Sutherland Highlanders, for not only providing me with an excellent daughter-in-law (with some assistance, it has to be said, from Mrs Steven) but also for recounting an army anecdote that was of help to me when wondering how I should have Robbie discover that the 'dead MacDonald' was not the MacDonald who'd appeared in court.

I'd also like to acknowledge the not-to-be-named court officer responsible for the incident that gave me the initial spark of an idea. For those who wonder how the wrong person could possibly appear in the witness box without anyone realising, the answer is: quite easily. A few years ago, I represented a man charged with assault. When the alleged victim took to the witness box his evidence was all over the place. It was as though he was talking about a completely different incident. Not only that, but he failed to identify the accused as his attacker.

Later in the day, my client having stood trial and been duly acquitted on a submission of no case to answer, it was discovered that the court officer had gone to the wrong witness room and brought back a man with the same surname, but who was waiting to give evidence in a completely different case. It's not usual for prosecution witnesses to be asked their address and are generally designed as c/o Police Scotland. No one noticed the mistake (though if my client did he never let on).

Something similar happened earlier this year when I was representing a client of mine at a deferred sentence diet. For once he was the subject of an extremely positive criminal justice social work report and I couldn't understand why the Sheriff didn't seem to agree with my view of it or that such a ringing endorsement deserved a non-custodial sentence. It was only after something of a heated exchange that my client was able to leave the building under his own steam. It turned out, when the next case called was also for the same client that I realised I had inadvertently represented a man with the same surname, but who hadn't bothered to come to court, presumably because his report, which the sheriff had been referring to, was so deplorable he knew he'd be sent to prison.

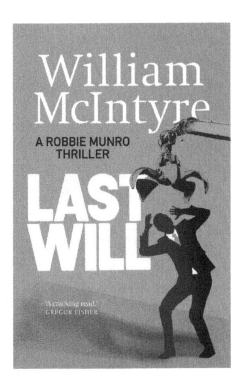

The trial of Robbie Munro's life: one month to prove he's
fit to be a father. Easy – apart from the small matter of a
double-murder in which Robbie's landlord, Jake Turpie,
is implicated. Robbie has a choice: look after his daughter
or look after his client...

'A cracking read.'   Gregor Fisher (*Rab C. Nesbitt*)

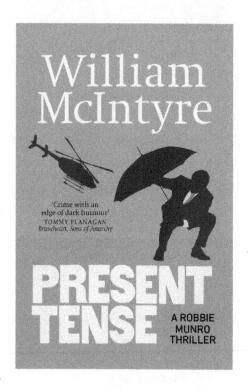

Robbie Munro is back home, living with his dad and his new-found daughter. Life as a criminal lawyer isn't going well, and neither is his love life. Then one of his more dubious clients leaves a mysterious box for him to look after. The contents will change his life forever.

'Crime with an edge of dark humour.'
Tommy Flanagan (*Braveheart, Sons of Anarchy*)

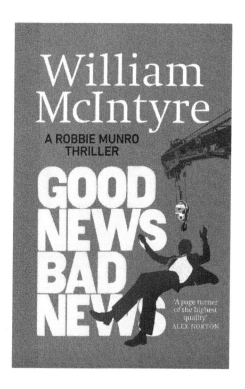

Robbie takes on a new client, only to find she's the grand-daughter of a Sheriff who hates him. His old clients are causing a few problems too, not to mention his shady former landlord. Yet the more Robbie tries to fix things, the more trouble he's in.

'Dry and pleasing wit which will surely see Robbie taking his place alongside Christopher Brookmyre's Jack Parlabane.'   *Sunday Sport*

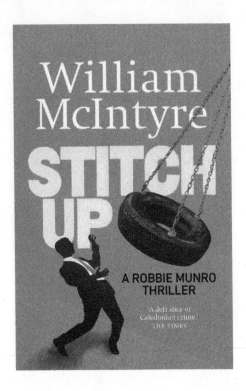

Newly-wed and happy, surely lawyer Robbie Munro can stay out of trouble. But a notorious child-murderer might soon be free because prosecution evidence was fabricated – and it was Robbie's dad who secured the conviction.

With time running out, can Robbie uncover the truth?

'A deft slice of Caledonian crime... rings viscerally true.'
The Times